MURDER BREAKS TRAIL

MURDER BREAKS TRAIL

AN ALASKA VINTAGE MYSTERY

EUNICE MAYS BOYD

First published by Level Best Books/Historia 2021

Honorable Mention: Third Mary Roberts Rinehart Mystery Contest

Author Photo Credit: Family Photo

Second edition

ISBN: 978-1-68512-256-0

Cover art by Level Best Designs

This book was professionally typeset on Reedsy.
Find out more at reedsy.com

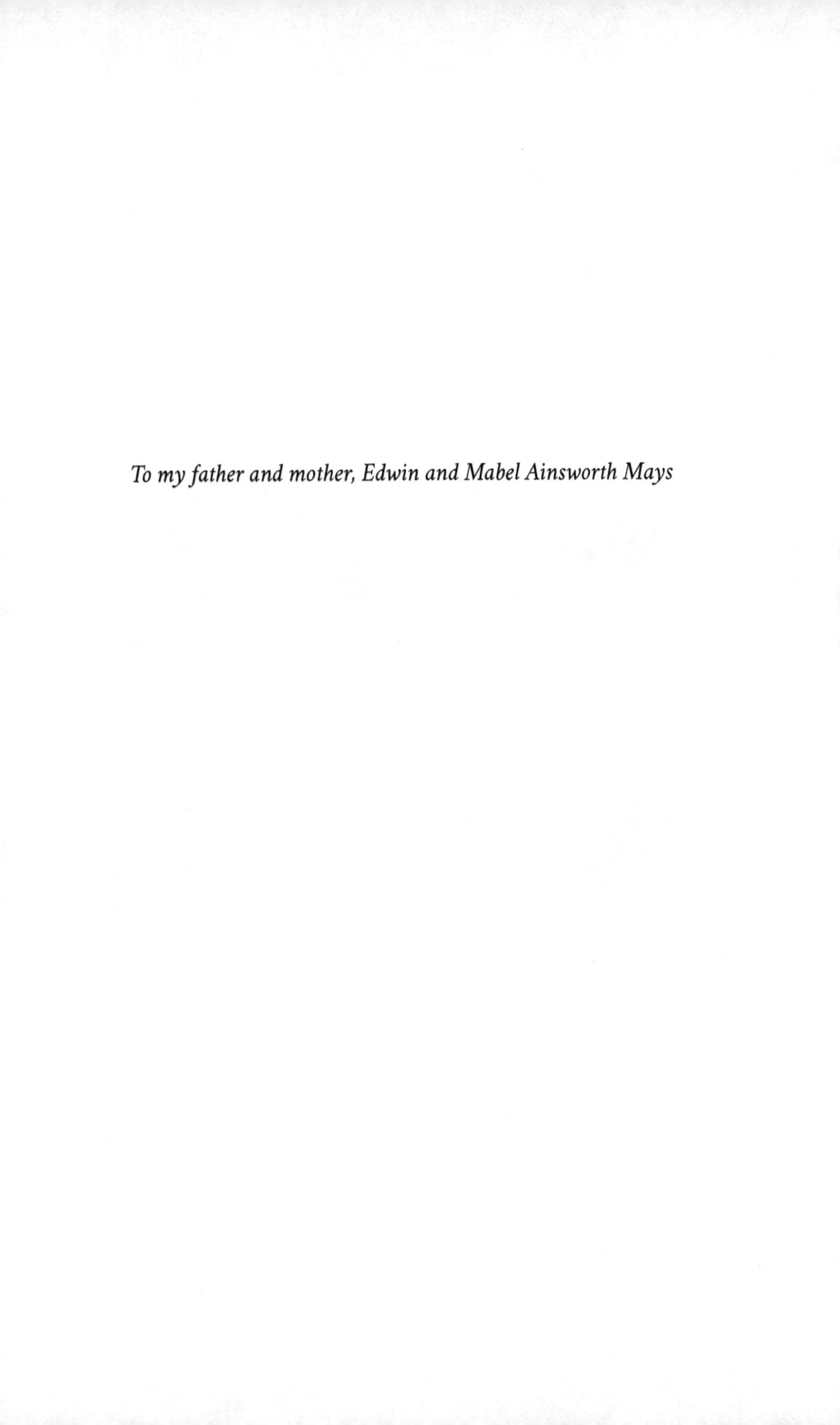

To my father and mother, Edwin and Mabel Ainsworth Mays

Praise for Murder Breaks Trail

"No scientific sleuthing this, but a blending of clues, coincidences and concentration by mystery-avid groceryman, Smyth, passenger on a plane, flying Alaska, carrying a Senator, Congressman and a Mayor. Forced to stay in a deserted settlement when gas is drained from their machine, murder and approaching winter produce near-panic among the castaways. Another killing and the problem of the mysterious skier, the abandonment of the colony, imminence of Japanese penetration and Nazi fifth column, add to the questions Smyth must solve before the Army takes over. A better than most brain workout."—*Kirkus Reviews* ca. 1943

"One of the most interesting parts of this story is the look Boyd gives us of Alaska during the war years and before the territory became a state. Smyth is not, perhaps, the swiftest of detectives—but he certainly does get there in the end and comes up with a plan to flush the murderer out (in lieu of direct of evidence). I did appreciate the set-up of the stranded party and thought the way they handled their situation was realistic and probable—with nerves fraying just the right amount and petty squabbles seeming more important than they should."—Bev (Goodreads)

"I found this little mystery in a second hand bookshop. It's great. F. Millard Smyth, a middle-aged grocer and keen reader of mystery stories, has managed to get himself included on a fact-finding trip to Alaska round about the time of Pearl Harbor. They decide to land at a remote settlement, which is when things start to go wrong."—Liz (Goodreads)

Chapter One

As she hurried from her station at the back of the plane into the pilot's compartment, the radio operator's blue-green coat brushed against F. Millard Smyth. He saw her blonde head bend towards the pilot, who was out of F. Millard's sight. He saw her lips move and her cheeks flush brighter pink. Turning, then, toward the six passengers, a straight little frown between her fair brows, she beckoned—F. Millard found himself supplying the adverb—urgently. In the seat ahead, Tony Webber, the Senator's secretary, unfasten his safety belt and swayed, with dancer's hips, into the pilot's compartment.

The senator raised his handsome white head, in a much publicized gesture. His platform voice boomed over the roar of the motors. "Who knows what treasure of essential minerals maybe hoarded in the vast, uncataloged store house of Alaska? Gold, platinum, mercury, tin, manganese, chrome—all these and more may yet await the plunge of the prospector's pick."

"Forget your work one day, Senator Lee. This is a picnic. Do you think it's time for lunch?" The pendulous cheeks of their host, Mayor Fletcher of Fairbluffs, quivered.

No one but himself, thought F. Millard—his small body in its large overcoat inconspicuously agog—was paying any attention to the conference up in the front. The others were all used to planes, maybe to such conferences too. With the feeling not quite downed that moving might rock the plane, he twisted gingerly about to catch the eye of the man behind him, marveling again that anyone so young, so engagingly homely, and only two inches taller than himself, could be a congressman. But Congressman Michael

O'Hara's gaze was fixed, as usual, on the senator's daughter across the aisle.

A cluster of black curls, one ear, and the firm, slender line of her jaw, were all F. Millard could see of Kilkenny Cordova Lee. Wrapped in aloofness as snugly as in her leopard coat, she was no more interested in that conference than the others.

With a sigh of relief F. Millard saw Tony Webber returning. But the secretary's ruddy face was as discretely expressionless as ever. Surely, he'd show some emotion if they were going to crash!

"Well?" boomed the Senator. "What is it, Tony?"

"The radio's out of order."

F. Millard released his breath. Only the radio; not a propeller, or a motor, or any other essential.

"The pilot wants to land on one of these lakes and fix it."

Everyone turned to the windows.

"We could have lunch ashore," beamed the Mayor, "while they work on the radio."

"There's a honey of a lake," pointed out Congressman O'Hara. "The one with all the water lilies at the narrow end."

F. Millard's spectacles bumped against the pane. The ground below was speckled with lakes. As big as turkey platters and as small as butter chips, they winked back at the drifting plane. The one Michael O'Hara had indicated was salad-plate size, with lilies a garnish of lettuce. A stream no wider than a thread, or a trickle of French dressing, glinted through trees at each end.

"A charming scene," declared Senator Thomas Jefferson Lee.

Mayor Fletcher's fat thighs strained against his safety belt as he pointed downward. "Smoke!"

F. Millard bumped his glasses again. Smoke, in this wilderness! Separated from the lake of the lilies by a tuft that might be a hill, splashed with autumn red and yellow, was a wide, dark blot like mildew. Sprinkled through the mildew gleamed scabby spots of dried grass. The little man felt an unaccountable revulsion. Then he saw what he was hunting. Near one of the scabs rose a thin, blue bristle of smoke.

"That's our lake," announced the Senator. "The one O'Hara suggested. It's nearest the smoke. I'll see firsthand how Alaskan prospectors live."

His daughter turned her gypsy-vivid face, a gleam of malice lighting topaz eyes. "Is it worth the trouble, Dad? There's a hill between the smoke and the lake. Remember: one prospector, one vote. And Alaska's not your district."

"Tony, tell the pilot that's our lake," the Senator repeated.

F. Millard choked down an impulse to grab the secretary's coat and hold him back. My gracious, he scoffed at himself, what could be more idyllic than lunch by a lake with water lilies and a girl like Kilkenny Lee? But that dark blot, that patch of mildew, came too close.

Tony Webber bent broad shoulders past the wall that hid the pilot. Too late to stop him now. Anyway, what could F. Millard Smyth do—a graying, insignificant grocer from Four Corners, Nebraska, sharing a congressional committee's holiday at the whim of the Senator's daughter?

The plane began to whistle earthward, its noisy heartbeats stilled. F. Millard found again the blue blade of smoke, just in time to see it puff white and disappear.

"It—it's gone," he stammered.

"What's gone?" asked the Mayor.

"The smoke. It disappeared."

"We're down too low to see it." The fat man's voice was impatient. "By the way, Senator—" Mayor Fletcher leaned forward.

The plane was low enough now for F. Millard to see that the green tufts, freckled red and yellow, were hills. Low enough, in another minute, so the lake with the water lilies was the only lake in sight.

The pontoons hit the water, motors roaring again as they taxied ashore. Gravel screamed, and the motors died.

Tony Webber, the big blond secretary, ceremoniously handed Hope Mullen, the small blonde radio operator, out of the pilot's compartment. Hope Mullen was as pretty as Kilkenny Lee, fair where the Senator's daughter was dark, short where she was tall, blooming with curves where the other girl was slight. F. Millard straightened his tie.

The pilot, Red Bailey, produced flaming hair and a grin and swaggered through the cabin to open the door. Standing on one pontoon he raised his arms to Hope and swung her to the beach. He looked at Kilkenny. She laughed and held out her arms.

F. Millard was the only one who got his feet wet. As he jumped ashore a rolled magazine fell from his pocket. He went in to his knees, but he got it before it sank. He flicked its damp pages, peered anxiously at the title, *Flatfoot*, and tenderly smoothed the grim mug of the great detective, Flatfoot Flannagan, on the cover.

Excitement needled through him as pebbles crunched under his feet. He was out in the wilderness now, treading where perhaps no creature save bear or caribou had set foot. No creature? What had made the smoke, and smothered it? He was certain it had been smothered, whatever anyone said. Sharply he scanned the country.

The lake had been poured into a shallow bowl of hills. Except where the lilies matted one end, it was neatly rimmed with gravel to the line where the trees began. Across from the lilies, a hundred yards from the plane, a rocky promontory jutted almost to the edge of the water. And beyond both lake and hills loomed a range of high mountains like a snaggle-toothed comb dipped in white paint.

"I'm all turned around," F. Millard blinked behind thick lenses. "Where did the smoke come from?"

Mayor Fletcher pointed to the promontory. "Over that hill. You can't see it from here."

Or anywhere, F. Millard's mind insisted stubbornly; there isn't any now.

"What are we waiting for?" demanded Senator Lee.

Congressman O'Hara grinned. "That's 'Do-It-Now' Lee, Mayor Fletcher. You can see where he got the name." He held out cigarettes to the girls. Hope refused, and he lighted a match for Kilkenny. Their two black heads bent over the flame.

Tony Webber and Red Bailey split another.

The pilot inhaled deeply. "Go ahead and look around," he said heartily. "I'll have a drag and help Hope with the radio."

"But aren't you coming with us, Red?" Kilkenny sounded disappointed.

F. Millard saw Michael O'Hara glance from her to the pilot, and grin.

"Please go, Red." Hope looked up quickly. She flushed and the troubled line came back between her brows. "It isn't as if I were your regular operator. When he couldn't come, I was so proud to take his place—and now I've already made a fizzle of it. I—I'll think you're sorry you took a chance on my brand-new license, if you don't let me fix it." Her chin quivered, and she bit her lip.

"We have to give in to the ladies, Bailey," said the Senator gallantly. "But we'll miss you, my dear," he told Hope. "You boys pick up the lunch, and let's get going."

"I—I—" F. Millard swallowed "—you may think I'm an awful fool, but I swear the smoke disappeared when we started to land.

"Disappeared" Thomas Jefferson Lee gave his best senatorial bark. "What do you mean, 'disappeared'?"

"Vanished, departed, went poof?" supplied Kilkenny pertly.

"That—that's what it looked like," F. Millard faltered. "The smoke was there—thin and blue—when we started to land, and then, as we dipped toward the lake, it turned white and disappeared—like someone put out the fire."

"Nonsense!" the Senator snorted. "Your imagination ran away with you. Or we dropped too low to see the smoke over the hill."

"Just what I told him, Senator," the Mayor said smugly.

"Come on! Can't you picture that prospector's face when he bites into a caviar sandwich?" Do-It-Now Lee flung up his theatrical head and swung along the beach.

Kilkenny glanced at the others and blew an expert series of smoke rings. "Whip up them mules, Paw," she drawled, "and hand me down mah sunbunnit." Her high-heeled alligator pumps slithered precariously through the gravel after her father. F. Millard caught a tantalizing whiff of the perfume that had scented all his dreams since he met the Senator's daughter.

The rotund Mayor bounced after her. Michael O'Hara glanced at Hope and Red, then scooped up a lunch basket and followed. Tony picked up the other basket and fell in line behind.

The big pilot looked down at the small blonde girl standing alone by the plane, "I feel like a dirty dog, picnicking while you work. But if that's the way you want it—sing out if I can help." His smile flashed, and he turned to F. Millard. "Come along, fella. You must be all goose pimples. September in Alaska's no time for wading.

F. Millard shivered. After his dip in the lake, perhaps the air was a bit brisk. But something more than cold had made him shiver—impatience to find what was on the other side of the promontory. He hurried to catch up.

Chapter Two

Where the spur of the ridge behind the lake jutted into the beach, the others waited.

Senator Lee gave F. Millard a small-boy grin. "Whatever happened to the smoke, here's a trail that shows recent use."

No path was visible in the pebbles, but their eyes followed a thin brown thread angling around the base of the promontory. Following past the headland, they saw where it made a crooked parting through a tangle of blueberry bushes toward a mass of heavy spruce shade.

For a minute they hesitated. Those evergreens, thought F. Millard, must be the mildewed-looking patch he had seen from the air. He glanced back at the sunlit lake with the red plane at its rim. His gaze returned to the spruce trees. No smoke rose from them now. No figure appeared on the path.

"Funny no one's showed up," the Senator remarked. "You'd think they'd have seen the plane land."

"I think they did," said F. Millard.

"Then why—?"

"That's why they put out the fire."

Kilkenny laughed. Do-It-Now Lee snorted and plunged up the trail. Single file, the others followed.

F. Millard trudged along, his eyes on the swinging tails of Tony's overcoat. Then he crashed into its tailored perfection. The line ahead had stopped.

Tony stepped aside, and F. Millard, with Red peering over his shoulder, joined in the general gasp.

Beneath the gloom of the evergreens huddled a handful of log cabins. The grocer saw a space that might have been a block-long street, with cabins straggling on each side. No wonder they hadn't seen it from the air. The splotchy shade made perfect camouflage—no roof of boards or shingles to attract the eye. Each roof was sod, and out of the sod grew dried weeds and tangled grass.

"We—we must have imagined that smoke." Kilkenny was the first to find her voice. "This little town is dead and buried in the shade." She shivered.

"Don't be like your Aunt Sheila," growled her father, "seeing ghosts and hearing banshees."

Michael touched her arm. "It's your Irish that gives you understanding, mavourneen; as you've taken your beauty from Spain; and the statesmen Lees of Virginia—"

"Our branch—" the bright line of Kilkenny's mouth hardened "—has sunk to politicians."

"This place must have been here since the Gold Rush," Red declared. "Some of the cabins have fallen in."

"But someone's keeping the trail open," the Mayor said practically. "It takes use to keep grass down."

"Where is he?" Tony asked.

They looked up the brush-grown street. No living thing stirred.

F. Millard cleared his throat.

The Senator said quickly, "We'll look in every cabin. No telling what might have happened to a man alone. Perhaps he's sick or hurt. He may have burned his last stick as we came along."

At the nearest door he raised his knuckles. The spruce-dark stillness of midday throbbed with the sound of his knock.

Quiet settled again. Quiet and gloom, the decay of the crumbling cabins, caught at the intruders, holding them still.

Thomas Jefferson Lee raised his hand to the wooden latch. As the door slowly creaked open, and dust and debris rained down, F. Millard began to tremble. My gracious, he sniffed, just because he slipped in the water—but he knew it wasn't damp trouser legs that made him shiver.

The Senator stepped over the sill, and the others trooped after. A Yukon stove was propped up on rocks in the middle of the room, a rustic table with a lantern, trailing cobwebs, three or four homemade chairs, two bunks built one above the other, made up the rest of the furniture. Dust and cobwebs were everywhere.

"Look! Look!" cried Kilkenny. "There's a woman's dress!" She pulled it from a nail and spread out its dark brown folds in billows of dust—high neck, a tucked and ruffled bodice, yards and yards of flounced skirt.

"Definitely not nineteen forty-one," she laughed.

F. Millard sneezed.

Kilkenny's smiling face suddenly sobered. "It's all going to pieces in my hands!" She hung it quickly back, dusting slim fingers on her leopard coat. "It—it's like walking on tombstones."

"Wasn't that the kind of clothes ladies wore in the Gold Rush days, Guy?" Red Bailey asked the Mayor.

Guy Fletcher's gray curls, escaping from his plaid cap, bobbed up and down. "Back in ninety-eight, when I came to Alaska. Though the clothes I remember were gayer."

Red grinned. "Tut-tut, Guy. I didn't mean the dancehall gals...I don't see how these roofs ever lasted from the Gold Rush," he went on, climbing to the upper bunk and reaching up. "Say, by gosh, this one has overlapping birchbark laid like shingles on the poles, and then a layer of moss between the bark and top sod! No wonder it hasn't fallen in." He slid to the floor. "Take a look at that place across the street, Guy. It's got a rock foundation!" The pilot shot out the door.

"What about lunch?" groaned their bulky host. "We bachelors have to depend on the restaurants, but I did order a good one."

Kilkenny patted his shoulder. "We'll enjoy it more for being hungry. I couldn't stop to eat, with all these other cabins to go through. No telling what we'll find. That dress—" her voice trailed back as she dashed outside.

The Senator followed. "There must be someone around here," he muttered, "sick, perhaps hurt, in one of these cabins."

One by one they left F. Millard staring at the cobweb-festooned relics. Years must have passed, he reflected to have laid down so much dust; years since some woman had worn that ruffled dress, and some man admired her in it. Years—but smoke had risen from among these very trees less than an hour ago!

He flicked the pages of *Flatfoot*, rolled once more, but still damp. Who would put out a fire when he saw a plane start to land? Only someone who didn't want his presence noticed. No detective would ever stand here dreaming; Flatfoot Flannagan would discover what that man was up to!

F. Millard stepped outside, and saw Mayor Fletcher in a doorway up the street, gazing dejectedly at the deserted lunch baskets waiting by the trail. Red Bailey strolled around the corner of the cabin F. Millard had just left and stooped to examine something near the ground. The grocer went on up the brushy slope that had been a street. Nine crumbling cabins—on his right, three were still standing, two on the left. He stepped into the nearest upright cabin. This one had a moosehide latchstring to open the door—new leather, he saw, with a quickening pulse. But only more dust and cobwebs coating more homemade furniture met his eyes in both of the musty rooms. He hurried on. A squirrel ran, chattering, from a jackstraw jumble of logs where once men had lived.

Now no one was in sight. He didn't even hear voices. If he hadn't seen the two Fairbluffs men, he'd have thought everyone had gone back to the plane, or that the Senator had them beating the woods to find an injured prospector.

The next cabin was the last on the upper end of the right-hand side of the road—one large room, four single bunks, more rustic furniture, more dust.

When F. Millard came up the hill, the Mayor had been in the lower cabin of the two still standing on the left-hand side of the street. Only the last at the upper end remained to be examined. It still seemed strange to F. Millard that he met no one else. What had become of all his fellow passengers?

Thoughtfully he approached the door, lifted the latch, and pushed. Instead of squealing and moaning reluctantly open like the others, this door flew wide. F. Millard stumbled in, blinking in the dim light. This cabin didn't smell musty, but it did have a definite odor. He thought of picnics and campfires. Then he sniffed again, suddenly remembering his store—the day the delivery boy upset a case of eggs and dropped a cigarette behind the pickle barrel. By the time the fire department left, the whole store smelled like this room.

And there was something else different about this cabin—it didn't have the closed-in chill the others had.

He made a dive toward the rock-propped Yukon stove and extended a careful hand. The iron was still warm!

While he stood staring at the stove, his eyes getting brighter and brighter, voices floated in through the open door. "But this is unbelievable, Senator! I've been teaching in Fairbluffs a year, and I never heard of a place like this."

Hope Mullen's voice. Then the radio must be fixed. F. Millard had momentarily forgotten that her regular job was teaching school, and her radio operator's license something on the side. It was hard to associate such capability with her ultrafeminine charm.

"I can't find Red," she went on. "I ought to report about the radio."

F. Millard dashed to the door. Hope and the Senator were walking up the trail.

"S-S-Senator Lee," he gasped, "I found where the fire was! The man was in this cabin."

"Hell's bells!" the Senator exploded. "I stuck my head in there, and didn't see anyone, and went on! Hey!" He raised his voice to a bellow. "Everybody here! Come on in!"

Guy Fletcher emerged from the same cabin F. Millard had seen him in earlier. Farther down the hill Red Bailey appeared at a loose-jointed lope. Behind him Kilkenny tore up the trail like a schoolgirl, the leopard coat streaming out from her smart black suit and yellow blouse. She passed the puffing Mayor just after Red. The young Congressman dashed from somewhere else. They all reached the cabin together and crowded through the door.

F. Millard opened the door of the stove, and heads bumped as they jostled to look. While the odor of wet charred wood crinkled their nostrils, Tony Webber came in, panting, his ruddy face hot scarlet.

"Someone poured water on the fire!" cried Kilkenny.

Hope Mullen drew away first. "You don't need a warm stove to prove someone's been living here. This cabin's clean."

Red straightened, bright eyes focused on Hope. "Radio okay. Now?"

Beneath her yellow curls, the new operator's doll-round cheeks turned deeper pink. "Oh, Red, I couldn't find you at first, and then I got so interested seeing the cabins—The radio—there's nothing we can do. The generator's burned out."

Red looked suddenly older, responsible, grave. "Okay, everybody, we'll have to get started back."

"Hey, wait!" yelled Michael O'Hara. "Here's another door!"

In the dim light admitted by the dark, crowding trees F. Millard hadn't seen the door at the back of the room.

The correct, blond secretary, still panting, reached it first, and pulled it open. "By Jove!" he exclaimed.

"Get a load of this!" shouted Michael.

The others pushed through. The second room, much smaller than the first, was filled with boxes, sacks, and cans. Flour, sugar, beans; cans of milk, vegetables, and meat; kerosene, matches, soap—cases of supplies lined the little room, and overflowed on the bunks.

"Why," gasped the grocer, "that's enough to feed a man for a year!"

"But where's the man?" asked Michael.

"Come on," said the pilot sharply. "We can't look any more now."

"Let's not go back yet," Kilkenny coaxed. "This is fun! Let's wait—"

"Sorry, Miss Lee," said the pilot firmly, "but we can't fool around here without a radio. This load of passengers is too important.

Do-It-Now Lee's daughter raised a stubborn chin. "Tell that to another load of passengers, Mr.—umm—Bailey, isn't it? Mick O'Hara used to have a pilot's license, and Tony Webber and I both have several hours toward one. We all know it doesn't take a radio to fly a plane."

"That makes it practically unanimous," drawled Red. His blue eyes had a glint as stubborn as her chin. "Hope has some flying hours to her credit too. But I'm pilot of this plane, and I'm not flying a congressional committee any longer than I have to without a radio." He turned to the others. "It's time to start."

Senator Lee's eyes glinted too, but with amusement. "Bailey's boss of this show, Kilkenny."

She appealed to the fat man. "Mayor Fletcher's our host. If he says we can stay—" She gave him an enchanting smile.

Guy Fletcher looked distressed. "I'd like to, Miss Lee, if you want to. But when Red—I guess what he says goes."

Michael O'Hara laughed. He slipped his hand under Kilkenny's arm. "Come on, Kenny. You're outvoted. Let's lead the way."

As Red herded his passengers out, F. Millard tried not to notice his scowl. People couldn't help doing things for a girl like Kilkenny Lee, and she couldn't help getting to expect it. But anyone who had done what Kilkenny had for him, must be as lovely inside as out. He remembered the moonlit decks on the boat from Seattle, the times she'd slipped away from the younger men and the dancing to hear about a forty-year-old dream: F. Millard thwarted longing to join the Nome stampede when he was a boy in his teens, and of how he had finally saved enough from the grocery business to make a trip to Alaska. It was she who had persuaded the Mayor to ask F. Millard on today's holiday plane ride.

Red hustled them down the slope.

Hope Mullen's voice, clear and young in the brush-grown tracks between the crumbling cabins, came back to F. Millard. "Did you see the clothes hanging up, and the blankets on the bunks? This dry climate must have preserved them. Why do you suppose the people who owned those things went off and left them?"

"Urgent business elsewhere?" suggested the urban-wise secretary, stooping for the lunch baskets.

"Elsewhere?" Hope laughed. "Where else, in an almost uninhabited country the size of this? And clothes and things must have been far more valuable those days than now, weren't they, Guy?"

"Just about literally worth their weight in gold," agreed Guy Fletcher. "I don't understand it myself."

"I saw the strangest thing," said Kilkenny, the same note of wonder and almost superstition in her voice that had been there when they first saw the village. "In one of the cabins I saw four hands of cards, lying every which way on the table. All the chairs were pushed back, as if the players had jumped up in a hurry. It's funny they didn't straighten the house before they left or take the cards. Do you suppose something could have happened to them?"

They had reached the blueberry patch. By common consent they all stopped to look back. The old cabins, crouched in evergreen gloom, stared after the intruders, a farewell as silent and secret as their greeting.

"What could have done it, Mayor Fletcher?" Kilkenny asked softly. "You were in Alaska when these cabins must have been built. Could anything have happened to a whole community?"

Fletcher eased his weight to his other foot. "Plenty of places were deserted when the strike was made somewhere else, but with women—it goes against their grain to leave things like clothes and coal oil lamps. I have heard of settlements getting wiped out—folks out in boats, and the storm came up and drowned them—or climbing through a pass and getting caught in a snowslide (note that'd hardly apply here)—and of course there were always epidemics."

Michael said dryly, "That'd do the trick."

"You think it might have been—disease?" Hope quavered.

"Might've been. Typhoid—diphtheria—smallpox. There's a place right now, out to the Westward, a fish camp or something, where the natives go every year, and some die with a sickness like meningitis. The Indians won't move camp—and neither will the germs."

"I wonder how long germs live?" Kilkenny's voice was husky.

The Mayor gave her a tight little smile. "I don't think these folks died in bed. We didn't find any bones."

F. Millard gulped.

Tony laughed harshly. "Why did we bring this up?"

"And why are we standing here?" Red broke in briskly. "We've got to get started, boys and girls. You can do your speculating flying back, while we eat that much-delayed lunch."

One more glance at the shadowed cabins, and, one by one, the eight visitors started down the trail through the blueberry patch. Down the trail toward the promontory and the lake, the plane, and the modern world.

"That's all very interesting," rumbled Senator Lee, "but I'm more interested in the fellow that's living there now. Finding that charred, water-soaked wood explodes my theory about a sick prospector."

Eyes on the trail, the little grocer walked on. Who was F. Millard Smyth to say "I told you so," in such distinguished company?

"Of course," Lee blustered, "that doesn't mean there's any shenanigans afoot. The fellow may have just been starting on a trip. There'd be no reason to change his plans because the plane flew over. He'd be busy getting ready and probably didn't even see us start to land."

"Can't you find an explanation to cover the whole village, Dad?" His daughter sounded tired.

Do-It-Now Lee disregarded the interruption. "Just coincidence. Or suppose it isn't. Suppose it's some native trapper, hiding when he sees us because he's got no right to be here."

"Those were a white man's supplies, Senator." Red spoke up at the end of the line.

F. Millard raised his head. The outthrust hogback hiding the lake looked suddenly menacing, the hills somehow nearer, the distant white mountains more cold—a barrier between this secret, dark place in the world.

They rounded the headland and saw the red plane on the beach. For no apparent reason F. Millard's heart lifted.

"Natives don't buy stuff like that," Red went on. "Usually don't have the price."

The crunch-crunch of shoes on pebbles emboldened the grocer to add, "They were all standard Pacific Coast brands—and all new."

Then he dropped his eyes to the coat just ahead, a blue-green, heavy wool, with Hope Mullen inside. Her ankles were as trim as Kilkenny's, her shoes the sensible kind. But he missed the alligator pumps and swinging leopard coat. Hope Mullen was a pretty little schoolteacher, the kind that there were lots of in Nebraska. Kilkenny Cordova Lee—to F. Millard Smyth, of Four

Corners, the Senator's daughter was a femme fatale, whatever that was, but he'd read about them.

He could hear her voice now, low-pitched for a woman, vibrating something within him: "I'm glad you wouldn't let us stay, Red. I really am. That place gives me the creeps."

By now they had reached the plane. Red jumped on a pontoon and held out his hand to Kilkenny. His arm stopped in mid-air.

F. Millard saw Kilkenny raise her head. Her lips parted. "I smell gasoline."

Gasoline? Hadn't he smelled gasoline somewhere else today? Apprehension clutched at F. Millard's throat.

Leaving Kilkenny with her hand outstretched, Red sprang into action. The noise of his progress thumped through the plane. Then even that was stilled.

The little company on the beach waited in breathless quiet. Illogical as his apprehension might be, F. Millard knew it had seized the others too.

Then at last the banging and clumping started again. Red's long legs swung back to the pontoon. His whole body was electric, his face as red as his hair. "Someone's drained the gas tanks—every compartment!"

F. Millard heard gasps and gulps. His own squeak was covered with a little scream from Hope. "But, Red! How'll we get back?"

"Good God, Red, we can't—" the Mayor stopped.

"You're crazy!" roared Senator Lee. "Look again."

Red drew a long breath. "Don't get excited, folks." His voice was as cool as his face was hot. "We'd been talking to Fairbluffs right along till the radio went off. They knew our course. A few hours after they stop hearing from us, they'll send out planes. They won't take any chances with passengers like you."

"The fellow that put out the fire," Tony grated between clenched teeth, "must have sneaked around and waited till the plane was alone!"

Red turned quickly to Hope. "How long had you been away from the plane, Hope, when I saw you in the cabin?"

"Oh, Red!" She looked almost ready to cry. "It never entered my head that anyone—it didn't take long to find the generator was burned out. So

I went to the village, but you were all scattered through the cabins, and I couldn't find *you* at all, Red. And then I got interested in seeing the cabins too, and—and when I finally found you, it must have been half an hour."

"Half an hour!" The pilot groaned. "The gas tanks could've been drained a dozen times."

"The important point," the Senator rumbled, "isn't if and when it happened—but how soon are we going to get back? I've no time to hang around this lake waiting for someone to find us."

Michael O'Hara's heavy black brows drew together. "We're not on one of the regular air routes, are we, Bailey?" He asked quietly.

Red's answer was brief. "Miles off. But we sent Fairbluffs messages all morning. They'll know near enough so it shouldn't take long to find us."

"Got an auxiliary radio?" Michael persisted.

"This isn't any airliner, Congressman O'Hara," the pilot drawled, "just a little six-passenger charter ship. We're lucky to have one radio—or we would be, if it worked."

Pebbles jingled noisily as someone shifted his feet.

"But, Red! My God, Red!" burst out Mayor Fletcher. "Don't you realize—?"

"Oh, Red, what shall we do?" wailed Hope.

Then they all began talking at once, all but F. Millard and Kilkenny. The Senator's daughter withdrew into aloofness, standing on a pontoon with her face toward the lake and her slim back to the babble of voices. F. Millard didn't dare open his mouth for fear his teeth might chatter.

Red Bailey's voice rose above the hubbub. "Take it easy folks. You may have to go without your toothbrushes a night or two but we're mighty lucky to have food and shelter. Why, we've got a whole village to sleep in!"

Kilkenny turned around wide golden eyes fixed on the pilot. They lifted slowly to the autumn-splashed hogback that hid the settlement. In spite of the sun and her leopard coat, F. Millard saw her shiver.

He shivered too.

"Well, Senator—" Michael O'Hara's impudent Irish grin dared the wilderness and everything in it—"we ought to turn in quite a report on Alaska's mineral resources. Not many congressional committees can do their prospecting in person."

"There's one thing we'll do in person," Lee said coldly, "and that's run down our friend who put out the fire."

"*And* the gas," added Michael.

"But surely—surely—" that panicky bleat was Mayor Fletcher's "—they'll find us right away. They'd never let an important party like this disappear! They'll send out searchers today. Why, they—we—they'll comb the Territory!"

"Of course they'll send out planes," agreed Congressman O'Hara. "Though maybe a senator won't look any bigger from the air that a reindeer herder."

"But—but they'll have to find us soon. They'll have to find us right away! Winter's coming on!" The Mayor's chubby face looked drawn.

"By Jove!" muttered the big, fair-haired secretary. "I hadn't thought of that." His ruddy color faded.

"Take it easy, folks," said Red again. "Let's get in the plane and eat that lunch we've been lugging around all day. No reason to get excited."

Kilkenny Cordova Lee brought her gaze back to the beach; eyes, brows, nose, and mouth all expressed bored contempt. "Who's excited, Mr. Bailey, except you and Mayor Fletcher and Miss Mullen? You Alaskans are the only ones I've seen excited."

Scarlet sprang into Red Bailey's face to merge in the red of his hair. Before words could rush out, Guy Fletcher cried, "Red, they've no idea! This is September. Winter is almost here! They don't know what they're up against."

The pilot closed his jaws with a snap that to F. Millard was as ominous as thunder. Red turned to climb into the plane. His answer to the Mayor was grim. "Maybe they'll find out."

Chapter Three

Lunch helped F. Millard's shivers, but didn't prevent his feeling that eyes watched from the hills as they made their way back to the village, or that eyes watched from the cabins themselves, as they wound through the blueberry patch.

Where the spruce gloom cut off the sun, Kilkenny stopped and pointed. "What's that? Those two little piles of rocks under that clump of spruce?"

"Look like surveyor's monuments," the Congressman said, "but they'd hardly have been so close together."

"They might mark a well," suggested the Mayor, "or quicksand."

Red swung his long legs over the bushes, and the others followed like sheep. They stopped by the miniature rock pyramids, one at each end of an oblong depression. The rotten edge of a weather board protruded from one stack.

"It's a grave," said the Senator sharply.

The shade seems suddenly cold.

"It—it must have been a child." Kilkenny's voice was soft. "It's too small for a man."

"Now we know what happened to one villager," Hope said matter-of-factly.

"Cheery welcome for the next inhabitants," observed Michael.

The Mayor grinned wryly. "Overnight guests not included—I hope."

"For the love of mud!" ejaculated Red. "Let's cut the comedy and get to work. Unless you folks like cobwebs, we'll have to sweep up."

"And air the bedding," added Hope.

"And pray it wasn't an epidemic that took off our predecessors." Michael winked at Kilkenny.

"Anyway, it hasn't got the fellow that lives here. He was able to douse the fire and clear out," remarked Red.

"And sneak back to get our gasoline," cried the Senator indignantly. "That's one fellow I want an interview with before we leave."

"But it doesn't make sense," F. Millard said slowly, his eyes on the grave at his feet. "Why would anyone who wanted to avoid his fellow man—who'd put out his fire and hide, so he wouldn't be seen—turn right around and do the very thing that keeps us here?"

"He must have changed his mind after he saw the plane land." Tony Weber's voice was equally thoughtful.

Do-It-Now Lee glanced quickly at his secretary. "You mean he recognized one of us, Tony?"

Hope looked up, pink cheeked, at the big white-haired man, her eyes blue and wide-openly admiring. "Anyone who reads papers would recognize your picture, Senator Lee."

The Senator's shoulders broadened. His daughter's brows arched, faintly disdainful.

"But there's no telling what sort of person this man is," Hope went on. "Suppose he saw a prosperous planeload—" her eyes rested on Kilkenny's leopard coat "—maybe the thought of ransom—"

"This still isn't doing any housework," broke in Red. "Whoever the fellow is, will have to shelter tonight."

As they moved away F. Millard looked back. Small, sunken, lonely under the trees, the grave, with its two little pyramids of rock, and the gleaming white mountains above the dark cloud of spruce, gave him a sense of foreboding. Almost unconsciously he reached inside his coat for a reassuring flick of *Flatfoot's* pages and hurried after the others.

In spite of protestations that the ransom theory was nonsense in Alaska, it was significant to F. Millard that they all chose cabins near together. Only two had more than one room: the one with the supplies at the upper end of the road, and the one diagonally across with the moose-hide latchstring. Kilkenny, who liked the latchstring, chose that cabin for her father, Hope, and herself. The three young men: the Congressman, the pilot, and the Senator's secretary, took the one next door, with four single bunks; F. Millard and Guy Fletcher the one across the street where the stranger had been living.

Red built fires in all three cabins, Hope heaped dusty blankets into Mayor Fletcher's arms, and Kilkenny handed the little grocer two kerosene cans for water.

His rolled magazine hiking up his overcoat above one hip, F. Millard swung the empty buckets up the trail. Where the old-time street ended in the woods the trail turned sharply past the last cabin and started downhill to the right. A clear, cold stream marked its end.

He slopped the full buckets back up the hill and was rounding the corner of the cabin when two tall man and a short one almost knocked him down.

"What are you boys up to? He demanded. "Don't tell me you've done your housework!"

Michael, Tony, and Red looked foolish. "S-sh," the young Congressman cautioned, "the girls aren't supposed to know."

"Know what?"

Michael grinned, lowering his voice conspiratorially. "We're on a man hunt! Didn't see anyone on the trail, did you? Or any traces to prove we are not alone?"

Water sloshed over F. Millard's shoes. He set the buckets down. "Have you got a gun?"

"Divil a gun. We've got to catch him barehanded."

"You kids may think this is funny," F. Millard said soberly. "But disabling a plane hundreds of miles from help is pretty serious business. Someone's up to something more than games. Did you look through the cabins? You might have found an old rifle."

"Not even a knife," Red told him. "Guess someone beat us to them."

Tony edged past the two full buckets. "We better get going, fellows."

The tall pilot and the wiry Congressman followed the blond secretary down the hill. Michael waved a debonair hand as they swaggered out of sight.

F. Millard stood looking at blank September trees: golden birch and alders, black-green clumps of spruce, scarlet high-bush cranberry shrubs—no movement, no sound to show that under the speckled shade three men stalked another. He had been left behind with the women and old men while the young men went off to fight. He bent forlornly for the buckets.

* * *

At the door of the Senator's cabin Kilkenny shaded her eyes. Her smart overcoat and hat were gone. The sleeves of her yellow blouse rolled above her elbows, and her black skirt showed smudges of dust. "I was beginning to think you'd run out on us, like Paw. Hope caught him reading a book in the mystery man's cabin. Where the boys are, God only knows. If it weren't for you and Mayor Fletcher—" she stepped inside and came out with an arm full of blankets. "Suppose you pop down to the blueberry patch and spread these in the sun on top of the bushes. Shake them first." She looked at him consideringly only, her eyes above the level of his. Then she gave him one of her rare, wide smiles, and reached out and patted his cheek. "You're kind of sweet. Did you know it, F. Millard Smyth?"

Under the load of bedding, he staggered out of doors, down the trail between the crumbling cabins, but now he staggered on air. Maybe the old men didn't have such a bad time when they got left in the village.

The nearest blueberry bushes already flaunted exotic woolen blossoms. Guy Fletcher stretched out a red blanket next to one checkered blue and white, and went puffing up the hill. The grocer wondered if Kilkenny's satin fingers had touched the other's cheek too. Peering at the Mayor's blue-black jowls, he decided that fastidiously they hadn't.

Kilkenny waved her broom as he panted back up the hill. "The boys' cabin next. I haven't had so much fun since Father broke his leg."

F. Millard looked at her shyly. "I certainly admire the way you pitched in, Miss Lee. You—you're not used to this sort of thing."

"Meaning I am?"

The gang glanced quickly at Hope. But the blonde teacher wasn't smiling.

"Oh, no, no, no, Miss Mullen. My gracious, I didn't mean—"

Kilkenny laughed and pushed him with her broom. "Hope doesn't have a corner on usefulness. Dad had a ranch before he went into politics and I went social. That was while Mother was alive." Her voice had a gentle tone he hadn't heard before.

Would he never learn to think before he spoke? He practically told Hope Mullen she was a scrubwoman. He'd reminded the Senator's daughter of what must be a sad recollection. Now if Guy Fletcher would just start whining again about winter coming on, everything would be perfect.

With a slim hand and shoulder Kilkenny pushed the door of the boys' cabin ajar. "Every time I open one of these squawky old doors, I wonder what could have happened to the people who used to live here."

"Ask Mr. Smyth. Isn't that a detective magazine in his pocket?"

F. Millard looked up swiftly. Hope's face was turned away, but her tone had an edge. Perhaps that scrubwoman crack rankled.

Before he could think of anything appropriate to say, she went on more naturally, "Don't you think it's funny we haven't seen Red or Congressman O'Hara or Mr. Webber all afternoon?"

"Dashed funny," the other girl agreed. "It's not like Mick to duck out when there's work to do. He plays his cards differently from Dad, but they both keep their eye on the votes."

Hope's blue eyes met Kilkenny's brown-gold ones. "You don't like politics, Miss Lee?"

"I do not." The Senator's daughter plunged her hands in a bucket of water.

F. Millard too had been thinking of the three young men. Surreptitiously he pulled out his watch. It had been two hours since he'd seen them swagger off—without a gun, to catch a man who might be dangerous.

When the sun was almost down the girls agreed it was time to bring in the blankets. They seemed reluctant to admit the creeping of the shadows, as if admission gave life to some unspoken thought. F. Millard and the Mayor twice trotted down the slope, and puffed back up with their arms full, the girls made all the beds, and still the three young men had not returned.

After a lesson from Guy in handling the piece of sheet iron that served for a draft in the pipe of the Yukon stove, Hope had set a pan of biscuits in the oven before the boys came back.

At the sound of Red's deep voice in the dusk outside, Kilkenny flew to the door.

"Okay, Kenny, relax." A smudge of dirt above one black brow gave Michael a rakish air, increased by a long scratch down one cheek. His thick black hair was matted with leaves and spruce needles. "We came back with our shields, not on them."

Well!" barked Do-It-Now Lee. "Did you find him?"

Red shook his flaming thatch and slumped into a chair.

"We found one place where he'd been hiding," said Tony, "on the spur of the ridge that cuts off the town from the lake."

"I suppose he hid there till Hope left the plane, and he could dump the gasoline." The Senator's face hardened. "So, he's still out there in the hills."

"Yeah, we'll have to latch our doors tonight," drawled Red. "And speaking of night—" F. Millard envied the one lithe motion with which Red pulled himself out of the chair "—suppose we collect the lamps and lanterns and fill them before it gets dark. This isn't the kind of hotel where you just flip a switch."

And again, after a dinner of biscuits and canned corned beef and peas, when the stranded passengers prepared to scatter to their cabins, Red paused with his hand on the door latch. "Don't open your windows, folks. See that little tin door like a porthole, high up in the wall? Open those tonight for ventilation instead of windows. Alaskans use them in the winter. And move something heavy in front of your doors." He grinned sheepishly. "Good-bye now. Pleasant dreams."

* * *

Pleasant dreams! F. Millard lay on his lumpy bed, staring into the musty dark. Pleasant dreams—in darkness peopled with ghosts? With every hill a possible menace, a shelter for that hidden presence that had drained off their gasoline? What of the woman who had worn the ruffled dress? What of the playmates of the child who lay beneath the spruce? What of the players of the interrupted card game? What had happened to those early settlers to make them desert their village? And where was the man who lurked there now? Where was he, and what was he planning?

Out of doors a twig snapped. Sweat dampened F. Millard's palms. Another loud pop. He need not have envied Red Bailey his lithe upward spring; in his lone bunk F. Millard stood straight up, without, as far as he knew, having twitched a muscle. Across the room Mayor Fletcher's bunk poles squeaked.

F. Millard whispered, "Fletcher, did you hear those sounds?"

The Mayor cleared his throat, but all he said was, "Yes."

"What do you think they were?"

"I hope—" the little man noticed the stress on the second word "—I hope it was only the cold. The thermometer must be pretty low tonight. The logs these cabins are made to expand and contract in sudden changes—"

F. Millard lay down again and pulled up the covers. No use catching pneumonia to complicate diphtheria or whatever germs lurked in these cabins.

You Cheechako don't recognize the most important factor here," Fletcher went on, "and that's cold weather, winter coming on—"

"Cheechako," repeated F. Millard softly, "Alaskan for tenderfoot."

"—so if we are found before snow flies, well and good. If not—" Guy stopped. F. Millard wondered if he'd scared himself. But he hadn't stopped for good. He returned to the subject that scared the grocer. "As for those sounds we just heard, they might have been logs popping in the cold—and they might not."

Then he really stopped. Rhythmic snores came floating through the dark. But F. Millard lay in his bunk with perspiration undried. The snores weren't loud enough to shut out the snaps and cracks. How about the bureau in front of the door? Would it withstand a determined shove? It might be animals—bears, wolves, some other four-footed prowlers. But—

He clenched his jaw. He had to stick it out. But he didn't have to spend the whole night in a sweat or a shiver. He'd force himself to think of something else. He felt for his clothes at the foot of the bunk. The bulky roll of *Flatfoot* reared out of his trousers pocket. Beneath his thumb the pages made a reassuring flutter. Suppose he were Flannagan. Suppose there were no mystery man. But if there weren't, why would they be here now? Who would have drained the gas tanks? It would have to have been one of themselves.

Just for the sake of argument, suppose one of them had a motive to prevent the plane's returning. Could he have slipped back while the others explored the town, and run off all the gas? F. Millard deliberated. After examining the first cabin together they had all scattered and run about like chickens. They were active people. Any one of them could have slipped back to the plane, opened up whatever drained the tanks, and dashed back without the others knowing he'd been gone. Every one of the younger people had flown a plane. Even the Senator and the Mayor were familiar with plane travel. Everyone but F. Millard himself would have known where and how to drain the tank.

Come to think of it, when they gathered around the still-warm stove here in this very cabin, where the fire had been put out, he'd heard a lot of panting. Tony Webber, the last to arrive, had still been panting when they opened the storeroom door.

Come to think of it again—my gracious, where was this leading?—while they were all crowded in this one small room, F. Millard had distinctly smelled gasoline. At the time he'd just connected it with one of the many peculiar smells about the deserted cabins. But what if it had been on someone's clothes—someone just back from the plane? In the sunny air it would have evaporated quickly. Who was it?

No, no, he told himself firmly, this was all nonsense, only a joke. It was the man who'd put out the fire and hidden who had drained the gasoline.

Chapter Four

Other puffy eyes at the breakfast table told F. Millard he hadn't been the only one who'd spent a restless night.

Michael O'Hara brought up the subject of the rescue plane. "Shouldn't we build a bonfire to guide them."

"Planes don't fly at night up here except in emergencies," said the pilot slowly. "Smoke would be the only value of a bonfire in the daytime, and we've got three smokes here in our three cabins. Whoever comes near enough to spot them will see our ship on the lake."

"Well, they better hurry up," the Senator growled. "This Alaskan mineral report is too important, with the Japanese situation what it is. We may be in the war ourselves before we know it."

"Compared to things like that, our own little affairs don't count, and yet—" Hope's blue eyes looked disturbed "—I can't help remembering that school begins next Monday. I'm a teacher, you know, in private life." She gave the Senator a rueful smile.

"There's a draft drawing coming up soon," said Red, "and my number may be called. Besides, I've got a flight to Wiseman scheduled tomorrow. But they'll find us in a day or two; we don't have to worry."

"And I'm supposed to be running a hardware store," the Mayor groaned, "when the city can spare me." His little black eyes almost hidden in his cheeks opened wide. "I tell you we've got to get out! They've got to find us right away! This is the tenth of September! Winter's only a jump away!"

"Take it easy, folks," soothed Red. "This party is too important not to be found right away. They'll have every plane in the Territory searching."

"If someone doesn't come today," said Tony slowly, "do you think we ought to try walking out?"

"Walking out!" Hope's voice and Kilkenny's eyebrows shot up.

"Damn poor idea if you're asking me," said Red promptly. "I've never been in this part of the country before. You haven't either, have you, Guy?" The Mayor shook his head. "By the time we fumble around these lakes and hills for a week or two, or three, Old Man Winter'll crackdown, and then where are we—with two girls, and no one but me dressed for the woods?"

"And we've got no guns," Guy Fletcher pointed out, "no way to kill game. We're hundreds of miles from anywhere. Eight people fresh from town, two of us women, three of us—" he glanced at the Senator and F. Millard, and struck his own pillowy chest "—not as young as we used to be."

"Besides," Red added, "when a search party comes—it's bound to be in a day or two—and we're not with our airplane, they're going to have one hell of a time finding eight little people on foot in a wooded country like this."

"Of course you Alaskans are right," agreed Senator Lee. "Walking is out of the question. Our best chance is to wait in the plane. We'll just hope they won't be long."

Red frowned. "Of course I might try walking. A man alone can go faster, and at least I've got shoepacks. But you folks will probably be back in Fairbluffs long before I get where I can send a message, though we might be playing safer."

"Nonsense!" Said the Senator briskly. "No reason for you to get caught by winter either. Besides, if we're stuck a few days, you might come in handy. Mayor Fletcher and you are the only Alaskans."

"How about me?" smiled Hope.

Red reached out a deep brown hand to ruffle her hair. "Guess you think you're a sourdough, Blondie, because you've been here a year."

But for all Red's cheerful grin, he took charge of the stranded picnic party in a very businesslike way. Just in case the rescue planes were delayed, he suggested they ration supplies. Adding the emergency rations from the plane, he also brought out fishing tackle and a rope, mourning the fact that the rifle he usually kept in the plane was at the gunsmith's for repairs, and that someone must have forgotten to return his emergency ax. But they probably wouldn't need a gun, he said comfortably, and one ax was enough; the man who cleared out had left his. While the Mayor expertly teased whitefish out of the lake; Hope and Kilkenny picked the remaining blueberries; the grocer, with the Senator's leaky fountain pen, inventoried the supplies they had found in the cabins; and Do-It-Now Lee impartially superintended and ranted about the delay—the three young men combed the woods for the prowler.

And always interrupting every activity, the face of each man and woman lifted to the sky, eyes raked it for planes, and ears strained for the drum of motors.

Just in case, Red said when they rationed supplies; just in case, when they cut fresh wild hay for each mattress; just in case, when they began to chop firewood. But two days passed and no plane came in sight. Red's "just in case" hit home.

The third day the cigarettes gave out, and Kilkenny's fuss was louder than her father's about his delayed report.

It was the fifth day that the Senator found the knife. "The granddaddy of all pocket knives," his daughter declared when he displayed the six-inch, horn-handled jackknife he'd unearthed in one of the cabins. Looking back later, F. Millard thought it unnecessarily ironic that the Senator should have been the one who found it.

About the same time F. Millard noticed that a change had come over Do-It-Now Lee. The Senator stopped yelling for plane service, he no longer joined the others in their hourly search of the sky and tabooed all mention of the overdue report. He spent hours rambling among the old cabins, and began, unaccountably, to look younger. In the middle of the day, when the sun was warm, he sat on the back step of the cabin that housed the supplies. There, in the days that followed, with no sign of the rescue plane, he gossiped and played mumblety-peg.

Red, Michael, and Hope were the chief runners-up for the knife-tossing title, though F. Millard made a close fourth. Mayor Fletcher, too, gave the old knife a frequent whirl, and traded brags with the bigger politician.

Only Kilkenny and Tony refused to play. They were the last to admit that a watched sky never boils rescue planes, and hunt for other occupation.

The day Senator Lee found the knife, the search for the mystery man was abandoned. "We've been tramping the hills five days," scowled Red, "and except for finding where he hid the first day, we haven't seen hide nor hair of him. I think he's cleared out. Maybe he just dumped our gas for cussedness to get even with our chasing him away."

F. Millard had no such hopes. As the days wore into a week, and the week slowly doubled, every time the logs popped or twigs snapped in the darkness, he considered all over again the staying power of the bureau in front of the door.

Then he found that the others had only been fooling themselves, that pretending the prowler had left the hills was only their way of whistling in the dark.

Two weeks after their arrival they were all sitting at breakfast in the boys' one-room cabin, which, being the largest, they used as a gathering place. Kilkenny pushed back her chair to refill the coffee cups. She stood for a minute with the pot in her hand, glancing around the table. Her voice, when she spoke, was strained. "Don't look now, but I see a bunch of tramps."

All seven leaped from their chairs to face the door.

The Senator's daughter laughed, but her laughter, too, was strained. "I don't mean literally. I'm talking about ourselves."

But F. Millard knew now how the others felt. They could no more dismiss the threat of the skulker's presence than he could. The man who had crippled their plane, even now probably hiding and watching, was as real to them all as he was to F. Millard.

"Just because we're stuck in the wilderness, do we have to go native?" Kilkenny was almost shrill. "There seems to be some of everything else in this metropolis. Didn't anyone find a razor?"

"Daughter," the Senator rumbled, "can't you find something better to do than criticize our appearance? Do anything—wash dishes—sweep the floor—but do it now!"

"If you hadn't been so 'Do-It-Now,'" she flared, "to get one prospector's goodwill, we wouldn't be here now!"

Sheepishly, the men ransacked the cabins. The early settlers, Michael remarked, must have run to beards. They went through cabin after cabin, finding stiffened leathers strops, but no razors. The Mayor finally came on an old-time, straight edged blade, rusted and age-spotted, beneath a rotting heap of red flannel underdrawers. F. Millard cut his chin, thinking about the strops, when they got the ancient blade sharp enough to use. Why were there half a dozen strops in the village, and only one razor?

The grocer had other things to consider too. He continued to watch and ponder the change in Senator Lee. It wasn't natural for such a man, at such a time of national crisis, to settle down with a kid's game on the back steps of a log cabin and be content to stay. What in the world could have happened? What could have caused the change?

The day after the shaving orgy the Senator got sick. He couldn't finish breakfast. He pushed his chair away from the table and went back to bed, his face almost purple, and his eyes unnaturally bright. His step, when he left the cabin, wavered like an old man's—the Senator, who was sixty-three years young.

Both girls spluttered after him. Hope came back in a little while, saying he'd been vomiting and seemed feverish and weak. The five men left at the table sought each others' eyes, and quickly averted their own.

That day their isolation rode on their very heels. Now they had a sick man to take care of, a sick man, and no doctor, no medicine, no knowledge of what to do. Still no speck appeared in the sky to grow into a plane, still no drone of motors could be heard above the village.

What if Guy Fletcher had guessed wrong about the fate of the settlers, F. Millard asked himself? What if no accident had carried them off? Could the Senator even now be coming down with typhoid, diphtheria, smallpox, or some mysterious plague? He wouldn't be the only victim. One by one the others would get purple in the face and strangely weak. One by one, until—when a rescue finally came, if it ever did, the village would have sunk once more into its ghostly silence. The little man shook himself. He hoped the girls didn't remember Fletcher's idle speculation.

The next day the congestion in the patient's face subsided, but violent cold symptoms developed. In terror of pneumonia, his seven companions, with fingers still crossed, persuaded him to rest a little longer.

Hope had taken cold shots before leaving Fairbluffs, and it was she, instead of Kilkenny, who became his nurse; Hope who spent hours plumping pillows, playing mumblety-peg with his big jackknife on a board, reading the few books they found in the cabins, trying to make tin plates of camp food look invalid dainty.

As his cold improved his other mumblety-peg cronies bent with him over the board on the bed, but his rest stretched on into days, and the Senator didn't get up. It was strange that it took him so long to get well, F. Millard thought. But he was getting well, wasn't he? He could see that nagging doubt in the others' eyes too. The Senator still had a cough, but he'd stopped his sneezing and blowing. He did look better. But if he really was better, why was a man like Do-It-Now Lee still in bed?

During his illness the northern lights began their winter witch dance, pale streamers at first like searchlight beams, deepening to red and green as the cold mounted. For the good weather had come to an end. F. Millard began to remember Guy Fletcher's terror of winter coming on. Sometimes like searchlight fingers, sometimes like writhing torches, or quivering scarves and curtains, the aurora raced across the night sky. And the day sky turned gray and heavy. The air was so knife sharp that the new residents of the village shivered in their overcoats. The creek froze. The lake froze. The plane's pontoons were now cemented to earth, and a hole had to be chopped in the ice to fish. The ground froze as hard as pavement, and a swooping, snatching wind screamed between the cabins. Winter was coming on, as Guy had said. This was just a sample. Winter was on the way, and the Senator still in bed, with blankets hung over every window to keep out the icy drafts.

The night he had been ill a week, a ten-minute spattering of snow as hard as pellets scratched the window panes and gave up before the wind that scooped it against walls and into corners. F. Millard had gone to his cabin early. Usually, he was the last to exchange the cozy hubbub of the boys' room for the unrestful quiet of his own. Guy Fletcher's snoring made it no less lonely. The first settlers, in their nightly sessions with F. Millard, didn't mind the snores at all, and the branch-snapping noises were louder. Lately the howling of the wind had added its eerie note. Tonight something had been wrong even with the boys' cabin. The Senator's protracted illness or the continued battering of the wind or the length of time they had been marooned had been getting on everyone's nerves. Tonight they didn't linger for gossip or a game with the old deck of cards. The few who sat down after dinner sat only for a minute and jumped up and went out again. No one person, by F. Millard's later tally, stayed in the house all evening. Neither did he. But coming in and out and jumping up and down, the choppy words that passed for conversation, at last upset him too. Briskly he walked from one end of the trail to the other, while northern lights played a wild crack-the-whip in the sky. He dropped in to see the Senator, tried once more to settle down in the boys' cabin, and finally giving up, stalked grumpily to his own.

Jamming a few more sticks into the stove, he stood over it, holding out his chilly hands and trying to keep his mind a pleasant blank. It wasn't so hard while the stove was glowing like this and the lamp lighted. But after dark, in bed—

The door behind him burst open and Guy Fletcher bounded in. "My God! My God, Smyth!" He cried. His overhanging cheeks were gray beneath black stubble, his small black eyes terror-wide. "He's dead!"

"Dead!" F. Millard gasped. "Who's dead? What are you talking about?"

Guy gulped twice before he could choke, "The Senator!"

F. Millard caught the back of the chair. "You mean he took a turn for the worse—and died?"

"No. He was killed."

"*Killed!*"

"Murdered—if you like that better."

Chapter Five

F. Millard was opening the door of the Senator's cabin before Guy Fletcher was halfway back across the street.

The room seemed full of people, but F. Millard's gaze went straight to Kilkenny. She stood with eyes squeezed shut, both hands clenched into fists. He looked hastily away and worked through the crowd to the bunk. Horror shriveled his stomach.

The Senator had been sitting up. Now he was doubled forward his face on top of the mumblety-peg board. From the side of his neck toward the back—the little man fought back nausea—protruded the big knife's horn handle. Blood stained the underwear he had used for pajamas, spread out in a blot on the blanket. But the blade had gone too deep for any telltale spurt to mark the murderer.

F. Millard clenched his own hands. "Didn't anyone catch him?"

Red Bailey shook his head. No name had been necessary. In everyone's mind "him" stood for the man in the hills.

"Who found him?" F. Millard demanded. Again, no name was necessary. All eyes turned to the bed and were hastily averted.

"I did," said Michael huskily. "I was coming in for a last game of mumblety-peg."

"Was everything the way it is now?" The little man's voice was suddenly alert, authoritative. "I'm not sticking my nose in someone else's business. A murder is everyone's business. We'll have to tell the marshal all about it if—*when* he comes, so the criminal can be punished."

"That's all right, Smyth," said Michael gently. "We appreciate your taking care of the job. No one's touched anything. The room looks just as it did when I found him."

Behind his thick-lensed glasses F. Millard surveyed the cabin. Blankets over the windows, the door to the girls' room propped shut with a rustic chair, the extra chairs for the Senator's visitors—the room was too full of people and furniture for a clear picture. His eyes found something white on the floor between the dead man's wide double bunk and the front door.

"Who dropped the handkerchief?" He demanded.

"It was here when I came in," Michael said. "I noticed it before I saw the Senator."

"It's evidence if the killer dropped it. Unless one of you did, just now." He picked it up and shook it open—a man's handkerchief, grayish from poor laundering, but unmistakably good linen—smeared with blood! "He—he must have used it to wipe off his hands after—afterward."

Was that an initial in the corner? F. Millard peered more closely, a nearsighted habit left over from a childhood without glasses. Once more his stomach contracted. He mustn't show emotion, he sternly reminded himself, just read the initial aloud. "Do any of you have a handkerchief embroidered with an 'R'?"

Each one refused to claim it. The little man pushed it quickly into his pocket. He steadied his voice. "I'll have to ask you to show me your hands."

"Show our hands!" Tony blustered. "What do you—"

"Say, fella," objected Red, "it wasn't one of us that killed the Senator."

"The man in the hills—" began Michael.

"Of course it must have been the man in the hills," agreed the little grocer, "but we'll have to tell the marshal we left no stone unturned... Look here, folks, didn't you just say you wanted me to take charge of the investigation?"

He waited. No one spoke.

"I'll admit I'm no detective, but none of you are either, and I've been reading detective stories ever since I could read. At least I know there ought to be one person at the head, and everyone should co-operate with him—if they want the case solved. You want it solved, don't you?"

Still no one spoke. Mutely, dazed, they stared at the little man.

"You want to be able to prove it's the fellow in the hills, don't you?" F. Millard asked slowly. "So none of you'll be suspected?"

At last the stunned silence was shattered by a murmur of assent.

"All right then," F. Millard stood as tall as he could. "I'm the detective. We'll begin by showing our hands. Let me see yours, Mayor Fletcher."

One by one they displayed their hands. The girls' and Tony's trembled as they held them out. The hands of the other three were as steady as a rock. None of them showed bloodstains.

F. Millard audibly released his breath and returned to his inspection of the room. It was then that he saw the watch, face down on the floor, a good five feet from the bunk. He scooped it up. "Isn't this the Senator's?"

Tony identified the watch he had seen come out of his boss's pockets so many times. Its hands had stopped at 9:24.

"9:24?" repeated Kilkenny sharply. F. Millard let himself look at her now, instead of trying not to. She was standing next to Hope, both girls ghastly white in the light of a kerosene lamp, but while Hope was white and shaking, the Senator's daughter was white and still, like a plaster of Paris woman. "I was in here at 9:15."

F. Millard swallowed. "You—you were?" He swallowed again. "Was everything all right then?"

"Da—My father was, if that's what you mean. But I felt there was something strange going on."

"Could you—could you tell us about it, Miss Lee?"

She drew a deep breath and for an instant shut her eyes. "I'd left Dad alone all evening, and knew it was time to put more wood in the fire unless someone had already done it. But with Da—my father in the condition he was I couldn't take any chances. I ran over here and reached for the latchstring—and couldn't find it. That scared me, and I pounded on the door and called. Dad's voice answered right away and told me to wait a minute. I was worried, so I listened very intently, but I didn't hear anything till he shuf—" her voice quivered "—shuffled across the floor and raised the latch. He had slipped his feet into shoes and thrown an overcoat over the underwear he slept in."

You say he opened the door. Was anyone else in the room? "

"No. That's what I couldn't understand. None of us ever pulled the latchstring except at night."

Was everything just as usual when you went in?"

"I didn't notice anything out of the ordinary. Of course, I mostly just looked at Dad. I did see he'd cleared off the table by his bed, and his watch and the cap of his fountain pen were lying on it. Since he was alright I just stayed long enough to put some more wood in the stove. And I pushed the latchstring back out."

"You say that it was 9:15?"

"Yes. I'd just looked at my watch. It gave me a jolt because I hadn't fixed the fire for quite a while."

Before he asked his next question, F. Millard hesitated. "Was the handkerchief on the floor when you came in?"

"I don't think so, or surely I'd have seen it. But I really didn't notice."

"Where was the mumblety-peg knife then, and the board?"

"On the chair where he always kept them when he wasn't playing, over near the bedroom door."

"You have to keep the bedroom door propped shut on account of the sag in the floor?"

"Yes. And I especially noticed it was fixed tonight because of the draft on—my father when it's open." Again her voice almost broke, but not quite.

"Was the door propped shut when you found him, Congressman O'Hara?"

"Yes. I was so excited I ran the wrong way and almost stumbled over the chair."

"What time was it?"

"Right after 9:30, not more than a minute or two."

A hush settled over the room. Mayor Fletcher broke it. "Miss Lee was here at 9:15—the watch stopped at 9:24—and just after 9:30 the Congressman came in and found him—dead."

Hope gave a muffled scream. "Oh, good Lord! Do we have to just stay here and talk? Can't anybody *do* anything?"

"Skip it, Hope," said Red gruffly. "What *can* we do?"

Silence again fell upon them all. As Red had observed, what could they do? Seven weaponless people—there had been eight—against a killer who knew the hills.

Michael stepped close to Kilkenny, though he didn't offer to touch her. "Won't you girls come away? There is nothing you can do."

For an instant she trembled before returning to inert plaster of Paris. "I don't like to leave him, by himself."

"Would—would you girls take our cabin?" F. Millard stammered. "And let us stay here tonight?"

"I'd like to be alone." That strange, controlled voice of hers made the little man want to cry.

"I'm sorry, Kilkenny." A time like this, F. Millard thought, was no time to notice that Red had stopped calling her Miss Lee, but he noticed it just the same. "I'm sorry, but we can't let anyone stay by himself, now, with this fellow loose in the woods."

"Darling—" that was Michael; this time he took her hand "—why don't you accept Mr. Smyth's offer? There are two bunks in the main room for you and Hope, and I'll sleep in the back room with the supplies. Then you won't be alone."

"But I want to be alone. Oh, well, all right—if that's the way it has to be. You can take me over, Mick."

Still holding her hand, he led her out. Hope followed.

The other four looked at each other. There was work to be done, and sorrowfully they did it.

When the Senator lay, long and straight, beneath a blanket, Red asked, "You're sure you don't mind staying, Smyth? Tony and I can bunk here if you'd rather."

"Oh, the Mayor and I won't mind," the little man said quickly. "We're so used to each other's snores we'd miss a change of tune. And I told Miss Lee I'd stay."

"Then I guess there's no use to hang around. We'll bury him tomorrow."

"Don't you think we ought to keep him a few days?" demurred the Mayor. "If a rescue party came—"

"We've been here three weeks, fella, and no rescue party's come yet." Red turned and walked out, with Tony at his heels.

"On which cheerful note," remarked the Mayor grimly, "we might as well go to bed."

The two men went into the girls' room, tying the door shut with a rope from the plane. The grocer climbed into the upper bunk with his clothes on and waited for Fletcher's snores. It seemed hours before they came. Maybe the Mayor was playing a waiting game too. Cautiously F. Millard pulled out the handkerchief he had found on the Senator's floor. In the darkness he raised it swiftly to his nose. Once more his stomach fluttered. He'd caught just the whiff, but now he knew it hadn't been imagination. The bloodstained handkerchief was strongly scented with Kilkenny Lee's perfume!

When the Mayor's rhythmic snoring began, F. Millard eased himself to the floor. Led by a crack of light, the groped his way to the door, untied the rope and squeezed through. Alone in the lighted room with the body of the Senator, he propped the chair against the bedroom door and leaned back for a moment on the wall.

The blanket at the windows served as a screen. Examining each one he found a small three-cornered tear in the blanket at the front window. Anyone out in the black night, with his eye to that hole, could watch what went on in the room. With a common pin from the back of his lapel where his mother had taught him to keep them, he pinned the snag together. He glanced at the front door. The latchstring was inside, as he and Guy had left it.

The room looked different, now that it was empty save for the still figure on the bunk and F. Millard in the middle of the floor, so very different that he stopped to reconsider each piece of furniture. The big corner bunk, of course, was just as it had been. He wished his eyes wouldn't keep returning to it. The stove was the same, except that the fire was low, as Red had told him to keep it, the wooden box beside it half-full. The two straight chairs were in their customary places, one holding the bedroom door shut, the other near it with the stained mumblety-peg board across it. One rocking chair stood in front of the bunk, the other at its foot. The lamp hung from the ceiling by a chain. F. Millard glanced briefly at the worn old suitcase the girls had found cleaning house. In it, the only receptacle with a lock in the village, he had put the mumblety-peg knife. The key was in his own pocket. Kilkenny—by rights the bloody handkerchief should be in the suitcase too. But no one had mentioned it when he put away the knife, and he prayed the perfume would evaporate before anyone remembered.

The handkerchief had been there—he dropped it between the head of the bunk and the door—and the watch over here. Tony had examined it and set it on the table. It was on the table now, the only object on the bare top. The books that the Senator had always stacked on the table were neatly arranged in two piles on the floor. The table hadn't been cleared for the mumblety-peg board; it had been in the Senator's lap when he—when someone—F. Millard returned by a detour—the board had been in his lap. Why had the books been moved? What had he used the table for?

The little man laid the watch on the floor where they had found it and sat down in a chair by the stove. Kilkenny had said the latchstring was in when she came to fix the fire. Had her father been doing something he didn't want discovered? Would it have any connection with the table being cleared? What could he have done with whatever he didn't want anyone to see before he let Kilkenny in?

Again F. Millard stared around the room: two straight chairs, two wooden rockers, a stove with a fire in it, one bare table. If the thing was small, he could have hidden it in the bedclothes; if very small, in his overcoat pocket; if it was large, he'd have had to shove it under the bed. He couldn't have put it in the girls' room, because it had been Kilkenny's voice at the door, and she might have gone into the bedroom—one place was eliminated. He knew there'd been nothing among the bedclothes when they arranged the body—another place eliminated. There was still the overcoat.

The Senator's suit had been hung in the girls' room after he got sick. Distasteful as it would be to go through a dead man's pockets, F. Miller thought again of the perfume on the handkerchief and steeled himself to do it. In the breast pocket were the Senator's pen with the cap screwed on, a map of Alaska, and notes on the mineral report; a handkerchief marked T. J. L. in one outside pocket; a pair of gloves in the other. Nothing for anyone to hide. That left only the space under the bunk, unless the murderer had taken the thing away.

Slowly the grocer approached the bed and got down on his hands and knees, slowly raised the edge of the blanket. He had no idea what he might find, except that it wouldn't be dirt; he'd brought water for the girls just yesterday, and when Kilkenny dropped her lipstick, and he retrieved it from under the bed, he'd seen, himself, how white the scrubbed floor gleamed in the last rays of the afternoon sun.

Reluctantly he put his head under and lighted a match. Nothing under the bunk—but there was! On the freshly scrubbed floor something dark caught his eyes. He reached, and his hand slid over smooth boards. He felt the place again. It wasn't something to pick up, but a stain in the boards themselves. It hadn't been there yesterday; he remembered the shining white wood. It was risky business, lighting matches under a bed, but murder was riskier business. With his hand he shielded the flame from the mattress and peered at the stain—a spot of fresh ink. Ink! If it had been blood—but this was ink!

Cautiously, still protecting the flame, he squinted at the floor, the wall, the bunk poles over his head. A tuft of fuzz was caught on a splintered pole. Dust accumulated fast in these decaying cabins, but this wasn't dust or blanket lint; it was threads, ravelings from some dark cloth. Flatfoot Flannagan had solved murders from nothing more than a smear of grease. Carefully F. Millard disengaged a few short threads. He'd better crawl out before cremation was added to murder.

Tossing the burnt matches into the stove, he took an envelope from his pocket and very gently slipped the threads inside. Could there possibly be anything else? If so, he must find it tonight. Tomorrow might be too late.

An ink spot on the floor, even if it was under the bed, certainly implied writing going on some place in the room. The table had been cleared off and the mumblety-peg board found in the Senator's lap. Probably he continued his writing on the board so he wouldn't have to sit up at the table. But if he had been writing, he wouldn't have been able to take away what he wrote, and F. Millard had already given the room a thorough search. A thorough search? He'd forgotten the books! A paper could be slipped in a book.

He squatted on the floor beside the piled-up books. From the next room came the whistling rumbles that proclaimed the Mayor still asleep. But his own snores might wake him up. F. Millard had to hurry. Not daring to skip a page he leafed rapidly through each volume. Short of paper as they were, the Senator might have written in the book itself.

During those flying minutes F. Millard forgot to feel queer, forgot the long, motionless shape beneath the blanket, the deserted, decaying cabins, and the man who skulked in the hills. For those minutes the stranded grocer from Four Corners was Flatfoot Flannagan's proxy.

Except for the inscriptions on the flyleaves no writing caught his gaze. But in the top book of the second stack he came across a small blotter, a crisscross of faded ink. Was it there to mark a place, or—

He held his breath while he turned the blotter over. On the other side—his heart thumped—leaping boldly through dim loops and scrawls, ran a line of fresh blue ink! If he had a mirror—but there wasn't time to get one now. He must hurry through the rest of the books before Guy Fletcher woke.

Involuntarily his spirits rose. You can't be really enraptured in a room with a murdered man, especially someone you've known, but he couldn't help a certain satisfaction as he kept meeting his favorite clues. The stopped watch, the dropped handkerchief, the ravelings, and now the blotter—frowned upon lately by *Flatfoot*, but all time-tested clues that F. Millard liked best. They had held his eyes on the printed page for many thrilling hours.

Finally, he closed the last book. He hadn't found a paper, but the blotter might be important. When those fresh, blue hieroglyphics turned into words in the mirror—excitedly he slipped the blotter into the envelope with the threads.

Creaking a little at the joints, he stood up. One more task remained, the most unpleasant. He must know if the Senator had done the writing, or someone else. Gritting his teeth he lifted the blanket and looked at the dead man's hands. On the second finger of the right hand was a smear of ink. Then the Senator had written something. What was it? And who had taken it away?

In the next room the snoring broke its rhythm. F. Millard shoved the envelope into his breast pocket, snatched up the handkerchief, and laid the watch back on the table. Gradually the rhythm smoothed and took up again it's full swing. But the little man had had his scare. Besides, he had collected every scrap of evidence he could. Now he must think it out.

He stuck the pin from the window blanket back in his lapel. As quietly as possible he removed the supporting chair from the bedroom door, slipped through, retied the rope, took off his outside clothes, and hoisted himself cautiously into the upper bunk.

Now was the time to think. But he lay there staring into the darkness, with his mind a jumble of words and pictures and flashes of almost-thought. What had the Senator written? Who had taken it away? Why was Kilkenny's perfume on the handkerchief, and whose was the handkerchief? What would he find on the blotter? If only he dared light the lamp and hold it to the mirror now. But he mustn't, with Guy Fletcher in the room. What was that ink spot doing under the bed? Could the ravelings have any connection with the murder? Why was the latchstring in when Kilkenny came to the door?

Now he remembered with bitter vividness that there was a dead man in the next room, that he and his companions were stranded in a remote, deserted settlement, that there was someone, probably a murderer, prowling through the hills. Guy's snores rolled out of the lower bunk, but something else was missing, some other sound he was used to. The wind! He didn't hear the screaming of the wind. Guy's snores stopped with a gurgle. In the strange, unnatural hush, death seems very near.

Chapter Six

The next morning F. Millard was late for breakfast. As he dressed, he thought of the room on the other side of the wall, where the Senator waited. With the bedroom door propped and the blankets at the windows—that tear—he slapped his head and knocked *Flatfoot* out of his pocket—the tear he pinned last night—the murderer might have peered through the hole to make sure the coast was clear. Some other curious observer might have seen something he didn't understand or was afraid to tell. With the spatter of snow last night—

F. Millard scooped up his magazine and dived for a window. The frozen ground still held a powdery white where the wind had filled depressions and flung the snow against walls. If there was snow beneath the front window—if the wind had stopped in time—there might be a track!

Quivering with excitement, F. Millard stepped outdoors. A thin scarf of snow lay beneath the Senator's window—and on it the prints of two shoes!

With trembling fingers F. Millard reached into his breast pocket, then withdrew his hand. He mustn't risk the precious envelope of clues even to draw a picture of the footprints. Besides, they might not be related to the murder. If he only knew when the wind stopped!

He pulled out *Flatfoot* and skimmed through it for a page not covered with print. At the end of a story he painstakingly copied the footprints—each wiggly, dim, concentric circle surrounding the faint star on the sole, the scattering of stars on the run-down heels—a man's shoe, medium-sized. *Flatfoot* would have to do for a measure too. He laid it beside the footprints— the length of a page, and about three inches more. He marked off the extra length on the same page with his drawings. Another line for width, and he straightened up. Now if he could get a ruler, and find out when the wind died down—

Someone called him to breakfast. He turned quickly, hoping his interest in the patch of snow had gone unnoticed.

No one had what could be called a hearty appetite for breakfast. They all wandered in at different times, sat down long enough to swallow some of Hope's coffee and biscuits, and hurried out. Even Kilkenny appeared for coffee, and crumbled a biscuit on her plate. She was as white and desperately controlled as she had been the night before. Hope's eyes were redder than hers. But she wasn't the kind to show her emotion in public, a girl like Kilkenny Lee. F. Millard thought of the perfume on the handkerchief. How could anyone else make a handkerchief smell like that? For that matter, how could Kilkenny after three weeks out in the wilds? Maybe girls carried perfume with them like lipstick, though he'd never smelled it on Hope. But Hope was more like ordinary people, more like himself, and maybe Red Bailey. Kilkenny was different, the femme fatale.

The day after her father had been killed wasn't the time to ask the Senator's daughter if she carried a bottle of perfume. Besides, F. Millard mustn't start speculation. But he had to ask two questions, and at the moment everyone was present.

"Has anyone seen a ruler? He began.

Two or three shook their heads. The others stared.

"There's a tape measure in the old work basket. I've been using," said Hope, "if that will do."

"Where is it?" He asked eagerly.

"In my—" she paused "—in the room where you slept last night."

Oh, dear, he hadn't meant to remind Kilkenny; still, he had to ask the next question. "Does anybody know what time the wind stopped last night?"

It was Kilkenny herself who answered. She looked up from her crumbled biscuit, and F. Millard saw there were no golden lights in her topaz eyes today; they were just dull brown. "I do," she said, her low-pitched voice as controlled as her haggard face. "It was between 9:15 and a few minutes later.

I felt a puff or two while I waited at the cabin for—for my father to let me in, but it was quiet as a church. That's why I could hear his steps. When I came out, after the few minutes it took to fix the fire, the wind had completely died down."

Died down—the wind wasn't the only moving thing that had stopped all motion soon after 9:15. F. Millard wondered how many of the others thought of that. But the wind—the wind had stopped just before the murder. Those tracks had been made some time last night. They might turn out to be clues. He pushed back his chair.

"Try to eat another biscuit, Mister Smyth," urged Hope.

He shook his head, stumbling over his own feet in his hurry to get out.

Red followed him to the door, his voice too low to carry across the room to Kilkenny. "We've got a fire built by that other grave to thaw out ground for the Senator."

F. Millard looked up questioningly.

"O'Hara and Webber and I took his body out before it got light this morning."

"Why, I didn't—"

Red gave a lopsided grin. "You were still asleep. Guy let us in. We wanted to get the Senator out of the cabin in case the girls had to go in."

F. Millard felt a flush creeping up his collar. What a fine detective he was! In his hurry to look for footprints, he hadn't even seen that the body was gone.

"We tore up some of those hand-sawed floorboards in a cabin down the hill," Red continued, "and made a coffin after daylight. We've got him there waiting till the ground thaws. You and Guy—"

Tony sauntered up to join them. Michael followed, and F. Millard saw both girls rise from the table.

Red saw them too. His speech quickened. "That devil isn't going to get away with this. Now it's too late, I admit we never should have stopped hunting. Well, we know now we have to get him. O'Hara and Webber and I—"

Tony stretched out his long legs, eying his oxfords and the expanse of thin sock between them and his trousers.

"Oh, I know you're not dressed for the woods," said Red impatiently, "But the snow won't hold off long. It's practically October, and when it settles down, we're stuck."

By now the girls had reached them.

"But after there's snow on the ground, all we'll have to do is track him," objected Tony.

"Track him!" snorted Red. "Once snow flies in this country, no man's going to get anywhere without skis or snowshoes."

"Then wouldn't he have to stay where he is, too?" F. Millard asked.

"That baby probably has skis *and* snowshoes," Red growled.

"I saw a pair of skis," put in Kilkenny listlessly, "on the rafters of the cabin down the street from the one with the provisions."

"You did!" Red shot through the door. "Wait a minute."

In five minutes, he was back, his eyes striking off blue sparks. "Now we *know* he has skis. He's beaten us to them."

Michael reached for his overcoat. "What are we waiting for?"

Just for you to get your legs covered, Mick. Are you coming Webber?"

"I—I'll come too," said F. Millard manfully.

"Look, Smyth," Red hesitated. "We can't leave the girls alone. Suppose you and Guy keep the home fires burning."

The pilot's words, intended to be cheerful, made F. Millard slightly sick. They were literally too true. But the fires were for a grave.

"What did you mean about covering Mick's legs?" asked Hope.

Red pointed to a heap of new canvas sacks they had found among the supplies. "He can pull those on over his shoes and tie them around his ankles and knees like mukluks. We can cut off strips for ties. Webber'd better wear them too. No one can stay out in this cold without protection.

As they started to work on the sacks, F. Millard turned back to the door. Once more he felt fingers pull at his sleeve and looked down at Hope who lifted a face like a distressed doll's.

"Are you going to—to his cabin, Mr. Smyth?"

F. Millard nodded impatiently. He'd wasted too much time now. The sun would soon melt the snow. Lucky he'd made a record of those tracks in his magazine.

"Then, please, Mr. Smyth, will you bring back our handbags? I do want to powder my nose, and I think the psychological effect of lipstick will be good for Kilkenny."

He nodded again and broke loose.

The house next door seemed a block away. A quick dash inside for the tape measure, and then—

He craned his neck as he hurried by the window—and skidded to a stop. Where the tracks had been was a patch of bare ground showing through the snow!

While he was in the house something—someone—had obliterated those tracks. In the place where they had been lay a branch as bare as a whip. Someone had brushed that branch back and forth till the snow was gone, someone who must not have realized the tracks were there till he was looking. One of the explanations advanced to account for the mystery man's wanting to keep the plane in the village had been that he recognized one of its passengers. The Senator, perhaps? Then might not one of the Senator's party have recognized the mystery man through the hole in the blanket, and fear for his own life if he told; fear enough to erase even the evidence of his presence at the peephole? Everyone except the girls had been in and out of the room while the grocer was eating breakfast. Perhaps the murderer himself, the mystery man – F. Millard highhandedly ignored the perfume on the handkerchief—had seen him examining the tracks and taken the desperate chance of returning to destroy them.

Slowly the little man turned toward the cabin he had left. Then he remembered Hope's request. Inside the Senator's cabin, with its significantly empty bunk, he found the girls' bags and started back up the hill. Kilkenny's bag—alligator hide to match her pumps—if she'd brought perfume with her, wouldn't she keep it in her bag? His fingers strayed to the catch. Then he shoved his hand into his pocket. He wouldn't spy on Kilkenny. When she had recovered from the shock of her father's death, he'd ask her openly and fairly about the perfume.

Back in the other cabin he found Michael and Tony tying the clumsy sacks on their legs. But this time the little grocer didn't feel so relegated to the ash can when the three young men started off. This time F. Millard had work of his own almost as important as theirs.

He could hardly wait to see them off, standing with the others in the bright, cold air, each with his head rigidly turned away from the slow smoke oozing from under flattened kerosene cans that threw the heat down on the ground—ground thawing for a new grave by the old one under the spruce. Above the smoke, above the spruce, under the curve of the hills, gleamed the newly white-washed mountains—cold, aloof, indifferent to human troubles.

When the girls and Guy started back to the boys' cabin, F. Millard muttered something about shaving and went on, trying to seem decently unhurried, toward the Senator's cabin.

Guy called and trotted after him. Oh, dear, was he going to come too? But what the Mayor urged in a hoarse half whisper was, "Don't be too long, Smyth. It isn't safe to stay alone."

With this warning echoing in his ears, he entered what he felt Flatfoot Flannagan would have called the "death cabin." The bedroom door stood open. There was no need now to keep it propped shut. F. Millard closed the front door and hastened through the first room. The packet of clues fairly tumbled out of his pocket on to the homemade bureau with the small mirror hanging above it. One last look at the loops and arcs and angles forming the line of fresh blue ink, then he held it up to the mirror. In the fading, sun-spotted glass three words stood out, distinct "and to my"; the rest of the line was a series of formless curves.

The little man leaned hard against the dresser. He laid the blotter almost on the glass, his cheek pressed close beside it, as if sheer force of will could drag more words from the blotter. But the broken snake track of new, dark ink maintained its illegible course across the desert of long-dead scrawls.

"And to my"—there was a devise-and-bequeath sound to those words. Could the Senator have been writing a will? "To my beloved daughter, Kilkenny Cordova Lee…and to my—" To my what? And what to my what?

Minute after minute passed while he worried his hair. At last, he began to shiver. He'd forgotten that they had let the fire go out; the cabin was already cold. His eyes traveled from the blotter in his hand to the envelope on the bureau. All done with mirrors—he'd been expecting a magician's trick when the blotter and a mirror came together. Well, maybe all magicians couldn't get rabbits out of hats. In his annoyance he wanted to throw the blotter away, but it had to be kept for evidence. And, after all, it had given him the idea that what the Senator wrote was a will. An idea though it might not be right.

He got up stiffly, filed the blotter in the envelope, and stood staring into the glass. The door into the other room, the Senator's bunk, and the outside door stared back. Suddenly he gripped the dresser. The outer door was beginning to open.

"Mr. Smyth," called a doubtful voice.

F. Millard jammed the envelope into his pocket and whirled to face the door.

Reluctantly, her step as uncertain as her voice, Hope's dainty figure appeared. Her eyes went straight to the Senator's bunk, swerved and found F. Millard soldered to the bureau in the bedroom. "O-oh," she drew a deep breath, "I'm so glad you're all right."

"You weren't worried, were you?"

"Oh, I—I suppose not, really, but after last night—" her words trailed off.

"There isn't any hot water here, is there?" she asked after a minute.

"Hot water?" he repeated stupidly.

"Yes. Weren't you going to shave?"

He remembered with a start. "Oh, my gracious, yes, of course. Now where did they leave that razor?"

He thought Hope looked at him oddly. After all, he'd said he was going to the cabin to shave. Goodness knew how long he'd been gone, and he hadn't yet found the razor. After the Senator got sick Tony's secretarial duties had been merged with a valet's. Too weak to shave himself, Thomas Jefferson Lee had still clung to his normal habits.

Hope's glance circled the room to the table where Tony had laid the razor after its final service to the Senator that morning. It lay in plain sight, the only thing on the table besides the broken watch. The books were still piled on the floor. Briefly her gaze touched F. Millard. Was it his imagination or did she take a backwards step toward the door?

"Oh—er—Mr. Smyth, Kilkenny said she thought we oughtn't to leave the suitcase with the –the knife in it alone in the cabin. She said we ought to take it to the other cabin where there's usually someone around. Would you mind bringing it back? I—I hate to touch it, even the suitcase."

He separated himself from the dresser and stood up very straight. Here was another lovely girl to protect, the only member of the party smaller than himself. He picked up the suitcase and heard the big mumblety-peg knife thud to the bottom. Something in his stomach thudded too.

Hope came back into the bedroom. "I'd better take my workbasket back with me. Kilkenny's snagged her suit. I never saw such ragged people as we're getting to be. I suppose it's these splintery old cabins and the homemade furniture. And then, of course, there are always branches and things outdoors."

"Are you the official mender?"

"I found the workbasket, so I seem to be elected."

While Hope chattered, F. Millard had been thinking of the ink spot under the bunk. How could ink have been dropped where it was—a big, round dot, like a splash? The Senator's fountain pen leaked—

Suddenly F. Millard stumbled. There was a way to account for that ink! He and Hope were just leaving the cabin; his stumble almost knocked the workbasket from her hands. He stammered an apology, and they hurried through the cold air to the next cabin. There might have been more than a paper and fountain pen under the bed while Kilkenny was in her father's room. There might have been a man!

That opened up a whole new field of speculation. If someone was under the bunk, it must have been someone the Senator knew, not the mystery man; no one would hide a stranger under his own bed. But wait! If the Senator's safety was threatened, he might have appeared to fall in with the other's plans, but being a man not easily intimidated, have intended to expose the fellow as soon as someone arrived. Then, when the person who came turned out to be his daughter, the Senator, in order to save her, had said nothing, and in the end had been killed.

Still, there was that other theory, that the stranger might not have been a stranger after all, at least not to the Senator. Oh, dear, it was very confusing. But one fact stood out clearly on the welter of conjecture like the line of fresh ink on the dim network on the blotter—someone must have been under the bed; the ink spot and the ravelings proved it!

Now he understood those bits of thread. He remembered his own difficulties in examining the ink spot with merely his head and shoulders under the bunk. No wonder that anyone going all the way under in a hurry, encumbered with an uncapped fountain pen and goodness knew what else, should have spilled a drop of ink on the floor. If he hadn't been in a hurry, he wouldn't have forgotten to cap the pen; Kilkenny wouldn't have seen the cap on the table, and there would have been no ink spot under the bed to start F. Millard's speculations. If he hadn't been in a hurry, he might not have caught his clothes on the splintery poles. That snag in somebody's clothes would be one means of identification. The three threads F. Millard had in the envelope were black.

Suddenly he raised his head and looked across the room at Hope, charmingly domestic with her sewing. She'd said Kilkenny snagged her suit—and Kilkenny's suit was black! F. Millard's heart dropped into his shoes. Then he took a firm grip on himself. The murderer was the mystery man. It was just coincidence that Kilkenny had torn her suit, as it was a coincidence that her perfume was on the bloody handkerchief. For the first time he thought about the clothes of the other members of the party: Hope wore a blue-green skirt that matched her heavy outer coat, and a black sweater; the Mayor wore black trousers with his gray sports jacket—he might as well say, F. Millard argued with himself, that Hope had torn her sweater or Guy his trousers under the Senator's bunk, as say that was how Kilkenny had torn her suit.

But her suit really was snagged. Well, maybe Hope and Guy's clothes were too.

He walked over to the side window where Hope sat. Kilkenny stood at the back window, her slim shoulders as straight as ever. She stood there, wordless, staring out of doors. Guy Fletcher overflowed the rustic rocker by the stove.

"It gets dark early these days," remarked F. Millard innocently. "Is it light enough, Miss Mullen, for you to sew on black?"

Hope held up the other girl's jacket. The snag, F. Millard saw, was on the shoulder. "I'll be able to finish it," she assured him, "but honestly, at the rate our clothes are going, if we aren't found pretty soon we'll have to wear what the ninety-eighters left."

"They ought to be becoming to you anyway." He smiled shyly. If she noticed his eyes running over her, she'd think he was admiring her curves. F. Millard blushed. He stepped farther to one side and his eyes traveled down her black sweater from the base of her honey-colored hair, up again—there! Right in the middle of the back of her sweater was a neat but unmistakable mend—so he could just as well say Hope had been the person under the bed as Kilkenny.

"Guy," he called to the Mayor, "come and see if you can make out anything moving on the hill. Your eyes are better than mine."

Hope jumped up too. Kilkenny didn't move. But it was Guy's black trousers that interested F. Millard. Almost at once he saw a snag on one rotund hip…. It could have been Guy who left the black threads on the bunk poles.

At last Kilkenny spoke from her window. "Here come the boys."

Michael, Tony, and Red tramped in dejectedly and made for the stove. The others didn't need to ask what luck they'd had.

"Of course we didn't find him," Tony scowled. "How could we see footprints on ground as hard as pavement?"

Hope's voice was barely audible. "Then we have to spend another night like this."

Michael blew on his hands. "I'll bet it's too cold to snow. Any takers?"

Red stared fixedly at the stove. When finally he looked up, his eyes, F. Millard noticed, sought Kilkenny first, but it was to Hope that he spoke. "No, we don't, Hope. We can't. I hate to suggest this; we won't be so comfortable.

But we can't run the risk of anything more happening. Are you all game to move into this cabin?"

For a moment no one spoke. Then Hope sighed, "Oh, I'd be so relieved."

"It's the biggest cabin except—" Red stopped. But no one would want to move into the Senator's cabin. "We've got four bunks here already. We can run up a few more tonight and hang blankets around those two in the corner for you girls."

"I'm for it," Mick said. "It would save a lot of wood chopping."

But first they had something else to do. The men went back outdoors. Red removed the tin reflector from the fire Guy had tended under the spruce. Then, with the old rusty picks and shovels they had found in the cabins, they dug a shallow grave for Thomas Jefferson Lee.

The girls joined the little procession that followed the crude coffin down the hill. The Senator, F. Millard reflected, was the first to leave the village. He raised his eyes to the crowding curves of wooded hills. For the living no trail had been blazed through that chaos of hills or broken through the snow of the ranges. But for the Senator, death broke trail.

When they turned at last from the high, rough mound by the sunken grave of the long-dead child, the men went into the woods to cut bunk poles, dragging white-barked, springy birch back to the cabin.

The four single bunks already in the cabin were built, head-to-head, in two diagonal corners. With the ax as their only constructing tool Red and Guy dovetailed frame poles for two more bunks in the corner nearest the door, and laid smaller, pliant poles across the frames for springs.

By the time the bunks were finished, Hope had dinner ready. Kilkenny made a pretense of eating with the others and insisted on washing dishes, with F. Millard and Red to dry them.

Hope's voice rose suddenly from across the room where she was spreading blankets on the new bunks. "Red, you've counted wrong. We're one bed short."

F. Millard looked at him sharply. The pilot polished a plate with excessive care.

"Two for Kilkenny and me in the far corner, "counted Hope, "two over there for Michael and Tony where they've been sleeping, two in the corner between—and one man out in the cold."

"I told him so," said Michael, "when we were cutting poles. He can't pretend it's poor mathematics."

"It hardly seemed worthwhile." Red picked up another plate. "I can sleep on the floor for one night."

Kilkenny let a dish slide back into the pan.

"Red! What do you mean?" cried Hope.

"Oh, well, all right." He laid down his towel and ran brown fingers through his rumpled copper-bright hair. "I can't help feeling responsible for you. If I hadn't brought you here we never would have been in this mess. If I'd stayed with the plane, no one could have drained the gas tank. If—"

For the first time in hours Kilkenny spoke, slowly, quietly. "What's done is done, Red. No use to look back and say 'if.' It was no more your fault than ours."

"Yes, it was. Guy was the only other sourdough. Hope's only been here a year. The rest of you were Cheechakos in my care, to take on a trip and bring back. And I fell down on the job.

"No, Red—"

"Yes, I did. I should have walked out and got help."

"Red, you couldn't!" cried Hope. "We're hundreds of miles from help.

"I should have started the day after we arrived. You'd have all been back in Fairbluffs by now."

"But we all thought—" began Michael.

"I know what we thought, Mick, because I thought it too—that a plane would come over any day, any hour. But it didn't. And now—"

"Listen, Red—" the Congressman's voice was strong and sure "—we talked it over and did what we thought was best. If you'd started out alone on foot, God knows where you'd be now, and the rest of us no better off; worse off, because we wouldn't have had you to help."

"You'll have to look out for them now, Mick, you and Guy and Smyth and Webber—because I've got to do what I should have done before."

"No... No, Red!" Hope caught his arm. "You can't walk out now! There'll be snow all through the mountains. It's going to snow here any day! You haven't skis. You can't! You'd never make it!"

For the first time in days F. Millard remembered that back in Fairbluffs, Hope had been Red's girlfriend.

Red kept his eyes on her hand. "Sorry, sugar, but I have to go."

Kilkenny came suddenly out of her trancelike state into pulsing life. "Red! Red! You can't go! You can't leave us—like Dad. We need you. I need you. I—I couldn't bear it."

With Hope's hand still on his arm, Red and Kilkenny met each other's eyes. "Please, Red," she said gently. "I—we really need you."

Michael swung abruptly across the room and stared through black glass into night.

"Couldn't we put it to a vote?" F. Millard suggested. "Would you let the majority rule?"

The majority ruled that Red should stay. Kilkenny lapsed once more into her apathy, and Hope got blankets ready for another bed, while the men went out with lanterns to cut more poles. But F. Millard didn't forget that scene in the cabin between Red and the Senator's daughter, and he knew that Michael remembered.

Chapter Seven

The next morning F. Millard woke in his new bunk to find the big room strangely dark. Red's bunk, at the foot of his, was empty.

The pilot stood by a window. "Well, it's caught up with us," he said. "If it keeps on coming down like this the fellow in the hills will have plenty of use for his skis."

F. Millard pattered to the window. The whole landscape seemed to be moving, tumbling over and over in downy, white fragments. On the untidy sod roof of the cabin across the road, snow was already piled a foot deep.

"I'm glad you're not starting out in this," he said impulsively.

"Me, too," admitted Red. "For several reasons."

Did those reasons, F. Millard wondered, have anything to do with Kilkenny Lee, or was Red thinking of Hope?

"A five-hundred-mile hike's not exactly a stroll when you run on to six feet of snow without snowshoes," remarked the pilot. "I figured I'd have to take along a couple of boards to ferry myself across drifts."

"You won't even be able to hunt for our man today, will you, Red, in the snow?"

Red tapped his fingers on the windowpane. "I think we'll have to try. It isn't deep enough yet to keep a man from walking. But at this rate, it soon will be."

Soon, chimed the words in F. Millard's brain, it will be too deep to walk.

"Want to come along?" invited Red.

The little man's heart gave a bounce. This time he wasn't to be left at home with the old men and the women.

It was Tony who stayed with Guy Fletcher and the girls. When Red announced that he and F. Millard were continuing the search, Michael gave him one brief, straight glance and said he'd go along; he didn't look at Kilkenny.

This time F. Millard, too, wore canvas bags tied on his feet and legs, and swaggered off with the fighters. He maintained the swagger while the village was in sight, but they hadn't gone a hundred yards before the falling snow blotted out the huddle of cabins. He and Michael and Red were like the only men in the world moving through a gray dream, and Michael and Red began to get too far away. He pulled at his makeshift mukluks and floundered faster.

They passed the dim white line that marked the trail to the creek and wove in and out among the trees.

The men stopped and F. Millard caught up. Red pointed to a blurred spruce clump on the hill. "That might be a cozy nook to keep out of the weather and overlook camp. I'll investigate." He parted the branches and disappeared.

"You go right, Smyth, and I'll go left," the Congressman suggested, "in case the fellow makes a break for it."

F. Millard settled his glasses and ploughed off to the right. But when he saw the branches shake off their burden of snow, it was only Red who backed out.

"No sale," said the pilot ruefully. "All I got was another rip in the pants."

Just below his sheepskin jacket was a jagged three-cornered tear. F. Millard bent forward. Red's breeches were plaid, black and dark green with a tiny thread of orange. Near the seam where they flared F. Millard saw another tear, small, on a wide line of black.... Black ravelings! Red Bailey's breeches could have left the threads on the Senator's bunk poles.

But why would an Alaskan pilot want to kill the Senator? Or why would the Mayor of Fairbluffs? Or a Fairbluffs schoolteacher? Would the Senator's own daughter want to kill him? Of course, she would inherit his property, unless there were other children—Kilkenny had said her mother was dead. Material gain was the greatest motive for killing in the world. The little man recoiled—not her own father—not Kilkenny Lee! There was still the mystery man, and some possible connection F. Millard hadn't discovered.

Red plunged on. Michael dropped back with F. Millard. The little man caught his sleeve. "Do you know if the Senator left much property?"

Michael started. He looked sharply at F. Millard. Then he said slowly and impressively, "Senator Lee was a very rich man."

F. Millard blinked.

"He had so much money," the Congressman continued, "that I had to work like hell to make a stake, so I could propose to his daughter."

"Oh," said the little man weakly. He had lost his taste for floundering in the snow. Still, he had never thought Kilkenny could be for him. Unimportant grocerymen nearly fifty-six years old didn't go about expecting beautiful girls to marry them. Michael O'Hara was a Congressman, and a nice young fellow, even if he was homely and only two inches taller than F. Millard. Anyway, Michael had only said he'd asked her, not what she'd answered. Maybe she'd refused him. And, engaged or not, she was still an orphaned girl who needed protection. If she didn't get it from her fiancé, he, F. Millard Smyth, would give it to her. He drew a long breath.

"Does the Senator have any other heirs?" he asked.

Michael's black brows came together. "Look here, Smyth—"

"I wouldn't suggest anything against her, Mr. O'Hara. Not against Miss Lee. You know that, don't you?"

The Irish blue eyes softened. "I don't believe you would at that. There's something about her, isn't there? By the way, she hasn't said 'yes' to me—yet."

They walked for a while in silence. But now the snow wasn't so heavy against F. Millard's legs.

"You wanted to know if there were any other heirs. Well, frankly, Smyth, I'm not sure."

"You're not *sure*? Are there any children missing? Did the Senator marry again?"

"He only *married* once. He has no heirs but Kilkenny, in the ordinary sense…. Look here, Smyth. I don't like to throw mud on a man's reputation, especially a dead man's."

"But it might be important," F. Millard cried, "and it's bound to come out. When a man's murdered there has to be an investigation.

"There's a rumor around, very hush-hush come re-election time, that the Senator has an illegitimate child."

"A grown child? A son?"

"Supposed to be older than Kilkenny. But I don't know if it's a son or a daughter. I don't know a damn thing, not even if the rumor's based on fact."

Michael stood on one foot to readjust his foot sacks, lost balance, and fell against a tree. When he righted himself, the low, prickly spruce branches held up his overcoat. F. Millard stared at Michael's jacket in fascinated horror.

The young Congressman freed his coat from the limb. "These clothes are the damnedest for the woods. Bailey's the only one who doesn't look like a fool outside the city limits. We'd better get going; he's out of sight.

The snow fell silently, relentlessly, in front, behind, on every side, shutting them off from the world. Half blindly F. Millard stumbled along the furrows Michael's feet ploughed in the snow. What the clinging spruce boughs exposed had shaken him. Michael wore a suit of mixed dark tweeds, mostly black. Michael O'Hara, who wanted to marry the Senator's heiress, had a snag in his dark tweed jacket.

Ahead, dim through the snowflakes, stood a man. What if it wasn't Red? Michael kept going. But the man was Red, waiting for them. And now F. Millard had four furrows to wallow in instead of two.

Red, Michael, Hope, Kilkenny, Guy—any one of them could have left black threads in the splintered pole beneath the Senator's bunk. F. Millard hadn't noticed Tony's clothes. Perhaps the secretary, too, must be added to the list. They were all so sure the murderer was the man who skulked in the hills. And so was he, F. Millard quickly assured himself; of course, the murderer was the mystery man. But why did they all have snags in their clothes? Why was Kilkenny's perfume on that unclaimed handkerchief? And why had those tracks been brushed away from beneath the Senator's window?

Once more, before they gave up the search, F. Millard spoke with Michael. This time the Congressman made the opportunity. His blurred figure leaning against a big, bare-branched alder gave the little grocer a start until he recognized Michael.

"I've been thinking," the Irishman began abruptly. "If you're trying to figure out about the Senator, perhaps there's something I should tell you. The other night, the night he was killed, I ran into something funny."

"Funny?" F. Millard repeated.

"Damn queer. I'd been out and came back through the woods. It was dark, but you know how your eyes get used to it, and when I came near enough to make out the cabins, I saw someone dodge behind the Senator's. He acted furtive, and, after all, we didn't know whether the fellow in the hills was still around or not, so I made a dash. He heard me and started to run, but I headed him off, and just as I grabbed, I saw it was Tony."

"Tony! What was he—?"

"That's what I wanted to know. He said he saw someone duck around the Senator's cabin and run. Tony said he was chasing him. But if you ask me, Tony acted a damn sight more like he was being chased."

F. Millard began to breathe faster. "Was that all you could get out of him?"

"Every word. It was right after that I found the Senator dead. I naturally supposed Tony'd seen the killer and tried to catch him. But today I got to thinking—" he stopped.

"What on earth were you doing out in the woods on a cold night like that, Congressman O'Hara?"

Michael's eyes suddenly sharpened. "Walking," he said briefly, and clamped hard jaws together.

After F. Millard went to bed, bone tired from his hours of floundering, he pondered the Congressman's words. The night of the Senator's death Tony Webber had been near the cabin, and run from, instead of chasing, a man who came out of the woods. That the man proved to be Michael didn't change the significance of Tony's flight. Congressman O'Hara's evening stroll, with the weather what it was, had its odd aspects too. Then there was the rumor of an illegitimate child.

Wild as the notion seemed, it might have been the Senator's natural son staying in the village, who had recognized his father and drained the gas to keep him there. That would explain Do-It-Now Lee's sudden content with his exile; why he had hidden the mystery man, if he had, under his bunk; even why he had been killed, if he made a will in his natural son's favor. But it might not have been a will the Senator wrote that night; perhaps that notion was as wild as the one about the mystery man's identity. "And to my—" might belong anywhere: "Send my old suits to the cleaner *and to my* tailor for mending"—"*and to my*self the idea has occurred that F. Millard Smyth may be nuts."

He flopped disgustedly on his side and went to sleep.

Chapter Eight

When F. Millard opened his eyes and stretched stiff muscles the next morning, the other men were up. Sunshine streamed in the windows, intensified a hundred times by the reflection on the snow.

A bronzed, flame-topped giant stood grinning by his bed. "Well, brother, want to come down to the plane—"

Every muscle screaming, F. Millard leaped to his feet. "The plane! Has it come?"

Red's grin vanished. "Sorry, fella. I didn't mean to raise false hopes. I just meant we'd better go down to our own plane and see if we can find it. This storm dumped five or six feet of snow on us. We'll have to get it off the plane so a search party can see it."

The little man sighed and reached for his glasses. This dazzling morning hadn't brought a rescue, only another day.

"Who said six feet of snow?" called Hope from behind the blankets that formed the girls' room.

"Come and see," Red shouted back. "We'll all help dig out the plane."

"But I'm only five feet two," objected Hope.

The pilot added softly to F. Millard, "It'll do Kilkenny good to get out in this swell air."

Michael and the grocer weren't the only ones thinking of Kilkenny. F. Millard sighed again.

They strained for gaiety on their progress to the plane. Down the road edged with snow-covered cabins as white and shapeless as a scallop of fungus bumps; down the trail through the blueberry patch where now only the tallest bushes made a smooth white swell, where the mounded grave and the sunken one were level and white; around the frosted loaf cake on the ridge that hid the lake; on over the snow-smothered ice to the mushroom that was the plane.

Watching unobtrusively, F. Millard saw Kilkenny trying not to blight the holiday atmosphere, trying to do her share of stamping snow as naturally as Hope, in the wake of the digging men. He could see Red and Michael pretending not to watch her too.

At the plane they made a wide clearing.

"The top's the main thing," said Red, "so they can see it from the air."

He heaved himself up on one wing. Tony stripped off his overcoat and swung up on the other. They were two of the best built men, thought F. Millard without envy, that he had ever seen.

Tony, in a dark tweed suit like Michael's, swung both arms and sent a huge stack of snow cascading over the side. F. Millard caught his breath. At the back of the secretary's shoulder seam was a gaping three-cornered hole. Tony, too, must be added to the list of persons who could have left black ravelings under the Senator's bunk.

That made it unanimous. Except himself, any one of the persons who had clambered into this plane for a holiday more than three weeks ago might have killed the Senator. They all had broken black threads in their clothes. F. Millard had smugly called himself "a symphony in gray" when he left the hotel—gray suit, gray coat gray hat, gray-streaked, mouse-colored hair. Now his color scheme gave him real reason for self-congratulation, all except the gray hairs. He glanced at Kilkenny's glistening black pompadour and sighed. For the first time he wondered what the mystery man wore. Would there be black in his clothes, too—black cloth, snagged?

As they shouldered their brush brooms to go back up the trail, F. Millard lengthened his stride beside Tony's. Of all the persons with whom he was stranded—including a Congressman, a Senator, and the Senator's beautiful daughter—only the Senator's secretary had a chilling effect on the grocer. F. Millard reminded himself that Tony had been the last to arrive at the cabin where they found the warm stove the first day, a Tony more out of breath than the people F. Millard had seen run up the hill. He remembered Michael's story about the night of the murder, of this correct young man dodging back of the Senator's cabin. The little grocer straightened his shoulders and addressed Tony's supercilious profile.

"How long have you been the Senator's secretary?"

Without turning his head, Tony answered, "Eight years."

"And you're how old now?"

"Nearly twenty-nine."

"Do you know the terms of his will?"

The secretary's profile looked haughtier than ever. "I really can't discuss his private affairs with strangers."

"You may have to one of these days—when we get to town." F. Millard paused, and added significantly, "It'll help our case if we have the information ready, when they catch the fellow in the hills."

At last, the secretary turned. His eyes held the expression F. Millard associated with mental arithmetic. "I'm as anxious to clear up this murder as you are, Smyth; more so, on account of my connection with Senator Lee. Perhaps you ought to know—the last will I saw, three years ago, left all his money to his daughter."

"Did he have any other relatives?"

"I really couldn't say."

F. Millard glanced sideways at the disapproving profile. No use asking Tony about an illegitimate child. The Senator's secretary had given his answer in advance.

"I imagine he's always been liberal with Kilkenny?" the grocer queried. "Made her a large allowance—all that sort of thing?"

"She had no allowance. Every penny she spent she had to come to the Senator for." Tony paused. "Of course, he might have made a new will."

"Why?"

"He might have wanted to establish a trust fund. And I must say I agree with him—now. Kilkenny was so—"

"Was she extravagant?"

"Washington, D.C.," began Tony loftily, "isn't Lost Village, Alaska. She had to dress well, and entertain, and ride, and play contract[1]. All those things take money. It wasn't those bills that made me agree—" he broke off.

"Then why did you agree with her father?" The grocer's quiet voice reflected none of his inner distress. Was he going to hear something about Kilkenny that would fit too well with the perfumed handkerchief?

"Don't misunderstand me, Smyth. I wouldn't dream of casting any aspersions on the Senator's daughter. I'm just telling you this to show that the Senator was justified in not letting her handle money, and because you've taken on the inquiry into his death. Two months ago, she asked me, as her father's secretary, for five thousand dollars cash—so she wouldn't have to run to her father, she said, for every little bill. I knew he'd insist on an itemized account, and I told her so. Finally, she admitted it was for contract debts."

"Contract debts!" F. Millard echoed.

"Her set doesn't play for a quarter a corner." Tony's smile was condescending. "But that seemed pretty steep to me. I told her I'd have to ask the Senator, and he demanded the names of the people she owed. She slammed out of the office but came back in a few days with a three thousand dollar bill from a clothing store. The Senator had me check and the actual bill was only a thousand. I checked her back bills then for a year (they'd been steadily getting larger) and found that for three months before she asked for that five thousand, the stores had been adding on a hundred here, two hundred there, even five hundred on one—it added up to fifteen hundred extra. You know how customers work that dodge, Smyth?"

F. Millard nodded miserably. He knew: back in Four Corners one of the spendthrift young women whose husband was strict had tried to get F. Millard to add on to the grocery bill. And Kilkenny, lovely Kilkenny Cordova Lee, had been reduced to such steps. A man with all the Senator's money—goodness knows, he hadn't looked tight. But five thousand dollars, and fifteen hundred before that—why had she wanted so much?

"She kept on trying it," said Tony, "up to the time we came on this trip. You'd think she'd finally give up."

Ah, Kilkenny, Kilkenny—her perfume on the handkerchief, and money the greatest motive for murder in the world! Like a robot, the grocer plodded on in the newly shoveled trail. In his heart there was no more warmth than in the cold sparkle of the sunlit snow, no more warmth than in the icy glitter of the far-away mountain slopes.

Tony glanced at him slyly. "You look as if the news hurts, Smyth." He laughed without amusement. "You've fallen too, I take it. They all fall for Kilkenny Cordova Lee."

F. Millard roused himself. He had something else to ask the secretary. "The night the Senator was killed, what did you see that made you run behind the cabin?"

Tony's ruddy face turned purple. "So Mick told you? I might have known it. Since I didn't catch the fellow, I thought there was no use crying over it."

"Tell me just what you saw."

"I was coming up the trail—"

"*Up* the trail? Where'd you been?"

"Just walking around. I felt restless that night."

How well F. Millard remembered that feeling the night of the murder!

"And I saw someone in front of the Senator's cabin, sort of hunched up at the window. If they hadn't all been covered with blankets, I'd have said he was a Peeping Tom."

"Did you get any idea of what he looked like?"

"Not the faintest. You know how dark it was. It was all I could do to make out a shape. But it was Mick that scared him away."

"Mick! I thought you said you chased the fellow."

"Well"—Tony hesitated—"as a matter of fact, the figure in front of the window looked so much like he was watching something, that I didn't start after him then. I cut back of the cabin to see if I could find a crack of light."

"And then Mick came out of the woods, and you ran away so you wouldn't be caught peeking!" finished the little man scornfully. "No wonder you didn't say anything! You didn't even try to catch the man at the window. You tried to get a peek too!"

"The Senator was my boss. I had a right to know what was going on."

"And so, the man, whoever he was, got away."

But it wasn't the man's escape, if Tony's story was true, or even the proof that the footprints had been made so near the time of the murder, that haunted F. Millard that day. It was knowing Kilkenny's sudden need of money. Kilkenny, who had sunk to padding bills; Kilkenny, whose perfume was on the bloody handkerchief.

One thing he accomplished in spite of his preoccupation. Unobtrusively he found out what each one had been doing the night of the murder; or at least he led the conversation in that direction and received some sort of answer, questioning each alone. Tony and Michael were already accounted for—unsatisfactorily. Red said he had spent the evening down at the plane hunting maps, producing the plane's broken flashlight as proof that at least he had been there long enough to get and break it. Hope said she had been walking, and though she said she'd been alone, F. Millard found himself wondering if Michael's mysterious stroll in the woods or Red's errand at the plane could have been connected with that walk. Guy Fletcher said he'd spent most of the evening in the boys' cabin except for a brisk turn or two on the trail, and Kilkenny made the same assertion for herself; Guy said he had been alone in the cabin, and Kilkenny said she had too. When Michael ran out of the Senator's cabin to tell of the murder, he had met or called to all the others, save F. Millard himself, on the trail.

When he went to bed that night the grocer was more bewildered than ever. He sat on his bunk without undressing, turning slowly over and over the contents of his change pocket as ideas churned in his mind. Mechanically his fingers recognized each key among the quarters and dimes: his store and house keys from Nebraska, the key with the tag to his room in the Fairbluffs hotel that he'd forgotten to leave at the desk, the little, rusty-feeling key to the suitcase that held the handkerchief and knife. He pulled them out and turned them over in his hand, looking without seeing. Someone yelled to put out the light. F. Millard automatically turned the wick down, blew out the lamp, and groped his way back to bed.

He spent a restless night. At what seemed his hundredth waking he had to have a drink; he couldn't wait till morning. Pulling on his trousers and slipping his feet in shoes, he again made his way to the lamp. His watch said half an hour to daylight. He stood by the water bucket, sipping slowly, once more turning over the keys. When he crawled back in bed he fell heavily to sleep.

He woke in broad daylight, the last man up, and hurried into trousers, his hand unconsciously seeking its former occupation. House key, store key, hotel key—one more, as soon as he could find it.

Instantly preoccupation vanished. The suitcase key was gone!

[1] Contract bridge, or bridge, is a trick-taking card game

Chapter Nine

F. Millard glared around the room. But no one looked at the little man standing by his bunk, fumbling in his pocket. Naturally, whoever stole the suitcase key wouldn't advertise it by watching F. Millard's reactions.

Guy Fletcher had the other bunk, head-to-head, in F. Millard's corner; Red's was equally close, the odd one, built at the foot of the grocer's. Michael and Tony had the two corner bunks to the left of the door, and the girls were diagonally across, on the grocer's right. Anyone, in that last half hour before light, while F. Millard was sleeping so soundly, could have slipped the key out of his pocket.

But, could whoever got the key have used it, in those few remaining minutes of darkness, with daylight so near and the room full of people?

The suitcase stood on a shelf above the washbasin. The towel hung beside it. Slowly F. Millard crossed the room, filled the tin basin, washed his face, and reached for the soggy towel. With a wide flourish he flipped it from the peg, and it landed on top of the suitcase. Stretching for the towel, he knocked off the bag, and heard the thud of the knife—whoever stole the key hadn't yet had a chance to use it. F. Millard drew a long breath and joined the others at breakfast.

No one hung back when Red reminded them that the frost must be swept off the plane. Everyone went to the caribou horns that hung by the door for coats and canvas mukluks.

They started down the trail. When they reached the last cabin, Michael turned back with an airy wave of his hand. F. Millard forced himself to keep on going with the others; it would never do for the Congressman to see he was being followed—Michael O'Hara, who had discovered the murder. What if it hadn't been a discovery, when he "found" the Senator dead?

A glance told him when the younger man entered the cabin. A few seconds more to give him time to look out of the window, then F. Millard, too, waved his hand and ran back up the trail.

When he burst through the door, he saw Michael bent over the open suitcase, lifting by a corner the bloody handkerchief.

"Trying to destroy the evidence, Congressman O'Hara?" F. Millard was proud of his own coolness, almost like Flatfoot Flannagan's.

Michael whirled. Color pumped to his face. "Why, I—I just wanted to look it over."

"I thought I was supposed to be the detective on the case." F. Millard swooped down on the little key in the rusty lock. "Just drop that handkerchief back in here, and I'll lock it up again."

The younger man's fingers slowly opened. The handkerchief fell into the bag. F. Millard turned the lock, shoved the key deep in his pocket, and put the suitcase back on the shelf.

"Fire would destroy fingerprints on the knife," he remarked. "Or were you planning to get rid of it completely?"

Michael's face darkened again, and his black brows meshed. "Look here, Smyth, you mustn't think—I wouldn't dream of taking the knife."

"Oh, you were just going to wipe it off and burn the handkerchief? Or perhaps you wouldn't dream of doing that—any more than you'd steal the key from my pocket?"

"Look here, Smyth," said the Congressman again. "I'm a lawyer, and I thought I'd better study the evidence. After all, you're a grocer; what would you know of legal matters?"

"Enough," returned F. Millard, "to know that anyone who'd steal the key to get the evidence to himself, instead of asking to see it in my presence, must have a mighty personal interest in the murder."

Michael batted his thick black lashes. Then he gave the older man a hard grin. "I didn't steal the key. I found it on the floor—where you dropped it—and you can't prove anything else!"

That was the trouble—F. Millard couldn't prove anything else. He knew very well the key hadn't dropped out of his pocket, but he could no more prove that Michael stole it than that the Congressman had intended to destroy the contents of the suitcase. He could only cut off a length of fishline to tie the key around his neck, and wait, hoping that time and the human formula would do the rest.

What was in the backs of their minds, he asked himself? Why had they all been so quick to fall in with his wish to take charge of the inquiry into the Senator's death, so ready to answer questions about the other members of the party, as long as it didn't involve themselves? Were they all co-operating for fear opposition would attract attention to themselves, or because they thought they could depend on him to muddle the case? Well, he set his jaw, he'd show them they could depend on him to solve it!

As the days crept slowly by, Kilkenny began to look more natural. She rejoined Michael, Tony, and Guy Fletcher at contract with the old deck of cards they had found and took her turn poring over the dozen worn books.

"It isn't fair" she complained, a week after the murder, "that out of the only twelve books here, three should be Bibles."

"And a hymnbook," chimed in Hope, "Plus a concordance."

Michael's eyes laughed. "You couldn't possibly deduce that the former villagers might have been a bit religious. Especially with *Stepping Heavenward* for light reading."

"Myself, I lean to *McGuffey's First Reader* and the *Primary Arithmetic*, grinned Red. "Nothing like a chance to brush up on your education."

"You kids are too irreverent," said the Mayor. "Those are all good books, especially the Bible and arithmetic."

"My sympathies are with the gal who wore the ruffled dress and had a couple of Marie Corelli's heart throbs hidden in her bureau." Kilkenny's determined smile was desperately pathetic to F. Millard. "*Thelma* and *Ardath* can almost make nineteen-forty-one hearts go pit-pat."

"Isn't it hell!" Tony burst out impulsively, circumspection for once discarded. "If it weren't for Bob Marshal's *Arctic Village* and that book on mineralogy, a fellow'd go crazy!"

"The mystery man's additions," F. Millard mused aloud. "But, as Congressman O'Hara said, the old books indicate something. We may never find out what happened to the people who used to live here, but at least we know they were religious."

"Do you suppose that's why only one girl wore flounces, and all the dresses were those drab, dark colors?" Hope's round blue eyes made her rosy face more doll-like than ever.

"Could be," the young Congressman smiled.

Kilkenny picked up one of the Bibles and began to ruffle its pages.

"How's for loaning me *Flatfoot*, Smyth? asked the Mayor. "Even if it has got a page missing. You wouldn't know how that happened, would you?"

F. Millard avoided Guy's bright black eyes; no one but himself could know that the page had been deliberately torn out, the page with the pictures and measurements of the footprints, now folded in the envelope with the ravelings and blotter.

"L-look!" Kilkenny gasped. "Here's a letter!"

Everyone jumped up, the grocer with a pounding heart. Could Kilkenny have found what he'd pawed through all those books for, the paper the Senator wrote? Flat between the pages of the Bible spread open on her lap lay an age-spotted sheet covered with faded writing.

F. Millard's pulse returned almost to normal. The Senator had only one Bible in his cabin. This must be one of the others.

"Listen!" cried Kilkenny. There was nothing faked now about her interest.

"July 3, 1899

    "Dear Sister:

    "Perhaps I shouldn't write this. Maybe it's complaining about the mercies of Providence, and about Henry, and the life he brought me to. But I can't help blaming this life for taking little Jud."

Kilkenny's breath caught. "That must be little Jud beside—beside my father." She steadied her voice and read on:

"If we hadn't had these privations, if he could have even had enough milk—no, I mustn't. It isn't fair to Henry.

"We're short of all food now. Henry sent some Indians to the post, but they haven't come back yet. Some way I don't trust this set of natives. Everyone laughs at me. I suppose I wasn't cut out for a pioneer woman. Or maybe it's little Jud's death. Maybe I really am getting queer. But it seems strange to me for Indians to have an Eskimo leader, and they haven't brought any squaws or children. Yet they've been unusually kind—taking over the hunting so our men can go on with their work, telling us where to find berries. It isn't their fault that game is scarce this year and the lake fished out (Even nature seems against us), though that many more mouths to feed helped fish it out. They've actually posted runners to bring back word of the salmon run.

"There's something I want to confess, Sister, knowing you'll understand, though many of our faith wouldn't. After little Jud left us, our isolation and all the conditions here nearly drove me out of my mind. I couldn't even take comfort in the Bible. Henry was worried half to death, and then one of our neighbors suggested that I learn to play cards. Don't be shocked, sister. She said her aunt lost all her family in a fire, and playing cards was all that saved her reason. She used to play with her aunt, and she taught Henry and me and her husband a game called whist. I know it sounds terrible, dear, but of course we don't play for money, and it's helped me. I know it has and pray God to forgive and bless those who are trying to help a bereaved mother keep her reason.

"I can't send this letter till the next time someone goes to the post. By then we should have our supplies and, God willing, I hope, a lot of smoked salmon, too. I'll have better news for you then. Will add more later."

But Henry's wife hadn't had better news for her sister. She hadn't added more later. The letter was never sent.

F. Millard wondered if that letter kept running through the others' minds as it ran through his own, crowding the Senator's murder for first place while they went about their daily tasks. There was a warning for the present in that echo from the past—this very lake on which they depended for food had once been fished out.

Clearing off the plane became as much a daily ritual as fishing. Each morning after breakfast, unless snow was actually falling, when even Red admitted they couldn't push it off as fast as it came down, all seven started out with brooms and shovels to keep the trail open. And each morning when the last of the snow or frost had been swept off the wings, and someone had chopped out the fishing hole and dropped in a line, their gaze raked the skies for a plane that didn't appear.

Time passed slowly, and yet the days were fairly full. Shoveling snow, cutting wood, carrying water, the everlasting cleaning and washing dishes and underwear, the niggardly cooking, all took time, but not the kind of time to occupy thought. The contract players shuffled and dealt till the old cards fuzzed at the edges. *Flatfoot* became as tattered as the old books. Hardly a day passed without some one's reviling F. Millard about the missing page. The story that couldn't be finished became the one everyone wanted to read. Questions were asked more sharply, answers were more tart in return.

Of the seven castaways, Guy Fletcher made the loudest outcry. He complained of the weather, of the work they had to do, of the incompetence of the aviators who hadn't found Red's plane. At first the others laughed uncomfortably, then they began to shush him and cover their ears with their hands, but when Guy loudly condemned Red for not having walked out for help ahead of the snow, Michael laid down the law.

"It was our own fault that Red didn't try walking out. And maybe our turning down his offers is all that keeps us from having his death on our conscience too. There'll be no more talk like this, Mayor Fletcher."

For hours Guy sulked by the stove, hunching his rocker close.

Before the middle of October walking had become limited to the path to the lake and the path to the creek and woodlot. All the rest of the exiles' world was buried in shoulder-deep snow. Red had been right when he said that first day of snow after the Senator's death might be their last in the woods. The snow kept up—days of snow, days of wind, and days of cold, bright sun, never a day of thaw.

But as day followed day Kilkenny grew more like herself. The morning finally came when F. Millard decided he could ask her one of the questions that had nagged him ever since the murder.

Michael was fishing that morning while the others stood around watching. Kilkenny's eyes sparkled when he pulled a flopping silver arc out of the ice.

It was good to see the golden sparkle back in her topaz eyes, good to see the gloss of her black hair against the snow, and the color the cold gave her cheeks. F. Millard sighed. It was hard to remember he wasn't as young as Michael and Red and Tony, that his interest in the Senator's daughter should be fatherly; in this case, business-like, too. He drew her farther up the trail and cleared his throat. "Would you mind, Miss Lee, if I asked you something?"

The sparkle disappeared from her eyes and the brilliant red from her cheeks. "Is it—necessary?"

In her suddenly whitened face, her eyes were as black as her hair, as black as the leafless branches waving above her head, mocking the upflung mountain range that cut off the civilized world. Was she thinking of her father? Of those strangely urgent debts? Or was it something else? F. Millard sighed again, and asked, "Do girls carry perfume around with them like lipsticks?"

For a minute she stared. Then her laughter rang over the snow. "Darling, what a question! Some do, and some don't. I do, as a matter of fact. In a tiny bottle in my handbag. I'll show you when we get to the cabin. And don't you know me well enough to call me Kilkenny? After all, we're living in the same house, and God knows how much longer we'll have to. I—I was afraid you were going to ask me—

"Look!" she interrupted herself. "Mick's caught another!" She pointed at the silver curved whitefish as if she hadn't seen five weeks of fishing or eaten five weeks' worth of fish.

As they watched, Hope stepped close to Michael and caught his arm. "Mick's beginning to notice Hope," said Kilkenny abruptly. "Have you seen them? It'd be a miracle if he didn't. She's making a dead set for him. I suppose it would be a good thing for him to forget me."

"How could he?" F. Millard exclaimed indignantly. "Why, even Red Bailey—"

Kilkenny smiled. Her skin had its natural hue again; her topaz eyes had recovered their golden glints. "He's sweet, isn't he? He reminds me of the cowboys on the ranch. I haven't known any one like him since I grew up. Let's go on back." She hurried in quick, graceful swoops toward the others, her smile embracing them all. "Today would be grand for skiing—" she stopped, and bit her lip.

F. Millard saw gravity descend on every face. Each one, he knew, remembered, as he did, that the prowler in the hills was the only one who had skis.

Red stopped that morning at the cabin with the supplies. "Well, folks, I hate to bring this up, but it's the middle of October. The stuff in this cache won't last forever. Someday we'll see a plane in them thar skies, but we've got no way of telling when."

"Hell, are you going to cut our ration again?" growled Guy.

But F. Millard drew a breath of relief. Those rapidly emptying shelves, to his grocer's eyes, had been alarming. He'd been afraid to talk for fear of starting a panic. But cutting down their ration was the only possible course.

That night it began to snow again.

Daylight showed snow still falling. It was hopeless to shovel the trail. The contract players picked up their cards right after breakfast. Hope, consistently refusing to play, kibitzed over Michael's shoulder. F. Millard took up his favorite stand by the window, staring out into the snow.

Red lounged over to join him. "So, you came to Alaska to see the country? What do you think of it now?"

Unconsciously F. Millard slipped back into his role of tourist, the inconspicuous, retired grocer from Nebraska, with the unbelievable luck to be asked on a picnic with a Senator. He smiled shyly. "I'm getting a different angle—what you might call an inside view."

Red's big hand fell with such hearty approval on F. Millard's shoulder that the little man rocked on his feet. "No one can say you're not a sport! I'd sure like to take you places. In a plane you can go in a few hours over ground it took my dad months to cover in ninety-eight. I'd like to show you how Eskimos live and take you up to Barrow. We could fly over Mt. McKinley, and I'd show you the Endicott Range."

F. Millard was lost again in boyhood dreams. Alaska, the land that beckoned, the land he'd had to absorb from travel books and adventure magazines! He was in it now—for a minute he forgot he couldn't get away— seeing Alaska as no tourist ever saw it.

"I'd show you fox islands to the Westward, and the sea where Bering crossed, the Kuskoquim and Kobuck, the ice pack in the Arctic, and Bristol Bay's platinum stampede."

F. Millard was breathing faster. The very names in this country were glamorous, the expressions these Alaskans used: "to the Westward," "the Interior," "Outside," "the freeze-up and the break-up"—glamorous to him, in the true, not the Hollywood, sense.

"—if we weren't stuck in this hellhole," finished Red.

The little man was jarred back to the present. He was in Alaska, all right, in where he couldn't get out. He felt almost guilty over his imaginary flight with Red, above the vast, exciting land. The strain of the murder and being stranded was harder on the others; F. Millard had work to do, the job of finding out and proving who killed the Senator.

"You're a great little guy, Smyth," beamed the pilot. "I'd like to call you by some other handle. Smyth isn't friendly enough. And Millard—well, if you'll excuse me, fella, it's kind of a sissy name—as bad as mine. Mom had me christened Vincent. Thank God I had red hair so I could get out of that. What's the F stand for in your name?"

Color surged up F. Millard's neck. He plunged his hands into his pockets. "I—I—my gracious, I can't tell you. It—it—"

"Worse than Millard, huh?" Red sympathized. "Tough luck. Suppose I call you Bud?"

F. Millard's clammy fingers, working among the matches in his pocket, closed on something else. Automatically he drew it out—a strip of mottled paper, torn and sloppily folded. Surprised, he began to unfold it. Inside, the paper was creamy tan with a line of cramped writing in pencil: *Ask Tony Webber—*

"Wh-what'd you say, Red?" He looked up from the paper.

"Suppose I call you Bud?"

*Ask Tony Webber—*eyes kept returning to those wobbly, penciled words. He looked up to see Red staring at the paper. Instinctively his hand closed. "You—you want to call me Bud? I'll be tickled to death."

The pilot looked at him curiously. "What's the matter, Bud? Put your finger in a bear trap?"

F. Millard grinned feebly while his thoughts ran in circles. "I—I made a list before I left Nebraska of some things I had to buy. And here I don't think of it again till I'm hundreds of miles from a store."

"And you weren't a professor either, were you, Bud, in that other life of yours, before you took the plane from Fairbluffs and landed on the lake?" the pilot smiled, but his keen blue eyes were on F. Millard's closed hand.

The grocer thrust it into his pocket. He stammered something he hoped made sense. Why was that note in his pocket? Who had put it there? How was he going to read it, with Red sticking closer than a brother, Hope wandering at large about the room, even the bridge players free to jump up at any moment? How did a man find privacy in a one-room cabin jammed with seven people, and the trails too deep for walking? But if he needed privacy to read the note, how much more had someone needed privacy to write it! Whoever wrote it had to be one of themselves. It was too far-fetched and wild to imagine the mystery man skiing down in a snow-blurred night and sneaking into a cabin filled with people to leave a note in anyone's pocket.

Standing by Red, staring into the falling snow, F. Millard's eyes fell on the butt of so many jokes, the little house in the back yard that took the place of plumbing—the only place in their intimate world where a man could be by himself.

But he mustn't rush right off. Red wasn't dumb. He'd accepted F. Millard's explanation pleasantly enough, but his eyes kept coming back to the jacket pocket with the little man's hand still in it.

Kilkenny called Red to the bridge table. The pilot had refused as persistently as Hope to learn contract, but they might want to change the game so the extra men could play. F. Millard went quickly for his overcoat and mukluks.

Wading through loose, fresh snow, gulping mouthfuls of air and snowflakes, he fought his way to the rough board door with the wooden catch that, for the moment, made him monarch of all he surveyed—all four square feet of floor space.

Not until he fastened the inside catch, did he dare pull out the note.

Ask Tony Webber why he isn't in the army.

What on earth? What difference would that make to anyone but Tony? Still, someone else was interested—whoever wrote the note. Had it been given to F. Millard to start something? Was it, for some reason obscure to him, intended to fan some smoldering ember into flame?

That was the first of what F. Millard came to call the "scandal notes."

Chapter Ten

Next morning F. Millard was the last to leave the cabin. Down the trail to the lake the three young men and the Mayor of Fairbluffs bent to the task of shoveling snow while behind them the girls tramped back and forth like mechanical dolls to pack the trail.

This was the first day since the Senator's illness that the weather had been warm enough for the men to leave off the tailored overcoats that looked so ridiculous in these primitive surroundings. The girls, F. Millard thought loyally, couldn't look ridiculous in anything. As a concession to the suddenly warm weather ("More snow," Guy had croakingly predicted as soon as he stepped outdoors), their coats hung open. Kilkenny's leopard skin and Hope's blue-green cloth fluttered like wings as they stamped.

Without the clumsy sacks, his feet felt strangely light. Glancing down he saw a woman's footprint—slim, high-arched, with a frivolous heel's tiny print—Kilkenny's shoes, of course. How like her to take advantage of the first break in the cold to discard her canvas too. The shoes that had made those small, muffled tracks must be Hope's, still prudently bagged. Here was a huge print all by itself that could only be Tony's or Red's. And this—F. Millard gasped—at the side of the trail where a fringe of new snow still remained was a replica of the track he had seen beneath the Senator's window: the wiggly concentric circles, the star in the center, the scattered stars on the heel!

Head lowered like a dog on a scent, he rushed about looking for more. In another fringe of new snow, he found one. That was all.

Ever since the morning he saw those tracks F. Millard had maintained an unobtrusive watch. But ever since that morning the ground had been so deep in snow and the air so bitterly cold that no one except Red in his shoepacks had been able to go outdoors without mukluks. The grocer couldn't ask to look at the bottoms of everyone's shoes or get up at night and light matches to examine them, without starting speculation. And when a man crossed his legs, by the time F. Millard got near enough for his nearsighted eyes, even aided by glasses, to make out more than the clearest markings, the other had changed his position.

Now here were the tracks again. Were they made by one of themselves—or had the skulker come back?

Both tracks were at right angles to the trail—F. Millard's head flew up— pointing toward the cabin that housed the supplies! What about their precious food? Would the mystery man—?

Tearing to the storehouse, he wrenched open the door. His practiced eyes flew over the shelves. He groaned. Can after can was gone—a sack of flour—a sack of beans—

He raced to the open door, shouting. Down by the spur Kilkenny looked back—Michael—Red. F. Millard wind-milled his arms, yelled again. Red began to run. The others streamed behind.

When they arrived, F. Millard could only stutter. "The f-food—he came back—look!"

They crowded into the little storeroom.

Red lunged to the back door and jerked it open—across the glistening snow-filled hollow that dipped away from the door and on into the woods led smooth, shining ski-track ribbons. Two coming, two going.

"God!" the pilot exploded. "If we only had skis too!"

Suddenly a dark streak shot past him, leaping into the snow. Then it was just a black dot floundering, head up, arms flailing like a swimmer's, fists doubled for a fight. "I'll get him! I'll follow those tracks! I'll—" Michael O'Hara choked on a mouthful of snow.

"Mick!" screamed Hope.

"Don't be an idiot, boy!" Guy Fletcher roared. "You'll get pneumonia. Do you want to make us more trouble?"

Michael raised both fists above the snow and shook them at the shining tracks, his face flaming red against the flat expanse of white. Then, as sharply as he'd leaped, he turned and floundered back.

Standing by the stove he shook himself like a dog coming out of the ocean. "God, I'm a damn fool," he mumbled. "Made a holy show of myself. If it did any good, I wouldn't care—but, my God, what can we do against a man on skis—in all this snow?

"That's just it," said Red. "He knew he was safe."

"Those tracks lead right to him," muttered Tony. He looked dazed. "And we can't follow."

F. Millard had had longer than the others to recover. "I thought our supplies were going fast! The fellow must have stolen dribbles, just enough to get along on, so we wouldn't be suspicious, and waited for the snow to get too deep for us—and slid in and loaded up."

"Slid in' is right," said Tony gruffly.

"And 'loaded up' is right," snarled Guy.

"We'll move it to the other cabin," Red announced.

"To—to the cabin where we live?" Hope began to giggle hysterically. "It's jammed to the hatches now."

"And a damn good thing!" returned Red. "Here, Hope, you take the rice. Can you carry the beans, Kilkenny? Come on gang, before that guy comes back and cleans us out."

With their arms as full as they could heap them, the seven people crossed the trail to the communal cabin. Dumping their loads, they hurried back for more, leaving the grocer to sort and rearrange.

It was nearly noon before he was through. If the room had seemed full before, now it was overflowing. Along every wall, wherever there wasn't a bunk, were stacked cases of kerosene and canned goods, sacks and cartons of food and supplies. F. Millard felt choked, as if he hadn't air enough to breathe, and yet when he glanced around the room, he found that only Guy and himself were left in it.

He stepped to the door. Hope and Michael were strolling up the hill. Far down the trail, almost at the hogback, he could see Kilkenny and Red throwing snowballs at each other. Faintly, through the still air, he heard Kilkenny laugh. Perhaps it wasn't just fresh air these two couples were looking for. To F. Millard Smyth came the unwelcome sensation of being elderly and lonesome.

He fumbled for a flick of *Flatfoot's* pages and felt better. What time did detectives have for romance? Now, while the weather was warm enough to leave off mukluks, was the time to check up on footprints.

A metallic clunk made him peer around the corner of the cabin. Tony was coming up the hill from the creek with two full water buckets, swinging them the way the grocer would if they were empty.

The little man stood watching. Tony Webber was a funny bunch of contradictions. He never shirked his share of work, apparently seeking to exert his splendid muscles. And yet, the night of the murder, instead of chasing whoever it was that he saw at the Senator's window, he had run behind the cabin himself, and the day after the murder he had tried to get out of searching for the skulker.

F. Millard's thoughts returned to the night of the murder. Michael said he had seen no one else around the cabin. Tony could have invented that figure at the window. Tony himself could have come out of the cabin and dodged behind it, in the hope that he hadn't been seen. But if that were the case, why had Michael stolen the suitcase key?

"Give you a hand with the buckets?" F. Millard offered politely.

Tony came up beside him and set the buckets down. He looked at the little man the way a greyhound looks at a terrier puppy. "Thanks, I can make it."

"I've often wondered," the grocer remarked, "how a fellow with muscles like yours ever came to waste them in an office."

"I wanted to go into the diplomatic service, and a connection with a senator seemed a good first step. I never got beyond it."

Bitterness in Tony's voice—he'd been with Do-It-Now Lee eight years and was no nearer his goal. Ever since he was twenty-one—was that significant? Tony was older than Kilkenny, as tall as her father—what if the Senator had decided to do something for his natural son when the boy reached twenty-one, taken him into his office—?

"Have—have you always lived in Washington, Tony?" F. Millard tried not to sound overeager.

Kilkenny and Red were nearer now, coming up the trail in spurts and dashes with a shower of snowballs and laughter.

"Always," Tony replied. "My great-grandfather used to be important there. His son—well, he lost all the money, and my mother had nothing but tradition to bring me up on."

"And your—your father?"

"He died before I was born. Mother and her sister had it all to do themselves. I've sometimes wondered if there'd been a man around the house instead of just two 'decayed gentlewomen'—"

F. Millard wondered too. That didn't sound like the kind of family tree with an illegitimate offshoot. And yet sometimes—

The scandal note dangled before the grocer's mental eye: *Ask Tony Webber why he isn't in the army.* "You've been lucky your work hasn't been interrupted by the draft."

Tony glanced down at him sharply. A mask slid over his face. "Not so lucky when you know the reason. My number was called, and the draft board turned me down."

"Turned you down! A grand specimen like you?"

Tony's ruddy skin darkened. "It's—my heart. They wouldn't take me."

Then he swung up both buckets and stalked on to the cabin.

F. Millard stared after the muscular figure, the long, strong arms lightly swinging the five-gallon buckets. He remembered how his own mother used to creep upstairs the last few years of her life and thought of Tony running up the trail from the lake, shoveling snow, chopping wood, tearing with his pick at the frozen sides of the senator's grave. Tony—with a bad heart?

Beyond the cabins the close hills watched, hills that fenced them in. Hills, and more hills, mountains. Slowly F. Millard swung toward the east where the range of jagged, unscalable spikes topped civilization's stone wall.

Bim! Something hit his shoulder. He whirled—and looked into Kilkenny's laughing face as she stood with arm upraised to throw another snowball. "Come on and play," she invited.

Behind her, Red's smile was only polite, not welcoming. Red believed that three was a crowd. And, so it was. F. Millard sighed. Besides, he had to check those footprints while the weather gave him a chance. He shook his head and watched them hurry on. There was no one like Kilkenny. He sighed again and bent his head toward the tracks. Those lovely, slim soles with such absurd heels! Kilkenny—F. Millard straightened. It was his job to find out who had killed her father and protect her from suspicion!

Red's shoes didn't make the pattern he was looking for. Anyway, they were too large, and so were Tony's. The grocer glanced down the trail to the creek up which Tony had just come with the water buckets.

Michael and Hope were abreast of him now, still sauntering.

"You must think it's summer," said the Congressman, "standing in the snow like that."

Hope smiled and said nothing.

"Better walk along with us and start your circulation," Michael suggested.

Hope's smile chilled. She didn't want F. Millard to make a third, any more than Red had. Well, she could set her mind at rest; all F. Millard wanted was a look at Michael's footprints. He waved them on and had his look.

The tracks beneath the Senator's window had not been made by Mick's shoes. They were near the size, but the soles were plain. Hope, he noticed, had taken off her canvas mukluks. The small tracks of her sensible shoes marched along by Michael's.

Of the men in their party, that left only Guy Fletcher. F. Millard turned back to the cabin.

But he couldn't coax Guy to come out. The fat Mayor sat by the stove in his favorite rustic rocker. "I've known men mush dogs at seventy-two below and get pneumonia and die when the thermometer went up to freezing," he declared. "That's the trouble with you Cheechakos, as soon as it warms up—"

Leaving Guy and Tony wrangling, F. Millard stepped back outdoors and walked up and down the trail. The mystery man had made another foray on the village. How long before he'd come again? How long could they live on the supplies he had left and the fish they could get from the lake? It was lucky for them that the storehouse shelves had once been crammed so full. Why had there been so much? Would a man want to stay here a year? How much longer would they themselves have to stay? There were eight of them when they came; now there were seven. When some cruising plane or wandering trapper finally found them, how many would be left?

He shivered. Something soft touched his face. Snow! More snow! How much longer were they going to be buried in this ever-deepening snow—with a dead man—and a killer?

Chapter Eleven

That night as Kilkenny, Michael, Tony, and Guy settled down to their evening's contract, the girl grimaced at the frayed, greasy cards. "Once we start playing, I forget about it, but every time I first pick up these cards, the room is filled with ghosts."

F. Millard turned quickly from the dark window where he'd been staring into the night. Hope looked up from her mending in Guy's favorite rocker by the stove. Red stopped his incessant pacing.

"I keep seeing these cards the way we found them, all laid out for whist, with the hands thrown down and the chairs pushed back. And the people—the people who jumped up in such a hurry—and never came back to finish the game."

F. Millard shivered.

"What do you suppose could have happened?" Hope again voiced the question they'd asked so many times.

"The place is cursed," Guy Fletcher croaked.

F. Millard jumped.

"Damned if I don't agree," said Red morosely. "This is a bad year for ptarmigan and rabbits all over Alaska, but we've hardly seen one since we've been here, and couldn't coax them into a snare. We haven't seen a porcupine. Since snow fell, the squirrels have gone; even the chickadees avoid this place. It sure looks cursed to me."

"What did you mean, Mayor Fletcher," the Congressman asked abruptly, "when you said the place is cursed?"

The fat man's answer was indirect. "Natives avoid a place they think's cursed. Why else didn't they move in and make it a native village?"

"There's one man the curse doesn't bother," said F. Millard. "The fellow who was here when we came was prepared to stay a long time, judging by his supplies." He turned to Michael. "Did you find anything, Mick, while you were hunting the mystery man that could possibly account for his interest in this place?"

The Congressman's mouth opened, then suddenly shut. He threw back his black head and laughed. "Maybe he's a long-lost child of the village come back to find out what happened to papa."

"He's a little late, "smiled Hope.

"One damn mystery after another," said Tony crossly. Then he, too, stopped abruptly.

Tony must have remembered the other mystery, F. Millard thought, the one so close to them all—the murder of the Senator. No wonder Tony stopped. But why had Michael?

"What about gold, Mick?" the grocer persisted. "Any evidence of a big strike?"

"No big strike, hardly a strike at all. There was one old shaft, but believe me, the pay dirt I took out wouldn't pay an office boy. But there's plenty about this place that looks queer to me." Michael leaned forward alertly. "Do you think there's any significance in our finding no guns and only one knife and razor in all these cabins? And the only ax was new?"

"But who would it be significant about," Kilkenny asked, "the mystery man, or the first settlers?"

Tony smoothed his already smooth blond hair. "That's another thing we don't know," he said glumly.

"I keep wondering," F. Millard muttered, "if there could be any connection."

"Between the mystery man and the first settlers?"

"Yes. I don't mean between their sudden departure—disappearance—whatever you want to call it, and the man who's here now. That's almost too much to expect. But do you suppose the people who built this village and the mystery man came for the same purpose?"

"I don't get you," said Guy.

"Suppose this is very rich ground—" the little man watched Michael "—even if Mick didn't find it out. Gold was the lure that brought stampeders to Alaska. If gold made this settlement, perhaps it brought the man who's hiding now."

Michael's eyes were very bright, but he didn't change expression.

"It's possible," said Guy, "but sure as hell not probable. There've been too many prospectors wandering around Alaska to let that much gold get by. Guess again, Mr. Detective."

"It's enough to give you the creeps when you get to thinking about it—just how much we don't know," Kilkenny said thoughtfully. "Why this settlement was made, and why it was deserted. Why the mystery man is here, and why he wanted to keep us here. Why—" she paused, then went on bravely "—why he had it in for my father. We don't even know what's going on in the world. We may be in the war."

"I'm glad Russia put in with England before we got marooned," said Hope. "It's pretty close to Alaska."

"So's Japan," said Michael.

"Pooh!" said the Mayor. "Japan would never dare to attack the United States. It's Germany we have to think of."

"I wonder what Congress is doing," mused Kilkenny.

"I thought you didn't like politics," Hope murmured.

"I don't. But that doesn't mean I'm not interested in the world. At least while Dad was in Washington, I knew what was going on."

"It's the middle of October," said Michael. "Hitler may have taken Moscow, or he may be getting a dose of Napoleon's medicine. We may be in the war. And yet we—we seven people in this God-forsaken sink between the hills—don't know any more about it than the bears in their winter sleep."

Gloom settled over the room, a stronger sense of frustration and isolation than F. Millard had felt since the Senator's death. He could hear the watch that had been his father's ticking in his pocket. The unnatural brilliance was gone from Michael's eyes, his heavy brows were one straight, black line of concentration above his blunt nose. Kilkenny's face was hidden by her hands. The Mayor drummed on the table. Tony, Hope, and Red stared into space.

Hope finally broke the spell. She sighed and picked up her sewing. "Well, there's no way we can find out—yet. We'll just have to wait and think harder than ever about what's going on here to make up for it."

"You wouldn't pull a Pollyanna on us, would you, Hope?" asked Red ironically.

The blonde girl flushed. "I was thinking about the mystery man."

"A subject well calculated to raise our flagging spirits." F. Millard's grin was wry.

Hope turned toward him. "What you just said about some connection between the mystery man and the first settlers—there could be one! I mean between their disappearance and the—Senator's death. This very man could have scared them away, and now he's trying it on us. Suppose he was young when they were here, in his early twenties. He wouldn't have to be much over sixty now. It must have happened somewhere around ninety-nine."

Red grinned. "You mean he's been living here all that time, a white-bearded lunatic by now, ready to scare off the second batch of intruders?"

"You understand, don't you, Mr. Smyth?" she appealed to F. Millard. "Someone with some strange obsession—?"

"I might agree with you," the little man hesitated, "if our gas tanks hadn't been drained. Surely no one trying to keep people away would deliberately force us to stay in the place he wanted to keep us away from."

Red grinned again. "You can't argue with a reader of *Flatfoot*, Hope."

"And besides," F. Millard added, "all the supplies were new. I've been in groceries too long not to recognize old canned goods and sacked stuff. All that was new. And there were all those new canvas bags we used for mukluks. And the ax was new, as Mick said."

"Looks like you're outvoted, Hope," said Red. "What about this curse Guy's been harping on?"

"I'll bite," Michael volunteered. "What about it?"

"Would the Indians think this place was cursed," the pilot asked, "if there was just one old man to haunt it, even if he's crazy?"

"It would be enough for me," said Kilkenny. "I don't know about the

Indians."

Red laughed. "I've lived in this country ever since I was born, and Guy was a ninety-eighter, but from all I've heard and what he says, it would take more than one lunatic to keep Indians away from a village with board floors and good bark-lined roofs like this. There's an ancient native battleground to the Westward where many people were killed. Now that's cursed ground to an Indian!"

"Well?" retorted Hope.

"What do you mean, 'well,' in that tone of voice, Hope Mullen?" Red bristled. "What sort of bloody wars do you think were fought here—with five cabins still standing, and clothes still hanging on the walls?"

"I didn't say wars. Wouldn't any mass killing be enough? With nine cabins here once, there must have been quite a few people. What became of them?" She stopped to catch her breath. "How do we know they weren't killed?"

Now it was F. Millard who caught his breath.

Red hooted. "You've been reading the wrong kind of books for a schoolteacher. Look, Hope, figure it out for yourself: nine cabins, eighteen or twenty people—one crazy man. Even if he was younger then, how in the name of God could one man kill off twenty people by himself?"

"Who said he was by himself? Maybe he had help. How about those Indians the letter spoke of?"

"Look, Hope—" Red wasn't a patient man, "—we started this argument on the theory that this guy's obsessed to keep people away. Well, a guy like that isn't getting help, or wanting it. It's people he wants to get away from, not go into partnership with."

"Then maybe he didn't have help. He could still have got rid of them—some way… Couldn't he, Mr. Smyth?"

"The lady ought to have the last word, Red," said F. Millard gallantly. "Besides, she might be right. It doesn't look reasonable. It hardly looks possible. And yet—some way, as Hope says, it might have happened."

Everyone was still. To the little man there was the same quality in the atmosphere of the cabin he had felt within himself, a sense of suspended breath.

Into the hush, like pebbles flung into a lake, fell Hope's next words. "Some way he got rid of them. And now he's begun on us."

F. Millard heard a gasp from someone and a sigh from someone else. Then finally Kilkenny's voice:

"There's one thing we must give the mystery man credit for, one thing that ought to make us most grateful. His hiding in the hills keeps us from being suspected—of murder."

"You mean—the Senator?" gasped Hope.

Tony's voice, sharp, almost shrill, rang through the room: "They won't suspect any of us, will they?"

All eyes turned to F. Millard, fastened on him, clung. The room was still again. This time with the hush of fear—hereditary fear—the fear of the hunted for the hunter.

The little man's own heart was pounding. His voice, when he could make it come, must be natural. He mustn't let them think he suspected any of them.

"Don't you see?" He took a deep breath. "That's why we have to prove it on the fellow in the hills. That's why we have to have our case prepared before the marshal comes."

This time the room rippled with sighs, F. Millard's own among them. He was over one hurdle—a big one.

"I'm so glad," said Kilkenny softly. "Living together as we have to, all in one cabin, it would be unbearable—each one spying on his neighbor—fearing him."

"But everyone's so nice," protested Hope. "Surely no one could suspect any of us!"

"Just one big happy family," murmured Michael. F. Millard couldn't see his eyes.

Perhaps Kilkenny could. "That's no joke, Mick," she returned. "Once we let suspicion start, and it doesn't stop. It keeps cropping up like fire in a grain elevator. With each one suspecting someone else, watching, setting traps—it's then our yellow streaks show."

"What yellow streaks, Kenny? Didn't Hope just tell us what nice people we were?"

"Darling, when you're suspected of anything as serious as murder, yellow streaks come out. We all have them. You know we do, Mick. In fact—they're already beginning to show."

F. Millard thought of the note on the marble-backed paper and agreed. Someone's yellow streak was cropping out.

Five days later he found another note.

Chapter Twelve

The second time F. Millard put his hand in his jacket pocket and found a note, it was snowing again. But this time, as soon as he felt a scrap of paper among the matches, he knew better than to pull it out until he was alone.

With a racing pulse he saw again the crabbed, uphill writing on the tan side of the marbled paper. *Ask Mick O'Hara what he knows about the Mt. Zion tunnel.*

What did these things have to do with the Senator's murder—Tony and the Army, Michael and a tunnel?

His chance for a private talk with Michael didn't come till two days later, when the snow finally stopped and the shoveling began.

In the meantime, F. Millard compared the handwriting samples he'd acquired with both notes. The card players had run out of backs of envelopes and letters for scoring. Now they were using the flyleaves of the books. It had been easy to get Red into a game of rummy with the rest and offer an unfilled page of *Flatfoot* for scores. It had been harder to get a sample of Hope's writing, but F. Millard finally asked her for the name of the doctor who gave her cold shots, and she wrote it in his magazine. None of the specimens matched the illiterate looking scrawl on the marble-backed paper, but it could have been done left-handed.

Hunting flyleaf scorecards the last day of the snow, Tony exclaimed, "Someone's beaten us to this one!"

He held up a book. The end paper glued to the cover was mottled; its companion flyleaf missing; the next page tan. F. Millard sucked in his breath.

The paper the notes were written on had been torn out of the hymn book.

When the snow finally stopped falling and they all reached for overcoats and mukluks, the grocer hung his coat back on the caribou horns. "My gracious, do you know what we're doing? We're leaving the gate wide open for that pack rat in the hills to come in and steal the rest of our supplies."

Six pairs of eyes focused on him.

"The least we can do is see that the cabin is never left alone. Someone ought to stay on guard every time we go out. In fact, I think two of us; we haven't any weapon, and for all we know, he may carry an arsenal."

"Right, Bud," applauded Red. "I should have thought of that."

"But he's just stocked up!" Kilkenny exclaimed. "Five days ago. He won't need more supplies for ages."

"Perhaps he figures that's what we'll think. He doesn't know how much longer we'll be here, any more than we do, and he may be forehanded." F. Millard turned to Michael. "How'd you like to take the first shift with me? Someone else can stay tomorrow."

Mick glanced at him swiftly. Then he, too, hung his coat back on the caribou horns.

"It's a shame to keep you in the house," F. Millard apologized as the others left. "We'll go out when they come back. But we can't take any chances—"

"Okay, Smyth," cut in Michael. "Why'd you want to see me?"

F. Millard blinked. "You—you knew I wanted to see you?"

"A child of three would have known. Spill it brother."

"Well, I—I—" the grocer's carefully planned approach was almost startled from his mind. "The other night when I asked you if you'd found anything to account for the mystery man's being here, you were going to say something, and then didn't. What did you decide not to tell?"

"You think I know something?"

"I think you do," returned F. Millard quietly. "And I have as much right to know it as you do."

The Congressman's glance was respectful. "You don't miss much, do you, Smyth? I found out something, all right, shortly after we got here. I told the Senator, but no one else. I don't know what made me keep it back the other night. I just felt it was no one else's business, and there might be some reason not to spread it. After all, there've been some pretty queer things going on here."

"Yes?" F. Millard encouraged.

"Maybe being in politics makes a man suspicious. Kilkenny says so. But, of course she's prejudiced. Still—"

"For goodness sake, Michael O'Hara, what did you find out?"

The Irishman's eyes sparkled. "We politicians learn the value of suspense. Okay, brother, listen. When we were hiking over the hills looking for the mystery man before the creeks froze, I did find out something." He reached into his jacket pocket and brought out a handful of smooth, brown pebbles, shoving them dramatically beneath F. Millard's nose. "Get a load of that!"

F. Millard looked, even sniffed at the other man's hand. "Looks like brown pebbles to me."

"My boy," said Michael grandly, "those aren't pebbles. That's tin! This ground is lousy with placer tin!"

"Tin!" the grocer gasped. "I didn't know Alaska grew tin!"

Michael grinned. "You'd be surprised what Alaska grows. They've found other tin deposits here, a few—but nothing like this. This is –this looks like something big."

"Do you—do you think that's why the mystery man—" F. Millard's mind jerked like his words.

"Maybe. Tin's a mighty valuable metal right now."

"But—the pioneers—could tin have brought them here, instead of gold?"

"Well, it must have been here then," Mick grinned. "Your guess is as good as mine."

"Tin!" Tin was something F. Millard had never dreamed of. Did tin have anything to do with the mysterious happenings among the crumbling cabins? With the murder of the Senator?

Michael walked to the window overlooking the trail. "They've dug through the blueberry patch. They're almost to the ridge."

The other man was jolted back to the present. The surprise he'd just received had knocked everything else from his mind. This wasn't all he'd planned to ask the Congressman.

"I've often wondered why you should have been chosen for this Alaska mineral report, Mick. Are you an engineer?"

The man at the window stiffened. "An engineer?" he repeated slowly, without turning. "Oh, you mean on account of my knowing minerals? I studied mineralogy some, but I'm a lawyer."

There were two things F. Millard wanted to find out from Michael O'Hara. But how could you—delicately—ask a man if his father had been married to his mother? Yet, of the two, that question might be less apt to antagonize him. "What sort of bringing up did you have, Michael? How did you live when you were a boy? I've often thought," he added hastily, "how interesting it would be to make a survey of the background of our statesmen."

Michael glanced over his shoulder. His eyes were like blue splinters wedged between smudges of soot. "Oh, yeah? Well, I was a farm kid. The usual political gag—farm to capitol."

"Your—your parents—" F. Millard stammered.

"Farm kids too. Both dead. Anything else you'd like to know?"

"Did—" F. Millard swallowed "—did you ever hear of a place called Mt. Zion?"

Michael whirled. "What do you know about Mt. Zion?"

"That—" F. Millard felt pale, but he stood his ground "—is what I'm asking you. What do you know about the Mt. Zion tunnel?"

The Congressman's face was greenish. "Who could've—how could you—no one knew it here except the Senator!"

So, the Senator had known—and had been killed! But it wasn't the Senator who wrote the note.

"Listen, F. Millard Smyth!" Michael O'Hara, Mick, the friendly young Congressman only slightly taller than himself, towered menacingly above the little grocer. "The Mt. Zion tunnel is none of your affair. Someday you'll learn to keep your nose out of other people's business! And you *may* learn it the hard way!"

Again, Michael whirled. He jerked his coat from the caribou horns, contemptuously kicked aside his canvas foot sacks, and stamped out the door.

F. Millard moved closer to the stove. Was it the icy air which billowed in like fog when the door was opened that made him cold? Or had he thought the younger man was going to hit him? Honestly, in his secret soul, he knew it wasn't the cold.

Chapter Thirteen

After finding two notes in his jacket pocket, F. Millard began to dither whenever he felt for a match. There was something nudging and pointing and slimy about those notes that almost made plain murder seem forthright and wholesome.

It was the 15th of October when he found the first note, the 20th when the second appeared. Then a week dragged by while he found nothing but matches in his pocket.

It was hard to believe that the Senator had been dead for nearly a month; as hard as it was to believe that less than two months had passed since their spying the Eden-like lake with the smoke rising from near-by trees, and landing their plane for a picnic lunch, a picnic that had ended in a funeral. It seemed as if they had been stuck in this deserted town site since time itself began.

The people who had stepped from that plane were now too thin for their clothes; even Guy Fletcher had had to tighten his belt. The clothes themselves were patched and darned and growing more tattered each day. The old cards were gathering more grease and turning more fuzzy at the edges, the old books getting more dog-eared and frayed.

October 20th, when F. Millard found the second note, had come on Monday. It was Monday again, a week later, when the little man's hand, thrust into his jacket pocket, brushed once more against paper.

His arms jerked back as if he had touched a snake. His flesh crawled as if the reptile had slithered up his fingers. What was he going to read now?

This time the trail wasn't choked with snow. He put on his overcoat and mukluks and hurried out of doors, waiting till he reached the field of snow that had been the blueberry patch before he let his hand seek his pocket again.

The marbled paper rustled into the open like the poisonous snake to which he had likened it, with brilliant scales and evil, watching eyes. Slowly the little man smoothed out the creases. On the plain side his eye caught Red's name.

Ask Red Bailey what happened to his first plane, the one he bought with Irv Cramm's money.

F. Millard dragged dejectedly back to the cabin. Tony—Michael—and now, Red.

Inside, the grocer reached up on the shelf by the door for the fishline. "Have you done your fishing today?" he asked Red.

The pilot nodded toward Michael. "Mick and Tony spelled me this morning. They caught a whole boxful"

"We can't catch too many, can we, as long as we keep them frozen? I was thinking that while it wasn't snowing would be a good time to get a lot on hand for the days when we can't get out. I—I haven't tried it yet. Have you time to show me how?"

Red grinned. "Time's what I've got most of, Bud. We can always use fish. Come along if you want to try."

It seemed to F. Millard, as he and Red went out the door, that Michael's eyes were sardonic.

As they walked to the lake, the little man chattered about whatever came to his mind, except the thought that loomed largest. The effect on Michael of the Mt. Zion tunnel note had been so startling, how would Red react?

He waited while the pilot knocked out the fresh ice that had formed at the bottom of the hole already chopped, speared a frozen piece of the morning's bait, and dropped the hook into the water. Then he cleared his throat and stammered, "R-Red, did you ever hear of a fellow named Irv Cramm?"

Red looked up quickly. "Yes." His tone was short. "Why?"

I was just curious. His name came up—"

"Who brought it up?" Red's eyes were like blue ice.

"I—I don't know." And certainly, he didn't know who wrote the note. Miserably conscious of his awkwardness, the grocer ploughed on. "I—they—it sounded like you might have had some connection with him."

"What do you mean, 'connection'?"

"Well, I—I—Look Red, your line's jerking. You've got a bite."

Red pulled up a fish, knocked it against the ice, cut it up, impaled a piece, and dropped the line back in the water. He glared again at F. Millard. "Well, did you come out to fish, or talk about a dead man?"

"A dead man?"

"You didn't know that Irv was killed?"

"Killed?"

Red shoved something into F. Millard's nerveless grasp. "Here's your fishline. Now what have you got to say about Irv Cramm?"

"Well, I—I just wanted to ask if you knew him."

"I knew him, all right. So what?"

My gracious, thought the little man, what a mess! He mustn't turn Red against him too, the way he'd done with Michael. "I—I just wondered," he finished weakly. Perhaps Hope could tell him about Irv Cramm, or he could ask the Mayor.

"After this—" the pilot's voice was as cold as his eyes, as cold as F. Millard's feet "—suppose you don't do your wondering out loud. If you catch too many fish to carry come up to the house for help."

He turned and strode away.

Dismayed, the grocer's eyes followed the angry swing of Red's shoulders, up the trail to the angling hogback hiding the village, along its base, and out of sight.

F. Millard felt a tug at his line. He pulled up a fish, rebaited the hook and dropped it back in the water. Soon another fish, another, and another flopped sluggishly in the box.

Everything was wilderness still. The ridge jutting out to the beach cut off the sound as well as the sight of habitation. Except for the smoke that rose, faintly blue, behind it, F. Millard and the feebly and more feebly flopping fish might have been the only living things for miles.

He pulled in another fish, threw back the freshly baited hook and listened to the silence, listened with straining ears. The ice felt colder to his numbing feet. The chill crept up his veins. Only the last fish now had any flop left in it.

F. Millard raised his head. The bushes that, before the snow came, had rustled when feet passed, were muffled and silent now. No twigs could snap on the ground. Suppose—what if he weren't alone? His spine prickled. Anyone approaching through this white, hushed world could slip right up behind him, silent as gliding wings, silent as death itself. A man on skis—was that something moving on the hill across the lake?

He jerked out his line, grabbed the fish box, and ran. It wasn't far up the trail, not if he ran all the way. Once around the hogback where he could see the cabins—

Gasping, he reached the shelter of the hill. The cabins were in sight. The huddle of crumbling shacks looked, at this cheering moment, like all the civilized world to the panting grocer. He made himself slow to a walk.

The first thing he saw when he stepped inside the door was Mick's sardonic face. The Congressman's bright eyes slid from the little man with his nearly empty fish box to the big red-headed pilot frowning at the stove. F. Millard felt, uncomfortably, that Michael knew what had happened. But no one, not even Michael, twitted him about the number of fish he'd brought back. Perhaps they'd wondered about him, down at the lake alone, after Red had returned.

When dinner dishes were washed and the card fiends settled around the table, Red pulled up another chair. "Will you count me in for a game? I'm feeling lucky tonight."

Kilkenny gave him a smile of welcome. "If the three of you join us, we'll play poker."

"Not I," said Hope quickly. "Thanks just the same, I'd rather watch."

F. Millard felt their eyes on him. At least two pairs were hostile. "I—I—no, thank you. I don't feel lucky tonight."

Into Michael's eyes came again that flash of grim amusement. Red scowled and looked away.

F. Millard moved off to his favorite place by the window to stare out into the night, the players reflected in the darkened glass. A step at his elbow made him jump. At his side Hope looked up, the only member of the group small enough to look up at F. Millard.

"Don't you ever play cards, Hope?" he asked. "It's a good way to pass the time."

She shook her soft blonde curls. "I wasn't brought up like Kilkenny Lee. She's never stopped playing games. I never had the time to begin, until now. And now it's too late."

"Too late to learn? My dear girl, you're just a child."

Her smile, brief and perfunctory, came and went. "Too late to get the spirit of the thing. Either a game seems silly to me, or it gets serious. That isn't the way to play. If a game isn't fun, then you'd better leave it alone."

"You're too young and pretty and—small, to have reached conclusions like that. You should have been protected from finding out such things."

"Protected!" Her low voice was momentarily harsh. "I grew up the hard way. I've had to earn what I wanted ever since I can remember. I didn't have parents to give me things—like Kilkenny Lee."

She looked back at the card table and F. Millard's eyes followed hers. The Senator's daughter sat facing the window. They saw her slim hand dart forward for a card. Her gay smile flashed on Mick across the table, flashed across the room to the watchers by the window.

F. Millard's eyes returned to the grave-faced girl at his side. In a different way, Hope was as pretty as Kilkenny, almost as young. Sometimes it didn't seem that things were divided as they should be. If Hope's parents— parents—was Hope Mullen one of those girls who didn't have a father? Mick hadn't known whether the Senator's natural child was a son or daughter.

"What—did something happen to your parents, Hope?"

"They were drowned—one of those times the Ohio went on a rampage. We lived in a little shack by the railroad tracks—the wrong side. When the flood came tearing down, it fell apart like matches. I was just a baby. You know how sometimes babies survive all kinds of disasters? I lived, and my parents both drowned."

Both, F. Millard reflected, both her parents drowned. Well, it hadn't hurt to ask. Maybe she could help him out about Red. "You've been in Alaska a year or so, haven't you, Hope?"

"A year in September. This is—would have been my second year in the Fairbluffs schools."

"Did you—" he glanced briefly at the card players. They seemed absorbed in their game, but he lowered his voice. "Did you ever know a man named Irv Cramm?"

Hope's blue eyes widened. "I didn't know him. He was killed before I came."

"How was he killed?"

"His plane crashed. He and Red were partners. Didn't you know?"

"I don't know anything!" cried the little man, exasperated. "You all act as if you mustn't let out a scandal. Did anything happen between him and Red?"

Hope looked thoughtful. "Did Red ever talk to you about it?"

"Once." She didn't have to know who'd brought up the subject. "But he didn't tell me anything except Cramm was dead, and he used to know him."

Her pink lips came primly together. "It's Red's business, Mr. Smyth. If he didn't want to tell you, I won't."

She turned abruptly and walked back to the table. He saw her lean over Michael's shoulder, pointing to the cards in his hand.

But Hope had told him something, F. Millard reflected. He knew now that Irv Cramm had been Red's partner and he'd been killed in a plane. No wonder Red didn't want to talk about it. But why would Hope keep still about it too? What was there so dreadful about a man's partner crashing, unless—unless Red had had something to do with it. Perhaps these notes were dynamite.

Chapter Fourteen

Four days passed without F. Millard finding any more scandal notes. November set in, the month of Thanksgiving and turkeys. He tried not to think of either.

The first night of the new month, when Kilkenny reached for the cards to start the contract session, Michael pulled them away. "Come on outdoors, Kenny. A walk will do you good before you settle down."

She hesitated. For a fraction of a second her topaz eyes flicked toward Red.

"Come on." Michael's tones held all the liquid coaxing of the Irish. "You haven't walked to the lake with me for weeks and weeks."

"How about this morning? And every other morning? I walk to the lake with you every day to clear off the plane."

"Me and a dozen others."

"Who're you counting twice?" grinned Guy.

Mick paid no attention. He and Kilkenny might have been alone in the room. "Come on, Kenny, I've almost forgotten what it is to have you to myself."

If he could just see them objectively, F. Millard told himself, like a scene in a play, he wouldn't think about its being Kilkenny that Michael was trying to charm right in front of his eyes. Considered objectively, how could any girl resist the compelling warmth in the Irishman's voice?

Kilkenny stopped trying to resist it. She walked toward the caribou horns for her wraps. Michael held out her leopard coat and knelt to tie her makeshift mukluks. Then he flung on his own things and the two stepped out into the night.

Guy grinned. "Well, that's settled. Or should I say just begun?"

"You shouldn't say anything, as far as I can see." Tony's ruddy brow creased with disapproval. "It's none of your business, is it?"

F. Millard's troubled eyes returned to the closed door. How dreadfully hard it was for seven people to live in one room. He felt, uncomfortably, that he'd had no right to witness that scene between Kilkenny and Mick. It should have been private between those two, not something to be stared at by five other people and grinned about later. Though Guy was the only one grinning. Red and Tony were scowling at the stove. Hope sat with her sewing in her lap, but she wasn't sewing. Her body was tense, her lips pressed tightly together. All of a sudden F. Millard remembered it had been mostly Hope he had seen with Mick lately; and Red who had been with Kilkenny. Funny, when they came, way back in September, it had been the other way, the way Mick was trying to make it tonight. And now look at them: Kilkenny going slowly, almost reluctantly, Red glowering at the fire, Hope sitting as tense as a patient at the dentist's.

The little man sighed. He hadn't changed. To him, Kilkenny was still the essence of all dreams. And the perfume on the bloody handkerchief? He bit his lip and reached for the cards.

The minutes limped by. Nervously F. Millard shuffled and laid the cards out for Canfield. It wasn't fair to play solitaire with the only deck. But he couldn't interest anyone else except Guy, and tonight he didn't want to play with the Mayor. Under the circumstances, with everyone living huddled up with everyone else, so slight a thing as curiosity ought to be forgiven, but tonight F. Millard wasn't in a forgiving mood; the Mayor's unconcealed interest smelled too rankly of the scandal notes. And since those notes began appearing in his pocket, the grocer's nose had become peculiarly sensitive to smells.

A sound from outside, too faint for identification, disturbed the stillness of the cabin. It came again, eerily, like a whine.

Hope jumped up and ran to the door, leaning out into the darkness. Her fair hair whirled around her head. "Wind!" she reported. "It feels right off a glacier. I wish they'd come in."

"Kilkenny and Mick?" drawled Tony.

She hesitated. "Perhaps if I call them—"

"Hell," said Red brusquely, "If they're cold, they'll come in."

But it wasn't their getting chilled, F. Millard knew, that bothered Hope.

The Mayor chuckled. To the grocer's hypersensitive ears, it sounded like a snigger. "If they're cold, love's young dream isn't what it was when I was young."

Red stood up, glaring at Guy.

"If you went downhill, Red, and Tony toward the creek," Hope hurried on, "you could find them and bring them back."

"My God, Hope," cried Red impatiently. "They aren't lost! You act like they were your dumbest first-graders."

The young teacher flushed. "I'd hate to add pneumonia to all our other troubles." She waited, and then, with a sidewise glance at Red, she added, "Kilkenny's so delicate looking."

But F. Millard was the one who was shaken. Kilkenny, so fine-boned and slim—

"Don't be a grandmother," the pilot growled. "She's got on a fur coat. If they've got private things to say to each other, who are we to interrupt them?"

Hope paled. She opened her mouth and shut it again abruptly. F. Millard saw her fingers curl into her palms. She turned and walked with quick, stiff little steps to the other end of the room.

Red lounged embarrassedly over to the table where the grocer sat with the cards. Tony silently pushed a chair at the standing pilot and drew up one for himself. Guy blinked at them all, then, uninvited, hunched his chair up to the table. F. Millard suddenly found himself deep in a game of stud poker.

They had played several hands before he noticed Hope's activity. She was moving efficiently around the stove, and he caught the rattle of dishes. Dishes? They'd had their dinner. People on short rations didn't go in for between-meal snacks. He craned his neck while the game went on. She was stirring something in a pot over the fire. On the shelf behind her he saw cups and saucers laid out.

Red gathered up the cards and started to shuffle.

"If you've finished that hand," broke in Hope, "will one of you get Kilkenny and Mick? Something hot ought to taste pretty good in weather like this, and waiting won't improve it."

Tony groaned, Red snorted, and Guy slumped back in his chair. But F. Millard was interested in the pan that steamed on the stove. "What'd you make, Hope?"

"Chocolate."

Guy sat up.

"Chocolate!" Tony exclaimed. "I thought we didn't have any more."

"We don't now," said Hope. "This is the last of the can. But we had to finish it sometime, and I thought with Kilkenny and Mick out in the cold—will one of you call them while it's hot?"

"Not me," grinned Guy. "Give the poor devil a chance."

"But the chocolate!" Hope protested. "We'll never have chocolate again— till we're rescued. It would be a shame for them to miss it. Tony, you go."

Emphatically, Tony shook his head.

Hope glanced briefly at F. Millard and reached for her coat.

The little man gave in. "All right, Hope. Don't let the chocolate burn. I'll get them."

She flashed him a radiant smile and hurried back to the stove.

He shrugged into his coat and tied on his canvas foot sacks. Outside the wind nipped at his face and neck. Trust a woman to get her own way. From the minute the door closed behind Kilkenny and Mick, Hope had wanted to bring them back. F. Millard grinned and felt the cold on his teeth. She'd been darn smart about it. She hadn't raised a fuss till the wind gave her an excuse. When the men outvoted her, she'd had sense enough to keep quiet till she thought of something else. Making chocolate was trumping an ace. With food as important as it was in their lives, if Hope had made chocolate and not called Kilkenny and Mick, it would have been a dirty trick. This way she got the credit for playing fair, and at the same time, got her own way. F. Millard grinned again and leaned harder into the wind.

Too bad it wasn't moonlight. In the white trail on the moonlit night he could have seen two black human dots clear down by the hogback, but in the murky gloom of this moonless, auroraless night everything was dark gray, shading into black. For all he knew, Kilkenny and Mick might have gone up toward the creek. But if F. Millard had been taking his girl for a walk, he'd have steered her toward the lake; the creek was too near the cabins. If he didn't find them before he reached the spur—he thought again of the day he had fished with Red, when the pilot left him there at the lake, alone. He remembered how the headland had shut him off, one helpless speck of a man in the bottom of that sugar bowl of hills.

He shuddered. That had been daytime. This was night. The wind moaned through the trees.

He passed the last cabin, then the last clump of spruce. Next came the blueberry patch. The hogback loomed very near. Out of the shadows it was lighter, but the wind snapped more viciously—snarled.

The ridge was almost on him. Faintly, over the moan of the wind, he heard another sound. He stopped, cupping his hands to his ears. Thin, fragile as an eggshell, it came again, a wind-stretched human voice.

He ran a few steps down the trail. The voice blew back to meet him in gusty jerks. "But—politics—you know—can't bear—"

Kilkenny's voice, blowing out of the grayness, from the black night thinned with white snow; Kilkenny's voice—he ran a few more steps.

It came again, stronger now, clearer. "I'm sorry, Mick. I told you I couldn't. How could we ever be happy?"

Michael's voice blew back to the panting grocer. "You didn't always act like I had smallpox, Kenny. Is Red Bailey the reason?"

F. Millard sucked in his breath and a mouthful of stinging snow spray. My gracious, he didn't mean to overhear anything like this. He still couldn't see the couple ahead, but if he was close enough to hear them so plainly maybe he could make them hear him. He cleared his throat.

"You should talk, Michael O'Hara!" he heard Kilkenny exclaim. "after mooning around over Hope!"

"Don't be like that, Kenny!" the Irishman's persuasive voice came as near to being sharp as F. Milliard had ever heard it. He wished he couldn't hear it now. He cleared his throat wildly again.

"You won't let this good-looking pilot make you forget—other things, will you, mavourneen?" Mick's voice was tender again.

Once more the little grocer scraped his suffering throat. The wind scooped up his "Ahem" and threw it back to home base. The wind—of course he couldn't make them hear, with the wind in this direction; he'd have to run and catch them or turn around and go home.

Suddenly his feet stopped moving. Every sense sprang alert. His mind gave no more reason for this electric tightness than the mind of a person wakened from sleep to frantic, unreasoning fear. Something instinctive, as primitive as the prickle of hair at the back of his neck, warned him of danger. Danger coming nearer—nearer—fast!

Involuntarily he faced the hogback, now directly above him. Distinct from the moaning of the wind, distinct from the human voices, his sharply attuned ears picked up another sound. Far off, faint, growing louder, an eerie *swishshshsh*. His straining eyes caught some motion on the hillside—a shadow streaking down! Growing blacker, larger as it came! Suddenly the shadow shot above his head, arms outspread like wings, the blur of long, pale skis between!

Plunk! He heard the slap of skis as the birdlike shadow hit the snow at the edge of the trail cut. He saw the blur of a face peering over a shoulder. Then the crouching figure straightened and skimmed on into the dark.

F. Millard drew a shuddering breath. He stumbled forward, running, gasping as he ran, "Kilkenny! Mick!" He must stop them. He must catch them. The menace from the hills was on the prowl!

Their voices still blew back, but now he didn't hear words. Now it would make no difference if Kilkenny were actually in Michael's arms. He had to warn her, save her. He forgot that there might be danger for himself, in his urge to get to her.

At last, a dark smudge appeared in the trail ahead. It separated into a man and a girl as F. Millard stumbled up. "Come back to the cabin!" he panted.

"The mystery man—"

"Is he back?" cried Michael.

"What happened?" cried Kilkenny.

"Has anyone—been hurt?" Mick's pause was significant.

"Not yet. I just saw him." F. Millard drew a deep breath. "I'll tell you on the way back. Hope made chocolate and I came out to call you, and just when I got to the ridge, something scared me, and I looked up. Something came flying down the hill and shot right over me like—like a bat out of hell."

"You mean—a bird—or—a man?" Kilkenny gasped.

"A man on skis. I couldn't see him well. He went by too fast. He jumped the trail and shot off across the snow. Here's the place. You can see his tracks."

They crowded to the side of the trail. At the edge of the snowbank above their heads were two sharply defined grooves like the tracks of wagon wheels set a few inches apart.

"So he's back again!" The Congressman's tone was as tense as his wiry body. "What does he want this time?"

They hurried up the hill and burst into the cabin. The event of drinking hot chocolate had to take second place beside the visit of the man on skis.

"What do you think he's here for now?" echoed through the room.

After telling his story once more F. Millard left the exclamations to the others. He stood by the stove, staring into the empty cup, that he had drained so thoroughly even sucking the rim brought no more taste of chocolate.

Not till the uproar subsided did the little man turn around. "Did any of you ever read about catching gorillas in Africa?"

"Catching gorillas!"

"Africa!"

"What on earth are you talking about?"

"I've been thinking about this fellow in the hills. I don't know what he came for tonight, maybe just to look around. I'll bet he was as surprised to see me as I was to see him. But it looks like he's keeping a pretty close eye on us. I've been thinking. He got away with those supplies the middle of October. That was two weeks ago. He can't have run short yet, but he must be getting low enough to stock up if he saw a chance."

"We're sure not giving him a chance." Red squared belligerent shoulders.

Michael's face lit up. For the first time since the Mt. Zion tunnel fiasco, F. Millard felt the warmth of the Congressman's smile. "By all that's holy, brother I think I see what you're driving at!"

The grocer's own eyes were shining. "Do you think we could do it, Mick?"

"What are you boys talking about?" Kilkenny demanded. "Let the rest of us in on it too."

"He must know the supplies are in our cabin. I'll bet he knows we leave a couple of guards when we go out. He must have noticed our daily expeditions to the plane, and fishing, and things. Well, if he sees we've stopped leaving guards—he knows how long it takes us to shovel out the trail and come back—"

"But I don't understand!" cried Hope. "You surely don't want him to get away with any more food!"

Michael laughed. "We don't want him to get *away* with it."

"You mean—some of you hide and catch him?" Hope's eyes were as round as her face. "What if he has a gun?"

"That's just it!" Michael turned verbal cartwheels. "He probably does have a gun, or two, or three. That's what makes the plan so good."

"Pardon my stupidity," said Tony, "but what is this wonderful plan?"

F. Millard looked eagerly around. "Don't you remember reading about digging pits to catch wild animals?"

"'Bring 'em back alive!'" shouted Red.

"Holy Moses!" muttered Guy.

"Do you mean you'd dig a pit out here in the trail," Kilkenny cried, "and hope the mystery man would come to get the food, and fall in it?"

"Right in front of the door," F. Millard supplemented. "And then we'd have him—at last."

"What about ourselves?" asked Guy. "What's to prevent our falling in first?"

"Well, of course, we'll have to have some sort of passage for ourselves, won't we, Mick?" the grocer appealed to Michael.

"We'll have the advantage of knowing where not to step," the Congressman grinned.

Red grinned too. "If we don't forget. You want to look out, Guy. They say a fall's pretty hard on a fat man."

Tony stood up. "When do we start?"

"But—but building a fire!" For the first time F. Millard heard Guy stammer. "How are we going to thaw the ground without the fellow seeing the fire? My God, you don't expect us to dig a pit with picks in this frozen ground?"

"My gracious," the grocer blinked, "I hadn't thought of that."

Red laughed. "And you living in Fairbluffs, Guy, ever since the camp was struck! What's the matter with water thawing? There're a couple of pipes right here in the cabin, and a stove, and several kettles. With boiling water and five men, and of course the picks and shovels, I don't know what's to prevent us getting that pit dug tonight."

That began a night of feverish activity. A glowing stove kept the water hot. The men scraped off snow the desired length and width of the pit, then, holding both pipes against the bare ground, they poured hot water down them. As, inch by inch, the earth began to soften, they drove in the pipes.

The first length underground supplied the first diversion.

"Where'd we put the picks," yelled Red, "the last time—"

He stopped. In the quiet night F. Millard heard a gasp. The last time they had used those picks was when they dug the Senator's grave.

"I gathered them together, "the Mayor said gruffly, "and left them in his—in the house next door."

They had to dig a trail, then, in to the Senator's cabin. Once more a light gleamed briefly in the room where a man had been murdered, once more winked out as the picks began their work.

Another pipe length down, and Guy straightened, mopping his face. "How deep do we have to do?"

Red grinned. "Ten or twelve feet, I guess. We don't want him climbing out before we get here."

"He ought to get a good shake-up when he lands," Michael added. "Don't forget he'll probably come heeled."

"Hope he breaks his leg," growled Guy.

"Make it his trigger arm," said Mick. "Wish Hope had thought of that chocolate now, instead of early this evening. I could eat a horse. Whatever possessed her to finish the can tonight?"

Renewed digging was his only answer.

They started the pit about nine o'clock. It was morning, though still dark, by the time they were ready to lay the false top. While Tony and Red fumbled their way to the woodlot, Michael, Guy, and F. Millard lined the banks of the trail with the dirt taken out of the hole and covered it with snow. Slender birch branches laid over the gap, snow smoothed on top, a plank to cross safely to the cabin, and at last, as a late dawn broke, the weary men were able to stack their picks inside the cabin and stumble to bed.

F. Millard hadn't even turned over in his bunk before Hope shook him awake. "You said you wanted to go down to the plane at the usual time, in case the man's watching, so he won't get suspicious," she reminded him.

The little man groaned. He heard answering groans from the other bunks, but finally they all grumbled themselves to the table.

"Now don't forget," cautioned Michael, wolfing biscuits, "after we've crossed the plank, we've got to take it with us, and sweep away the marks. Everything's got to look normal."

"Business as usual," grumbled Guy, "however we feel after last night's exertions."

"Look out crossing that plank, Kilkenny," warned Red, as they started. "Give me your hand."

They made themselves walk slowly to the plane and spend their usual time sweeping off the wings and fishing. They made themselves not hurry back around the spur, up the slope. But the snow above the gorilla pit remained white and unbroken.

Neither did the mystery man rise to the bait next day. Morning after morning the seven cabinmates walked down the hill and hurried breathlessly back to find the branch and snow platform still whole.

But something else happened one morning. Eight days after digging the pit, F. Millard found another note.

Chapter Fifteen

As soon as he felt a fold of paper in his pocket, F. Millard scurried, like a rabbit from its burrow, down the trail, alone. Only he was careful not to be alone too far from home, careful to stay on the town side of the spur. Once in the snow-covered blueberry patch, his hand slid reluctantly inside his overcoat.

Ask Hope Mullen how her aunt is living… So the notes had begun on the girls!

"What do I care," F. Millard asked himself aloud in the empty, dazzling white of the one-time blueberry patch, "how her aunt is living?"

And yet, look at the apparent inoffensiveness of the question about the Mt Zion tunnel, and the devil it had roused in Michael! Look at the effect on Red of the question about his first plane!

F. Millard pulled the pocket of his overcoat wrong side out and picked at the thread till it broke. Then he worked his fingers into the hole to make it as wide as his hand.

By the time he returned to the cabin, Michael and Tony were starting to cut wood.

"Let's all go while the sun's out!" cried Kilkenny. "God knows we seldom see it."

Even Guy reached for his canvas mukluks.

"Not me," said F. Millard, hanging up his overcoat. "I've just been out. Besides, I've got a hole in my pocket—my coat pocket—" he paused, and his eyes made a swift circuit of the room. Was it his imagination, or were they all listening intently, far more intently than so simple a remark warranted?

"Since Hope's going out, maybe she'll lend me her workbasket."

Hope pulled off her improvised mukluks. "I'd rather go some other time." Her glance just touched Kilkenny. "If you'll take off your coat, I'll mend it."

"Not my suit coat; it's my overcoat." Again F. Millard's eyes circled the room. No face had changed expression. But he knew he must have set one mind at rest, the furtive mind responsible for the notes. Whoever had been putting them in his pocket needn't be afraid they'd gone through.

Kilkenny and the Mayor stepped outside, but the three younger men lingered.

Red glanced from Hope to the grocer, and his eyes sharpened. "Better come with us, Hope," he urged.

"Some other time. Just think if Mr. Smyth lost his gloves through this big hole in his pocket!"

"Let him mend it then," returned the pilot. "Look, Hope, you don't want to stay in today. See how bright the sun is!"

His urgency was out of all proportion to the subject. His eyes met F. Millard's, and the little man saw they were as hard as granite. Michael's had again that grim, sardonic glitter. Tony scowled over Mick's shoulder.

This was the first sign of mass hostility. The night a few weeks ago when Tony had demanded to know if any of them were suspects, F. Millard had felt antagonism, fear, as palpable as a wall, rise up in the room between himself and them. That had been his first hint of solidarity among the others, of himself as standing alone. Now it was plain for anyone to see. If he paid no attention, if he went ahead and got Hope's workbasket—

He made a half-blind snatch at something on the table that he recognized as Hope's.

"That's my handbag, Mr. Smyth. But don't bother to hunt the basket; there's a needle and thread in here. Be seeing you, Mick." She smiled at the Congressman and waved out the three young men.

F. Millard heard the door close. With a sigh he dropped into a chair. Hope opened her bag and took out a card wrapped with different-colored threads, a needle woven through them. This was almost domestic.

"Talk about forethought!" F. Millard applauded. "You're going to make some man a wonderful wife."

"I don't know about that—" Hope looked attractively self-conscious "—but there's many a time when a needle and thread may keep a girl from going home in a barrel. I always carry a mending kit. But it's lucky we found a workbasket here, or I couldn't even try to keep us mended."

"You don't see many domestic girls these days. Someone did a good job of raising you, Hope."

Through the window the nearly horizontal winter sunlight made her hair a golden nimbus above F. Millard's gray coat. "My aunt brought me up." She sighed. "She did the best she could according to her means."

"Is she still alive?"

Hope nodded, and bit off the thread.

"Is she a schoolteacher, like you?"

The overcoat slid to the floor. Hope's "N-no," was muffled as she bent to pick it up.

"Just a housewife?" he suggested.

She didn't answer. He reached down to lift the coat.

"How does she earn her living, then?"

At last Hope raised her head. All the color slowly drained from her face. "Who told you to ask me that?"

"Why—why—"he stammered "—is there any reason why I shouldn't?"

The girl's hands doubled into fists. F. Millard saw she was shaking. "Yes—yes, there is!" she burst out. "Can't I ever get away from it? Even in Alaska? Even teaching school?"

He dropped the coat and caught her arm. "What do you mean, Hope? What are you talking about?"

She began to sob. "I'm t-talking about what you asked me about. Even if the way she earns her living is—humble, what business is it of yours? You're not on the Fairbluffs School Board."

"Hope, listen, I didn't mean to upset you. I only wanted to know—"

"What if I didn't want to follow in her steps? Is it a crime for a girl to be ambitious? The way my aunt makes money doesn't have anything to do with me! It never did, I tell you!"

"My dear girl, I never said—"

"Then who did?"

Wretchedly, F. Millard felt as if his hands and feet and tongue had all been tied in knots. "I never dreamed—I only meant to ask—"

"Then ask someone else. There's someone here who knows or he never would have put you up to asking me. Ask Red! Ask Guy Fletcher! Ask anyone—but me!"

Hope jumped up and ran across the room to her bunk. From behind the hanging blankets, F. Millard heard her sobbing. "My gracious," he muttered weakly.

He scooped his coat off the floor and plunged his arms into the sleeves, jerked the canvas on his feet, and hurried out. He couldn't go on listening to these sobs.

When the others came back—what would they think when they found the blonde teacher in tears? He hoped to goodness she'd be straightened up by then. When they came back, he'd take Guy off in a corner. Whatever there was about her aunt, Guy and Red would be more likely to know than the others. He couldn't ask Red, but Guy hadn't turned against him—yet. Guy—could Guy have written the scandal notes? F. Millard himself, Guy, and Kilkenny were the only ones who hadn't been attacked.

Whoever wrote those notes—it would be like dealing with a snake. Though anything less snakelike than the bulbous Mayor would be hard to imagine, F. Millard thought, waylaying him as he waddled down the trail. Guy still had enough stomach left to bounce.

The grocer wasted no time on preliminaries; he wasn't digging into the Mayor's private business. He took Guy's arm and propelled him toward the creek. "I'd like to ask you a few things, Guy. You've lived in Fairbluffs ever since there was a Fairbluffs. Was there anything fishy about Red Bailey's partnership with a fellow called Irv Cramm?"

"Fishy?"

"Shady. Crooked. Off-color. Was there anything like that about their partnership?"

"Not that I know of." The mayor shook his plaid cap and escaping gray curls. "Plenty of things were said about Red when Irv crashed, but nobody claimed there was anything crooked about the partnership."

"What do you mean by 'things said about Red when Irv crashed?' Did Red have anything to do with it?"

"Well, I don't know. They were pretty hard up right then, and the plane was insured. So was Irv. And afterwards Red didn't seem as drunk as the woman claimed."

"What on earth are you talking about? For gracious sake, Fletcher, begin at the beginning and tell it right straight through. In words of one syllable if you can."

Guy flashed his gold teeth indulgently. "Of course you won't hold this against Red. Some folks did, but he was only a kid, and he had to sow his wild oats. That's all I believe it was—just a kid's wild oats, and not—why, what they claimed happened would be no better than murder."

"For gracious sake, Guy—"

The Mayor's crowns gleamed again. "Guess murder's a two-syllable word, hey, Smyth? Well, the point was the two kids were starting out with a one-plane transportation company. Irv put up the money and Red the experience. Irv didn't know how to pilot a plane, but he was learning from Red. Well, the boys were hard up, and the business all going to companies that had radios in their planes and more than one ship and one pilot. Irv took out his worry in trying to drum up trade, and Red took out his in whisky and women. Well, there came along this night when all the planes were up, and Wiseman sent in an emergency call to come and get a sick man. But that night Red was in this woman's cabin roaring drunk, or so the woman said. Irv went there and argued with him, and finally Red told him to take up the plane himself. That's what Irv finally did. Well, the kid had never flown at night and didn't know much about flying anyway. He crashed. The plane was a total loss, and so was Irv."

"But—Red—"objected F. Millard "—why would Red—?

"That's just it," Guy declared. "When word got back an hour after Irv had left, Red showed up as sober as a judge. He was right on the dot to collect the insurance, too. But you know how people talk."

F. Millard swallowed. Red—could Red Bailey have sent his inexperienced partner up in the night—for the sake of the insurance? These notes—the Senator's death—surely not Red?

The Mayor cleared his throat. "Did you want to know anything else?"

F. Millard tried to shake the cobwebs from his brain. He must ask his questions now and do his thinking later. What was the other thing? Oh, yes—Hope. Had she finished her cry by the time the others got back? "Did you know Hope Mullen had an aunt in the States?"

"Is there anything queer about that?" the Mayor asked cautiously.

"Well, I did hear something." Guy hesitated this time. "Of course, I'm not a member of the school board, so I wouldn't hold it against Hope. As a matter of fact, I haven't told anyone in Fairbluffs."

"Very noble," the little man commented. "But I'm not a member of the school board either, so it ought to be safe to tell me."

"You understand I didn't see the aunt myself. I talked to a fellow who was Outside last winter and stopped off in Cincinnati. He went to a house of joy there, and the madam said she had a niece in Fairbluffs. Well, that woman turned out to be Hope's aunt."

Poor Hope. No wonder she'd been upset. "That wouldn't be Hope's fault, would it?" F. Millard asked defensively.

"Her aunt says so. She says she only went into it to bring up the girl, and she'd have given up the business long ago if her niece would have helped support her. But Hope's an ambitious little piece. Acknowledging an aunt like that would cramp her style"

Ambition to rise above such a background, if Guy's story was true, would only be commendable, F. Millard thought. And to make herself a teacher and a radio operator as well—Hope was not only ambitious, she was capable.

"The woman said she'd been sick," went on Guy. "She looked it, my friend said. She claimed that she wrote Hope, and Hope never sent her a line, let alone any money."

The tourist from Nebraska felt sick himself—Hope, refusing to help the sick aunt who'd brought her up even though the woman's business shamed her—Red, sending his partner up into the air and the night, to his death.

What sort of people—wait a minute, how did Guy know all this? Guy knew all the answers. Was it Guy who had written the notes? F. Millard whirled on him. "What do you know about the Mt. Zion tunnel?"

Guy didn't change expression. "There's no Mt. Zion around Fairbluffs, and no tunnels, except mine tunnels, for half a day on the railroad."

Maybe it hadn't been Guy. That was one answer he didn't know. And the note about Tony—what would Guy know about that? How could he get the lowdown on the people from the States? For that matter—this information he'd just been passing out—the part about Hope was hearsay, the part about Red, the worst part, was only surmise.

Chapter Sixteen

But the notes with their unsavory innuendoes took the edge off F. Millard's excitement in watching for the mystery man. Red, Mick, and the girls treated it like a game. They couldn't wait till the fishing was done and the plane swept off before one of them dashed around the spur to see if their trap had been sprung. Tony should have been in the hound pack too, F. Millard reflected, but the blond giant seemed to hang back, almost as if he waited to hear that nothing had happened before he quickened his step to join the others.

For two weeks after digging the pit it looked as if their labor had been useless. Then, one morning, Red, with their newly filled fish box under his arm, was first around the promontory. F. Millard saw him stop. He heard a shout. The pilot dropped the box and disappeared at a gallop. Leaping over the scattered fish, Mick flashed after him. F. Millard broke into a run. Rounding the spur, he saw Red and Michael tearing up the trail. The girls were running too. The patch of snow in front of the cabin was too far off for the grocer to see detail, but something must have happened. He put on a burst of speed.

Just when he thought he couldn't drag another breath through his raw lungs, the four in front of him stopped. Red and Mick held out both arms to bar the trail.

F. Millard was near enough now to see the pit. Something had broken through the false cover. Branches and snow lay scattered about the gaping hole.

"You girls stay here," said Michael firmly. "He's probably got a gun. Even if he is ten feet in the ground, his trigger finger may be working."

"Where's Tony?" cried Kilkenny. "Can't all you boys jump on him at once?"

F. Millard looked back. Tony was making no better speed than the steaming Mayor. They pounded up, side by side.

"Is he there?" gasped Guy.

"Has he got a gun?" asked Tony.

F. Millard looked curiously at the Senator's secretary. He was breathing easily, not panting like the Mayor. The purple that running had pumped to his face was fading to his normal high color, but he didn't look his normal self.

"All right, fellas," said Red. "Let's go. You girls wait here."

Mick was already advancing up the trail. A few yards before he reached the pit, he stopped and lifted his voice. "Hi! Do you want to come out?"

The pit remained as still and portentous as a waiting grave.

"Hi, in there!" called Mick again. "Anybody home?"

He met F. Millard's eyes and winked. "You got a gun?"

Still no answer.

"There's one way to find out," muttered Red. He started forward. Mick caught his arm. The two men whispered together.

"Gimme your hat!" Mick nudged F. Millard. "Your broom, Tony!"

The secretary still held the brush broom that he used to sweep off the plane's wings. He handed it to Michael and F. Millard held out his hat. Mick stuck the hat on the broom handle and slowly started to raise it.

Whang! Something *zingggggged* over their heads. The five men stared at each other. Mick had his answer. Some one was "home," all right. And he had a gun.

Mick and Red whispered again. The Congressman beckoned to Guy and reached for the Mayor's plaid cap. He pulled it over the brush end of the broom. Red stepped to the side of the trail, inching forward along the bank. He stopped, nodded at Mick. Once more the Congressman raised the broom.

F. Millard's eyes flew back and forth from the cap on the broomstick to the tense figure of the pilot by the snowbank. Then three things happened at once. Another *zing* came out of the ground, the cap fell, and Red and Mick sprang into the pit.

Grunts and sounds of scuffling rose from it. Tony hurried by F. Millard, paused, then he too leaped in. F. Millard came to life. They were overpowering the mystery man down there and he must help.

But as he reached the hole, Michael's wild black hair, with a face red and joyous smile below it, shot up above the snow. "Gimme a hand, Millard!" he shouted. "Gotta get ropes!"

His jerk left F. Millard still teetering on the edge of the pit as Mick banged the cabin door.

"No use you coming down, Bud," grinned Red. "Tony and I'll hold him till Mick gets back with the rope. He's all tired out anyway."

F. Millard peered over the edge. Red and Tony were sitting on a man flat in the bottom of the pit—the mystery man at last! Another blond, was the little man's first disgruntled thought; he should have been dark, like Kilkenny. The hair and a square forehead were all he could see beyond the spread of Red's big body sitting on the man's chest. Then Red leaned forward, and F. Millard had a brief glimpse of a flushed face, a blond mustache and shorter beard, sullen blue eyes staring up. Nothing in that face like Kilkenny Lee's.

Guy and the girls had reached the pit by now and were bending over too.

Red straightened, brandishing an automatic, which he slid into his hip pocket. "Boy! We've got a gun!"

"We don't need it now!" cried Hope. "We've got the man now!"

Not need a gun, F. Millard repeated to himself? Not need protection? Because they'd caught the mystery man. But had they caught the murderer?

"What you looking so sour about, Bud?" Red grinned again. "You want to come down and sit on him too?"

Everyone was joyous, F. Millard saw, except himself. Red was calling him Bud again, Michael had taken him back into the fold, Hope leaned sideways and squeezed his arm, Tony looked up and smiled. Apparently, all was forgiven. The notes, and the enmity his questions had aroused seemed to be forgotten. Everyone was happy now, everyone but F. Millard. They'd caught the menace that threatened from the hills.

F. Millard had to see the man's clothes, he had to see his boot tracks. He had to know who he was, why he was here, and what he wanted with them. He had to know—oh, he had to know a million things. Would Mick never get back with the rope so they could bring the fellow up and look him over?

Michael popped out of the cabin, almost into the pit. He waved Hope's scissors and some canvas sacks. "Hey, you guys, help cut these up for ropes!"

"The rope from the plane's in the Senator's cabin," F. Millard cried, "to tie the bedroom door shut!"

He flung himself through the new snow not yet clogging the unused path since clearing it out to get the picks when they dug the pit.

Fumbling with the knot in the darkened cabin, he finally pulled it loose and ran back to throw the rope into the pit.

"Here, you don't have to jerk like that!"

F. Millard jumped, not only at the venom in the stranger's voice as Red and Tony bound his hands, but at the mere sound of a voice different from the six to which he had grown accustomed.

"Okay, above!" Red called. "We'll hoist him up if the rest of you'll haul him out."

The stranger's head rose into view, the red face and fair whiskers, a brown jacket. The three men in the trail caught his arms and pulled.

F. Millard's eyes ran quickly over the man who now stood beside him— medium tall, so erect that he seemed taller, dark blue flannel shirt, brown breeches thrust into high leather boots. There was no black in any of his garments.

The little grocer stepped awkwardly sideways, swayed, and pushed against the stranger. Glaring, the man retreated a step.

"Sorry," said the smaller man politely. He ducked his head as if embarrassed. In the snow where the stranger had been standing was the track of a plain leather sole.

"You don't have to be so rough!" the fellow snarled.

"You should kick!" cried Michael, Irish eyes blazing "How about the guy you croaked?"

"Croaked!" The man's face lost its sullenness, sharpened. "What are you talking about?"

"I knew it!" For an instant Tony's head and shoulders popped like a jack-in-the-box out of the pit. As they disappeared, his voice came up. "He has an English accent!"

"Don't put on an act," the Mayor said wearily to the prisoner. "No use pretending not to know."

"But I don't!" The stranger's voice was like a whip crack. "Are you accusing me of murder?"

With a boost from below Tony climbed out of the pit. He gave a hand to Red, and they joined the group around their quarry.

"Who the hell are you, anyway?" demanded Red.

The man stood even straighter. "I am—John Smith."

"And how is Pocahontas?" murmured Michael.

The stranger's furious eyes lashed briefly at the Congressman and returned to Red.

" 'John Smith!' " sneered the pilot. "John Doe will do for the jury—when you're held to answer for murder!"

"Will someone be good enough to explain this murder charge?" The mystery man's haughty gaze circled the group around him, this time including the girls.

F. Millard's glance followed his. All eyes were intent on the stranger. There was no softening in any watchful face.

"I suppose you didn't even know there'd been a funeral here." Guy Fletcher's tone was heavily sarcastic.

"Certainly, I saw the funeral," the man returned coolly. "But how was I to know the corpse had been murdered?"

"How indeed?" jeered Tony. "Any more than you'd know how the gas was drained from our plane!"

The man who called himself John Smith whirled on Tony. F. Millard saw his hands strain at their bonds.

"The petrol was drained from your plane? Drained deliberately?"

"Don't push me too far, big boy," Red grated between clenched teeth, "or I may forget myself and take a poke at you.'"

"But if someone deliberately drained off your petrol, he must have meant you to stay here!" The man's tone was incredulous.

Red stuck out his jaw. "So what?"

"You haven't seen us leaving, have you?" asked Michael softly.

"But, I say, that proves it wasn't I! Because I didn't want you to stay."

"Sez you!" barked Red.

"Wait a minute," F. Millard interrupted. "Mr.—er—I wish you hadn't chosen Smith, because that's really my name, except possibly the spelling—why do you say you didn't want us to stay?"

"Because, naturally, I didn't."

"Why not?"

The stranger looked haughty again. "I came here to be alone."

"You came to a good place," the Congressman murmured.

"Why did you come here to be alone?" the grocer persisted, accenting "here."

"I am a writer."

F. Millard heard quickly indrawn breaths and something that sounded like a giggle. "Wouldn't it be just as easy to write in a city, or wherever you came from?"

"Not for my work. I am doing a book on skiing."

F. Millard remembered the birdlike shadow that had soared above his head while he stood that night in the trail. "I imagine you're well qualified," he said politely. "But did you have to come so far out in the wilderness to write a book on skiing?"

"My book is on Arctic skiing," the man said stiffly.

"That's his story," broke in Michael; "if he wants to stick to it, we can soon checkup, now that we have skis."

"Skis?" echoed Kilkenny.

Mick nodded up the hill. The others pried their gaze off the stranger long enough to look. A few yards from the pit, through one of the steep snowbanks that lined the trail, a passage had been cut. There, toes pointed for a quick getaway, lay a pair of skis with two poles upright in the snow beside them.

"This is one time we'll be able to follow the ski tracks." Michael's tone was triumphant. "And we may find a pot of gold at the end of the rainbow. Anyway, we'll find something. Want to change your story?" He turned back to the man who had called himself John Smith.

The stranger's eyes were sullen again. He shook his head and stared moodily down into the pit that had trapped him.

Michael looked at the others. "Now we've got him, what shall we do with him?"

"Do with him?" repeated Hope.

The Congressman laughed. "Don't get upset. I didn't mean a necktie party, or anything so final. We won't try taking the law into our own hands—" he paused "—unless we have to. I mean shall we bring him into our cabin, right into the bosom of the family, or shall we have a separate cell for prisoners?"

"Why, Mick!" Kilkenny exclaimed. "I hadn't thought of that! We don't all have to live in the same cabin anymore!"

"Kenny, I'm hurt," Michael protested, smiling. "Don't you like our big, happy family?"

"Don't be silly, Mick. You know how cramped we are as well as I do. But don't you see—we don't have to huddle in one cabin for protection anymore! Each of us can have a cabin all to himself if he wants to! We don't even have to sleep with the provisions any longer! We've caught the man who made it dangerous."

As he watched her eager face, F. Millard sighed. He looked around at the enthusiastic group and sighed again. "I don't believe we ought to, Kilkenny. We may be a little crowded, but we've got our bunks built now, and we don't have to keep up so many fires, and—besides, he might get away," he finished lamely.

Silence fell on the chattering group, one of those thinking silences that had fallen so often lately.

"Do we have to take him in with us, the way we did the groceries?" Hope asked plaintively. "It's hard enough the way it is without adding a criminal."

"I very much object to that term!" declared the prisoner fiercely. "If one of your party, really has been killed, the criminal is among yourselves."

F. Millard disregarded him. "I'm so sorry, girls. But we'd never forgive ourselves if something happened to anyone else after—after what did happen. Perhaps every thing would be all right, but maybe not. He might get away, and then we'd have to face it all over again. Can't you make yourselves stand it a little longer?"

"If we knew it would only be a little longer—" Guy began.

"Of course, we can stand it," Michael interposed. "The girls have been swell sports so far, and they're not going to spoil their record. I suppose we could tie the fellow up in the cabin you and Fletcher had, couldn't we, Smyth? The provisions are out of it now. Then he wouldn't interfere with our privacy."

"Privacy!" said Tony bitterly. "When you say that— smile!"

The Congressman did. "You'll tell the world a gold fish bowl is a hermitage, I suppose? Well, do you fellows want to dig into the other cabin and build a fire, while I take the skis and see what Mr. John Smith left at the end of his trail?"

Red asked suddenly, "Why should *you* take the skis?"

"Why not?"

"You're always out in front when anything interesting happens. And it was you that started to parley with this bozo before we could see in the pit."

"And it was you that would have been shot if I hadn't!" the Irishman said hotly.

"I've been thinking you know something you're holding out. Why should you be the one to find the stuff this fellow's cached?"

For an instant F. Millard's eyes met Michael's. So he hadn't told Red about the tin?

"And it was you, Michael O'Hara, who found the Senator!"

"Red!" both girls gasped at once.

The two men glared at each other—rangy, redheaded pilot; quick, dark Irish-American.

"By the way!" the Congressman snapped. "The guy had a gun when we got to the pit. Where is it now?"

Red's hand went to his hip pocket.

"Oh, you've got it, have you?" Mick sneered. "Or were you reaching for a handkerchief?"

"I'll use you for a handkerchief, you little runt!"

"Red! Mick!" cried Hope. She darted forward and caught the pilot's arm. "Don't you dare hit him! You're twice as big as he is!"

Kilkenny began to laugh. "Mick's been trained by champions, Hope. If you've got to worry, maybe you'd better worry over Red."

Michael looked from Kilkenny to Hope, Red from Hope to Kilkenny.

F. Millard stepped between the two men in a way that he hoped was firm. "Take it easy, boys. We haven't time for this sort of nonsense." He stopped to clear his throat.

In the momentary pause he heard Guy Fletcher's stage whisper to Tony. "Time's all we have got, to my notion. I wouldn't mind seeing a good fight."

"This isn't the place for it, either," F. Millard added quickly. "And while we're arguing, it might start to snow and cover up the tracks." He turned his back on the dazzling sun. "Let's compromise. Suppose I take the gun and Tony takes the skis."

"The only joker," Tony drawled, "is that I can't ski."

Behind his glasses F. Millard did some rapid blinking. He glanced at Guy who vehemently shook his head.

"I can," volunteered Kilkenny.

"So can I, a little," Hope offered doubtfully.

"You girls can't go in those skirts," objected Guy.

"Besides," F. Millard continued, "there may be a lot to carry."

"I hope a lot of food," said Tony fervently.

"I've never been on skis in my life," said the little grocer, "or I'd go. I guess there's just one thing to do. If Red gives up the gun, wouldn't it be fair, Mick, to let him take the skis?"

Michael gave in with unexpected grace. "Fair enough, if he wants the job of moving the fellow's camp. I only offered because I've done a lot of skiing, but maybe not as much as Red."

The pilot's tension also relaxed. "I've set a lot of planes down on skis, but never used them much myself. Guess I'll make plenty of landings between here and the end of the trail. Here's the gun, Bud. You want to take charge of it?"

He handed F. Millard the efficient-looking automatic that had been knocked from the stranger's hand.

"Why should Smyth have the gun?" demanded Guy. His plump jowls, shadowed with blue-black that shaving couldn't remove, looked like the wattles of a turkey cock. His gross body swelled like a turkey's feathers. "Why not give it to me?"

F. Millard's fingers tightened on the pistol. Give it to Guy? Give it to any of his six fellow castaways? Five of them might think that the captured man had killed the Senator—but the sixth? You had to be sure before you handed over a lethal weapon. You had to be sure you weren't paving the way for a second murder—or a third—or—my gracious, what couldn't happen with a gun in the wrong man's hands!

Guy Fletcher had his nerve! Guy Fletcher—why, now that F. Millard had seen the mystery man's tracks, unless he had an extra pair of shoes in camp that were marked with concentric circles and stars, the grocer knew it was Guy who had left the footprints beneath the Senator's window! Guy who had made the footprints and rubbed them out the next day.

And not only Guy—how could F. Millard have left the gun with Mick, who had stolen the suitcase key; or Tony, who had run from the Senator's cabin; or Red; or even one of the girls? Each had something to his or her discredit; each wore black clothing that had been torn.

The little man's hand closed tighter on the butt of the automatic. He couldn't give it to them. He wouldn't give it to them! For one wild, heady moment he knew the feeling of power. In his own hands he held the only weapon in the crowd. If anyone tried to take it away, he'd let him feel its bite.

Michael shrugged. "It's okay by me for him to have it. With a prisoner to guard, someone has to carry the gun. Millard's been looking after the detective work; so I think he has the right."

"I think so too," Kilkenny said warmly.

The others agreed, Hope, Red, and Tony doubtfully, Guy still muttering;

but they agreed.

F. Millard slipped the automatic in his pocket, patting the bulge with a sigh of satisfaction. It was good to know he had a gun. As for letting any of the others feel its bite, how could he turn it against Red or Michael, Hope or Tony, even against the Mayor? How could he turn it against Kilkenny? But someone had killed the Senator—the mystery man or one of the other six. The gun might have to be used.

"Well, boys and girls," said Red, "daylight doesn't last long in the middle of November. I better get going to follow these tracks. If you can't make our boy friend come clean—" he nodded toward the man whose hands were tied "—maybe I'll bring back the dope."

He fastened the ski straps as well as he could about his shoepacks, picked up the poles, gave one mighty shove to push up the slope the mystery man had cut; then he was off across the snow.

The others stood watching as long as they could see his head above the snowbank. F. Millard wondered if they envied Red as much as he did this chance to leave the shoveled trail and strike off, free, into the hills. The little man sighed. His fingers pressed the automatic in his pocket, and he stifled the sigh. Red might have the trip on skis, but F. Millard had the gun.

The prisoner refused to talk. He, too, had watched Red leave, but when the new-penny bright head vanished beyond the snowbank and the others turned back to him, he refused to enlarge on his skiing book; refused to tell where he had come from; persistently denied all knowledge of the murder, or of the drained gasoline.

Giving up, the four men cleared a path to the cabin that Guy and F. Millard had occupied before the Senator's death and built a fire in the cold stove.

The mood of hilarity had passed. Everyone remained keyed up, trying to pump the stranger, running to the window to watch for Red, but it was nervous tension now not gaiety.

When the long-closed cabin warmed up enough to move the prisoner inside, they tied him to a bunk and left him in disgust.

As they jounced across the plank that bridged the pit to the communal cabin, F. Millard said hesitantly, "We ought to fill this hole while we're waiting for Red, before one of us falls in."

"Oh, hell," Guy grumbled, "we've done enough work today. I'm going to park in that rocker by the fire or know the reason why."

The others agreed, and the fat man was already parked, with his coat and mukluks off, by the time F. Millard, who had stopped to stare at the gaping pit, followed the others inside.

Suddenly the grocer was tired of shilly-shallying. He had seen the track of every man's shoe except Guy's. Now—

He darted forward, caught the Mayor's plump ankle. "Wait!" he cried sharply. "You've got something on your shoe!"

He raised the fat man's foot. There were the dim circles and stars—there on the sole of Guy's shoe!

For an instant the Mayor's black eyes met his. The little man saw defiant knowledge in their muddy depths— Guy knew that F. Millard knew who had made the foot prints beneath the Senator's window.

The grocer dropped Guy's foot. He turned and walked out of the cabin. Until actually seeing the shoes with the circles and stars on Guy Fletcher, F. Millard did not realize how much he had counted on Red's finding them in the mystery man's camp.

Of course the fact that Guy had made the tracks beneath the Senator's window didn't necessarily mean that he was the murderer, F. Millard reminded himself. He might have been a witness. But if he had witnessed the killing of Thomas Jefferson Lee, why hadn't he told? Was he afraid? Was he in partnership with the murderer? Or was Guy the murderer himself?

F. Millard craned his neck. On the skyline the mountains were dim and ghostly, and Red not yet in sight above the snowbank. How much longer would it be before the return of the pilot gave him something else to think about? The sun had already set. Twilight was turning to dusk. Soon it would be dark. He went to go inside, to sit beneath the kerosene lamp, looking at Guy, trying not to give away his thoughts—

A match flared in the communal cabin as someone lighted the lamp. Across the street smoke came out of the house where the prisoner was quartered. F. Millard looked at the gaping pit, at the long, cleared walk to the lake, at the deep indentations in the snow before the Senator's cabin where he had wallowed, himself, a few hours ago, to get the rope. Ever since he had found those black threads beneath the murdered man's bunk, the grocer had played with the idea of an experiment. Now, while he waited for Red, while he wanted to avoid the others, while the path was still open—now was his chance.

F. Millard turned toward the Senator's door and raised his hand to the latchstring.

Chapter Seventeen

Inside the Senator's cabin everything was dark. The blankets still hanging at the windows, as they had hung in the statesman's life, shut out the fading daylight. In spite of the musty odor that had returned since its recent brief occupation, in spite of the weight of snow now pressing against its walls, F. Millard was carried back a month and a half. It might have been the last few days of September, with the Senator sitting up in bed playing mumblety-peg with the Mayor, or Mick, or Hope, or Red. F. Millard might have been coming in to take Guy's place at the board. Or it might have been September 30th, with the room full of people and the Senator doubled across the board he had played on, the knife he had played with plunged deep into his neck.

The little grocer shuddered, longing for a switch beside the door to flood the room with light and lay the ghosts. He fumbled for a match. One of his overcoat pockets held the automatic; he gave its sinister shape a friendly pat. Through the heavy cloth his hand grazed *Flatfoot's* bulge. This he patted too, a sop to Flannagan whose help he badly needed. At last he found the pocket with the matches. Selecting one from the jumble, he felt something else—the sharp edge, the smooth texture of paper—something small and folded. His heart landed with a thud against his stomach. It couldn't, surely it couldn't be another note!

His hands shook so he could hardly strike the match. Its flame showed him the lamp still hanging by its chain from the ceiling. His fourth match ignited the wick. One glance assured him that the Senator's bunk was empty, as it had been for a month and a half. His hand went back to the pocket with the matches.

The ghosts in the cabin might not be real, but the note in his pocket was. Once more the mottled paper leered with evil eyes.

Ask Kilkenny Lee what she knows about the handkerchief that was found on her father's floor.

Kilkenny—the handkerchief—someone else had found out! Her perfume rose again to F. Millard's nostrils. Once more the month and a half rolled back, and the room was packed with horror.

The little man shook himself. Now wasn't the time to think about this new note and its implications. Now was the time for his experiment.

The blankets had been folded at the foot of the bunk. He wouldn't put them back on the bed; he didn't have to make things so realistic for himself, and he'd avoid the hazard of tangling. The handkerchief wasn't necessary either, but a watch—he couldn't use his own. There was no jeweler to fix it if it was broken too. The Senator's, stopped at 9:24, was in the other cabin.

He looked around the room. On the flat top of the Yukon stove, he saw the thick saucer the Senator had used for an ashtray. Would that take the place of a watch? F. Millard carried the table to the place beside the bunk where it had stood the night of the murder and laid the saucer on a corner.

A search of his inner coat pockets revealed only the envelope with the clues; he ought to have some other papers to scramble together in a hurry. *Flatfoot* would have to do. He laid the magazine on the table beside the envelope, his pencil beside that, gave one quick look at his watch before he jammed it back in his pocket, swept the two papers and the pencil hastily together, and dived beneath the bunk.

There wasn't any room for bobbing up and down. He felt his shoulder rub against the poles that made the spring. His shoulder—it had been the shoulder of Kilkenny's jacket that was torn. He pulled up his hips and felt his buttocks bump on the poles. Guy and Red had torn their trousers at the hip.

The Senator's bunk was double width. From where F. Millard crouched against the wall, the frame and poles above his head cut off most of the room. He couldn't see the front door at all, only the crack at the bottom of the bedroom door, the rocks that held up the stove and the legs of the table and chairs. The books had since been carried to the main cabin, but the night the Senator was killed they were stacked on the floor by the table.

The snag in Michael's suit had been at the bottom of his jacket. The hip-rolling exercise could have made it Tony's was near the back of his armhole, and Hope's in the middle of her back. Either of the back tears could have been made on these poles, though Hope's sweater had been mended before the grocer started looking for snags, and she didn't have the workbasket till late the day of the funeral. He remembered her coming for it while he was examining the blotter in the Senator's empty cabin.

That covered the situation. He lit a match to make sure there was no gray fuzz from his own clothes on the poles where he had found the black. Once more he saw the ink spot on the floor, now coated with dust. He almost expected to see the poles sag with the weight of the Senator's body.

Slowly he began to wriggle out; then increased his speed. Whoever had been under the bed must have felt the need for speed before someone else came to the door. Hurrying, it was more natural to kick the spot where the books had been piled and imagine the toppling stack. He hit one rickety table leg as the books must have hit it, and sent the saucer, which should have been a watch, crashing to the floor.

Sprawling half under the bunk, clutching in one hand his papers and pencil, in the other the leg of the table, the saucer in fragments about him, F. Millard jerked up his head. Outside—the crunch of snow—a smothered voice—

The door burst open. Michael plunged into the room. Guy and Tony followed. Kilkenny and Hope hovered in the doorway.

"What's going on here?" demanded Mick.

"What the hell are you doing?" sputtered Guy.

With all the dignity he could summon, the grocer crawled out. He stood up and brushed off his knees. "I—I—" he fumbled for his pockets, and his fingers closed around the automatic; after all, *he* was the man with the gun. "Just experimenting, boys," he finished grandly.

Were you looking for me?"

"Experimenting?" queried Tony sharply. "What do you mean by that?"

"Oh, just working on a theory." F. Millard tried to make his voice offhand, but even the possession of a fire arm didn't show him all the answers.

"If it has anything to do with the killing of Senator Lee, I thought we had a theory." Tony's words were slow, deliberate, spaced. His eyes gleamed through narrowed slits.

"Well—mmm—" the little man faltered "—we did, didn't we?"

"Why, Tony," exclaimed Michael, "didn't we decide it was the mystery man?"

"*We* did." The secretary's voice was charged with meaning. His hard blue eyes met F. Millard's. "But did you?"

"Why—why, of course; that's what I meant." His words stumbled over each other. "I was just checking up on—on our theory about the mystery man."

Kilkenny spoke. Her face was almost as pale as the last time F. Millard had seen her in this room. He could hear in her voice the effort she made to speak lightly.

Your experiment seems to have been pretty hard on the saucer. Do you want to pick up the pieces and come back to the other cabin?"

Hope stepped back from the doorway. "Mick, come here," she called excitedly. "Did you ever notice the hole in the blanket at this window? I wonder how long it's been there? What if—"

Kilkenny turned around. Michael started for the door followed by the others.

Before they reached it, Hope flew back inside, her eyes round and big pupiled. "If the snow wasn't there, you could look right into the cabin! Does anyone know—" she glanced suddenly at Kilkenny and lowered her voice "—was that hole there the night the Senator was killed?"

While Hope was still asking her question, F. Millard told himself he must not let his eyes seek Guy. If Guy wasn't the murderer himself, then, on account of his special knowledge, he was in danger. Now that F. Millard knew it was Guy who had made the footprints, he knew also they had been made almost at the time the Senator was killed between 9:15, when the wind died down, and 9:30, when the body was discovered. Guy had been with him every minute after that until F. Millard himself closed the peephole in the blanket.

Guy moved restlessly. The motion drew F. Millard's eyes, and their glances meshed. At last the grocer forced them apart. Hours seemed to have passed, and yet Michael was just answering Hope's question. Maybe that long stare, while speculation tumbled over speculation in his mind, had been neither so long nor so conspicuous as he had feared.

"I didn't notice," Mick was saying, "while the Senator was alive. But it was the light shining through that hole that made me investigate tonight."

"Was it there the night of the murder, Mr. Smyth?' Hope persevered. "I know *you* must have noticed."

No use to lie about it now, the grocer thought. The damage had been done. Guy must have realized it too. His glance scuttled from face to face. "Yes," returned F. Millard slowly. "It was there." But maybe it wasn't too late to cover up. "Of course, that doesn't mean anyone happened to be on hand at just the right time to look through it. If anyone had, he'd certainly have told us."

"Of course," the Congressman agreed. "I'd like to find out how much you could see through it, though."

"M-me too," stammered Guy.

"I'll get a shovel," Tony volunteered.

The others followed him outdoors. F. Millard was amazed to find that it was dark. No wonder the small star of light shining through the blanket had caught Michael's sharp eyes. He'd been in the cabin longer than he realized. Red ought to be back by now.

Tony brought the shovel and flung snow about like flour. A funny contradiction, that young man, the way he both sought and avoided physical exertion.

A passage was soon dug to the window, where every one took turns applying an eye to the hole, everyone but Kilkenny. She stood in the trail, gazing off in the direction Red had gone.

This might be only satisfying idle curiosity for the others, F. Millard reflected, shivering, as he waited for his turn; perhaps only he and Guy knew how important it was. He and Guy, if Guy was the murderer; he and Guy and someone else, if Guy had been a witness.

A surprisingly large portion of the room showed through the gap, he discovered when his turn finally came. He could see from the bedroom door to the stove. But no matter how he twisted, the Senator's bunk, built into the front corner on the other side of the door, the table, and all the space around them were hidden from view.

Out in the trail Kilkenny gave a cry of welcome. "Red! Here comes Red!"

Everyone rushed forward. Through the darkness something blacker loomed above the snowbank.

"What'd you find out, Red?" Tony called.

"My God!" The pilot's voice was clear. It sounded closer than his shadow looked. "My God, I haven't had time to find out anything. All I am is a pack mule. Come and unload me and we'll go over the stuff together."

He slid down the slope the mystery man had cut in the steep bank, gliding into the waiting group, his outline distorted with bulges. In the darkness F. Millard made out a sleeping bag, a suitcase, something tied in a blanket like Santa Claus's pack.

They all started for the communal cabin. F. Millard heard their voices and the creak and pop of their passage over the cold plank across the pit. The little man stopped and turned back. He'd left the lamp burning in the Senator's cabin, and they mustn't waste kerosene.

As he stepped over the threshold into the empty room he heard behind him the crunch of snow. He whirled, his hand leaping to the pocket with the gun.

The Mayor appeared from the darkness. "Listen," he began abruptly, "don't go jumping to conclusions. You've got to look into things first."

F. Millard was still too startled to speak.

"Why was Tony Webber's heart too bad for active service? What was Mick O'Hara's connection with the Mt. Zion tunnel disaster? How much does Kilkenny Lee know about that handkerchief dropped on the Senator's floor? Find out—"

F. Millard choked, "It was you who wrote the notes!"

"What if it was?" the Mayor barked. "You've got to know what sort of folks you're dealing with. They're not all sweetness and light. Take *off* your rose-colored glasses!"

"What a low-down, dirty stunt!" For once the tremor in F. Millard's voice came from earnestness, not strain.

Guy made a sound that was half snort and half stage laughter. "Anonymous letters aren't in the class with murder, you know. Think it over, brother. Get wise to what you're mixed up in."

He stepped out into the night.

Chapter Eighteen

With hands that shook, F. Millard turned down the wick of the lamp and blew out the flame. He closed the Senator's cabin and hurried to the lighted house next door.

The table was littered with papers, Kilkenny, Mick, and Tony bending eagerly above them. A suitcase stood open on the floor. Red was still unloading. He pulled a hatchet out of his belt and laid it on a blanket on the floor, beside a heap of groceries.

He looked up with a grin as the door closed behind F. Millard. "Where you been, Bud? Thought you'd be right in pitching when it came to getting the dirt. Tell him what you found out, Kenny."

Kilkenny raised topaz eyes now black with excitement. Mick and Tony didn't even lift their heads. "That man's no more English than I am!" she cried. "His name's Rudolph Schrenk. And he's a Nazi agent!"

The Congressman looked up. "Now we're really getting somewhere. 'John Smith,' my eye! And a book on skiing! I suppose he figured we'd never be able to get at him, so he didn't destroy his papers. We found maps, and a German passport, and letters from Nazi officials, proving he's an agent. He had a camera too."

"What the hell would a Nazi agent be doing out here all by himself?" growled Guy, once more established in his rocking chair.

"There might be several reasons," F. Millard answered slowly. To himself he added, a German agent—tin— Japan—anything might happen.

Red held up a weighted canvas sack. "Does this look familiar, boys and girls?"

"I know the face." Michael's forehead puckered. "But I can't remember the name."

Kilkenny jumped to her feet. "Our canvas mukluks!" she cried.

Red grinned. "And look what's in it!" He pushed the papers on the table to one side and dumped out a stream of brownish pebbles.

"That's what those bags were for!" exclaimed Tony. But F. Millard's eyes met Michael's.

"You know what this is, Congressman O'Hara?" The red-haired pilot grinned down at the man in the chair. "Correct me if I'm wrong, but weren't you making a mineral report on Alaska?"

"Do you know what it is, yourself?" countered Michael.

"Sure I do. An aviator gets around."

Mick glanced once more at the grocer, who nodded.

"From where I'm sitting—" the Congressman's voice was very clear in the quiet room "—it looks like placer tin."

Kilkenny, Hope, Tony, and Guy leaped to attention.

"Tin!" gasped the Senator's daughter. "Is that why there's a German agent here?"

"Could be," said Michael.

"Could be," echoed Tony.

"Tin!" Guy muttered. "I wonder if the poor devils who used to live here knew about it?"

"If there's much of it," cried Hope, "think how important it would be, with the situation what it is in the Pacific!"

"Any government that can name tin among its resources," said the Congressman solemnly, "is damn lucky."

"Have any of you thought about how close we are to Japan?" F. Millard asked.

Hope suddenly paled. "Do you mean—you don't mean—"

"This man is a German agent. Japan and Germany are partners. Figure it out for yourself."

"Oh, no!" she cried sharply. "We're not at war!"

"Maybe we are," said F. Millard.

"We were damn close to it," said Michael, "back in September, when we dropped out of the world."

"Well, anyway—" Kilkenny brought an end to the baffled silence "—we've got the mystery man. We know his name and business. That's one whole set of worries we can cross off our trouble list."

F. Millard's glance flicked to Guy, and hastily withdrew. Why not rejoice over snaring the mystery man, instead of seeing other dangers larger and nearer than ever? Maybe his own speculations were leading him the wrong way. Maybe all danger was centered in Rudolph Schrenk. Maybe, by capturing him, they had drawn the fangs of the lurking menace. If he could only believe that, the little man sighed.

His glance fell to the jumble of articles on the blanket spread out on the floor. "The bad thing about catching the fellow is that now we have to feed him. He must be pretty hard on groceries, if this is all he had left?" He looked questioningly at Red.

"Every can and bean, worse luck," returned the pilot.

F. Millard picked up the hatchet he had seen Red take from his belt. It was bright and very sharp. "The little brother of our ax," he said idly, "I suppose he brought them both. Well, it may come in handy someday." How handy, he didn't know, then.

He joined Mick and Tony at the table. They were still poring over the Nazi's papers when the girls said dinner was ready.

"I'll carry over Rudolph's supper," F. Millard offered. "I wouldn't mind another little talk, now that we knowwhat we're talking about."

"Count me in too," said Mick.

"And me," said Tony.

Kilkenny's eyes sparkled. "I want to see his face when you tell him what we know."

"But let's make him wait for the second table," said Hope.

When the prisoner's plate was ready, everyone but Guy started for the other cabin. The fat man stayed in the rocker by the stove. F. Millard looked back and saw him sitting there alone. Something fluttered in the grocer's chest. "Aren't you coming with us, Fletcher?"

The Mayor shook his head, and rocked on.

"I don't—I hate to leave you by yourself." F. Millard hesitated. "I don't think you ought to stay alone." His glance was full of meaning.

"Good God!" Guy wriggled impatiently. "Why not give me a bottle with a nipple, and be done with it?"

F. Millard glanced behind him. The others had all gone out. He could see them across the pit, headed for the prisoner's cabin. The grocer lowered his voice. "Things are different now, you know."

"Because we caught this Rudolph fellow?" Guy sneered. "More personal than that—for you."

"What do you mean?"

But F. Millard saw the other man's hands tighten on the rustic chair arms. "I think you know what I mean. But in case you don't—has it occurred to you that the murderer didn't guess until today that he might have had a witness?"

"What—?"

"There's no use bluffing, Guy. Even if you did brush out those tracks in front of the Senator's window the morning after he was killed, what makes you think I was the only one who saw them? If the murderer didn't know about that snag in the blanket till tonight, he may be pretty busy now putting two and two together. Are you coming? I'm in a hurry."

His face a purple-tinged gray, Guy got up, though force of habit brought one more protest. "You might have left me the gun."

"The gun," said F. Millard firmly, starting across the street, "stays where it is…. Who did you see, Guy, through the hole in the blanket?"

Guy's fat face looked knowing. "That'd be telling."

They paused at the door of the other cabin. "Then tell me this," said F. Millard: "when you looked in, were the mumblety-peg board and knife on the chair by the bedroom door?"

Guy considered. "No," he answered finally. "That chair was the closest thing under my eyes, and I remember noticing a knothole in the seat, and wondering if it wouldn't be uncomfortable to sit on. I couldn't have seen that knothole if the mumblety-peg board had been there."

Inside, the room was crowded. The prisoner stood by a bunk, facing his captors. Hands still bound, one leg tied to the bunk with a longer rope to allow him freedom of movement, this man had a very different air from the surly captive who had refused to talk, different from that of the more voluble author of a book on skiing who called himself John Smith. Tied like a dog on a loose-running wire, like a goat staked out to graze, yet this man was insolent, arrogant, disdainful of his captors.

"Have you told him?" F. Millard asked.

It was the prisoner who answered. "Your friends have told me that I no longer need to dissemble, to hide behind a name and nationality repugnant to me."

"Repugnant?" F. Millard repeated.

Michael grinned. "Even the British are mud beneath the heel of the Teutonic Aryan."

"Better turn your profile, Mick," Kilkenny giggled, "so he won't make any mistake about that wavy black hair."

"Kilkenny Lee!" reproved Hope. "How can you joke like that, when this man killed your own father?"

The Senator's daughter caught her breath sharply. Red laid his arm across her shoulders. Mick turned away from the tableau. Hope took a quick step toward him, and then drew slowly back.

F. Millard sighed. He returned ostentatiously to the prisoner. "But you do have a British accent, even now when you say you don't have to pretend."

"That's one reason they chose me for this job. With Canada Alaska's nearest neighbor, my accent would pass unchallenged." Now that his status was established, Rudolph Schrenk seemed to enjoy the superior position of passing out information. "I went to school in England."

"You're making a fine return for a liberal education," said Michael scornfully. "The way your country did in Norway, where they sent so many German boys after the last war."

"When one country is so much more intelligent, it ought to rule. And it will! You'll see!" A fanatical gleam lit the German's eyes. "It won't be only Norway and England; your own United States will come under our domination!"

Red dropped his arm from Kilkenny's shoulders and doubled up his fists.

"Why, even Alaska—" rang out the German's voice.

F. Millard caught the aviator's elbow. "Wait a minute, Red; I want to hear—yes, Mr. Schrenk, you were saying—about Alaska—?"

The German looked from the little grocer to the truculent redhead. His glance traveled over the semicircle of faces, and a thin-lipped smile lifted the blond mustache above his teeth. "Alaska is filled with our agents. There isn't a town of any importance without one: Ketchikan, Juneau, Anchorage, Fairbluffs, Nome, and a hundred other places; spots you may never have heard of, like this, but spots that have their interesting features."

"Tin deposits, for instance?" queried Tony,

But the smile that looked like a snarl on Rudolph Schrenk's face remained superior. "So you found that out too? You're not so stupid as most of your countrymen."

Red started forward, but F. Millard's fingers tightened on his arm.

"You supplied us with samples," said Michael O'Hara suavely.

F. Millard looked at him keenly. For once it wasn't hard to imagine the young Irishman in Congress.

"Ninety-five per cent of the people in Alaska are too ignorant to tell placer tin from any brown pebble in a stream bed," declared Schrenk. "All they think of is gold."

F. Millard's ears burned. His eyes fell on the covered tin plate that someone had laid on the stove while he and Guy argued in the other cabin. "My gracious, we forgot to give Mr. Schrenk his supper."

No one seemed to care except the prisoner; so F. Millard dragged a table to the bunk and laid on it the scantily filled plate. Schrenk jerked at his bonds.

"But—but he can't feed himself!" exclaimed Kilkenny.

"He won't get fed by me," said Hope grimly.

F. Millard looked at the men. Every face was forbidding. "Why not untie him long enough for him to feed himself? I'll stand by with the gun."

He took the automatic from his pocket. Tony untied the prisoner's hands.

Grudgingly watched by everyone in the room, Rudolph Schrenk flexed his arms and ate.

"I wouldn't be on short rations if it wasn't for you!" He pushed aside his empty plate and glared at his captors.

Kilkenny turned her back. "There've been times when I've felt almost guilty about eating another man's supplies. But now I know he's a Nazi agent, it makes me feel he has no right to American food."

"Maybe this isn't American food," Schrenk growled

"What do you mean?" F. Millard asked quickly.

The prisoner turned sullen again, clamping his lips together.

"If we nail the nearest windows shut," suggested Guy, "why not leave his hands loose so he can keep up the fire for himself?"

"There'd be too many other things he could do for himself," returned Red, "including laying for the first man in the door with a piece of stove wood. While Bud's here with the gun, we can untie him to eat. Or else he can root for himself in the plate."

"Like—like a hog!" cried the pink-cheeked school teacher. "Like Hitler and all the Nazis!"

"Hope!" Kilkenny gasped.

"Good for you, Hope," Michael applauded.

"Careful, Mick," warned Tony. "That kind of talk leads to war."

"Where we belong," muttered Michael.

"That's all right for you to say," retorted Tony. "A Congressman wouldn't be drafted."

"A man doesn't have to be a Congressman, I understand," said Michael meaningfully, "to get on the deferred list."

"Any insinuations?" Tony blustered. "A disability—"

"Oh, for God's sake, boys," broke in Kilkenny, "let's forget it and go back to our bridge game."

"Second the motion," Guy muttered.

Red tied up Rudolph Schrenk again, while the German scowled and swore. Michael jammed the stove with wood, and the jailers trooped back over the plank to their cabin.

There were other things F. Millard wanted to ask the prisoner, but they were things that required putting out feelers, perhaps some delicate fencing. The little man sighed for the finesse of Flatfoot Flannagan; well, he'd have to do the best he could, when the time came. But with everyone on edge the way each was tonight, with nationalities and personalities already clashing, now was hardly the time.

But even away from the upsetting presence of the German, that night the personalities didn't settle down. The bridge game broke up in a quarrel. The girls kept darting poisoned arrows through blowguns aimed at each other. The men, except for F. Millard, acted as if they were in some sort of conspiracy, not only against him, but against each other as well. Two at a time, heads close together, they kept going off in corners or outdoors; seldom the same two heads together twice. The girls got into it too. *Flatfoot* in one-hip pocket and the heartening automatic in the other were poor compensations to F. Millard for the feeling of being left out. Red's big hand on Kilkenny's arm, Hope's fair head close to Mick's dark one, Tony and Guy hobnobbing together, gave the little man sitting by the stove a feeling of forlornness. A constant reshuffle of partners left him still alone. The buzz of low voices, the nervous tramp of feet, made him uneasy too, reminding him uncomfortably of the night the Senator was killed.

When at last Kilkenny announced, with an enigmatic topaz glance at Hope, that she was ready to call it a day and go to bed; and the teacher, with an answering blue glance at the Senator's daughter, followed her behind the hanging blankets; F. Millard drew a long breath. Perhaps now all the clashing personalities would rest.

Tonight, he had one more possession to take care of before he went to sleep. Each night since the Senator's death, F. Millard had removed the envelope with the clues from the breast pocket of his jacket and disposed it neatly beneath the underwear he slept in. Slipping it under the pillow would have made it too easy for someone else to slip out. Now he had a gun to think of too. He laid it under the covers between himself and the wall.

The other men settled down slowly. Michael kept the lamp on, sitting at the table for an hour or two after F. Millard lay down. Red and Tony talked for a while in low tones, and then Red and Guy. Presently they went to bed, but Guy's snores were filling the room before Mick blew out the light.

The restless spirit that pervaded the cabin that evening still hovered about it at night. F. Millard slept fitfully. Every time he woke it seemed to his anxious ears that the door had just opened or closed, that footsteps had just died down. The last few times he wakened, toward morning, he didn't hear Guy's rhythmic snore. *Oh, well,* he thought drowsily, *seven people in one room—you can't expect—*he turned over, felt for the automatic, and slid once more into sleep.

When he opened his eyes in the morning, the other men were up. Mick and Tony were dressing in their corner across the room, Red stoking the fire; Guy's bunk, with its head to the grocer's, was empty.

As F. Millard sat up, Red nodded toward the Mayor's rumpled blankets. "Even Guy's out early this morning. Doesn't that put you to shame?"

Hope's voice called from the curtained corner. "Are you men dressed? I want to come out and start breakfast."

F. Millard grabbed for his trousers. "Wait! Wait!" he begged. "Just a minute, girls."

He scrambled into his clothes. He had reached the coat stage, one hand fumbling for a sleeve, the other for the gun in his bed, when someone called "The coast is clear," the girls emerged, and breakfast preparations began.

A breakfast as scanty as theirs didn't take long to prepare. The biscuits were out of the oven twenty minutes after F. Millard began to struggle with his jacket. As they gathered around the table, one place was still vacant.

"Guy sure must have important business," Red remarked, grinning. "This is the first meal I ever knew him to be late to."

Guy—F. Millard's flying glance counted faces. No one else was missing. He allowed himself to exhale. If one of the others had been gone too—but Guy should be safe alone. "He must be—" the little man stopped. A painful blush surged up past his collar. In the week and two months since their party had been stranded, in the more than six weeks since they had all been living in the same cabin, there was still one thing he couldn't mention before the girls. His unwilling eyes pivoted toward the window that overlooked the backyard.

Red laughed and shook his head.

F. Millard's blush vanished. He leaped to his feet.

"How long's he been gone?" he snapped.

The other looked up blankly.

"His bunk was empty when I got up," Red volunteered.

"I haven't seen him all morning," said Mick.

F. Millard's chair crashed to the floor. "Come on! Quick! We've got to find him!"

"What's eating you, Bud?" demanded Red. "Guy Fletcher's been in the Territory over forty years."

"Why all the excitement?" drawled Tony.

"Smyth, you don't mean—?" Michael leaped to his feet.

"Yes, I do mean something may have happened to him! We've had one murder already! Guy may be next!"

Now they were all on their feet, snatching wraps. The men didn't stop for mukluks. F. Millard panted up the trail and down to the creek, Red tore on through the woodlot, Tony ran to the prisoner's cabin and back across the street to the Senator's, Mick dashed for the lake.

It was Mick who found him. F. Millard, returning, half frantic, from his fruitless errand to the creek, met the girls coming out of the communal cabin with their makeshift mukluks just tied, Tony shaking his head as he closed the Senator's door. Faintly, far down the hill they heard a shout. At the base of the spur jutting out to the lake the black figure of Michael, no larger than a bug, gestured and called. Tony shot off like a greyhound, Kilkenny close behind; F. Millard and Hope pelted after.

By the time the last two reached the spur, the others were out of sight. Red yelled coming down behind them. All three swept around the hill together and slowed to a sickened stop.

Just past the promontory, where the trail crossed the beach, Kilkenny knelt by a prone figure, dark against the snow. Mick and Tony stood beside her, looking down.

"Guy!" F. Millard wheezed, struggling for breath. "Is he—?"

Silently Tony and Michael stepped back.

Though the body lay on its face, there was no mistaking its bulk. Guy Fletcher, one-time Mayor of Fairbluffs, sprawled, stiff limbed, in the path. From the side of his neck, toward the back, protruded the Nazi agent's hatchet.

Chapter Nineteen

"My God!" cried Red. Staring down at the dark huddle with the appalling patch of crimsoned snow beside it, he clenched both fists. "How'd he get untied?"

"He wasn't tied," Kilkenny whispered. "Why would anyone tie up Guy?"

F. Millard whirled on Tony. "The German—Schrenk— you looked in his cabin! Was he there? Tied up?"

Tony nodded. "Just like we left him last night."

"Oh, you mean was *he* still tied? I didn't think—why, of course, he'd have to get loose to—do this, wouldn't he? But if he's still tied, then how—?" Kilkenny stopped. Her face paled. Her eyes were round black dollars. "Does that mean—?"

The sound of breathing was the only sound in the white wilderness of lake and hills.

"That means," said F. Millard grimly, "that it has to be one of us."

Their breaths caught in a gasp.

Suddenly Michael jumped. "Maybe there's someone else! Maybe Schrenk wasn't the only one in the hills! Someone else may have slipped in and done this."

"We can soon find out," shouted Red. "You go the rest of the way to the plane, and Tony and I'll go back up the hill, each side of the trail. No one could come without leaving tracks!"

It didn't take long. F. Millard had only started to ask Hope about Guy's connections in Fairbluffs before Michael came back.

Guy wasn't married. She said he had no relatives there, and, while he knew casually nearly everyone in town, he had no special cronies.

By then Red and Tony were back. "No tracks," Red said briefly.

The grocer bent over the body. "Does anyone remember where that hatchet was last night?"

"I picked it up with the other things Red brought in," said Hope, "and laid it on the shelf by the door."

"Right where it was handy."

"Oh, Mr. Smyth, don't say that! I never dreamed—"

"No, no, Hope, of course not. I only meant—well, it was handy, for someone."

Again, that breathing hush closed in around them.

F. Millard sighed. "I suppose there's no use asking if any of you were up in the night and saw Guy." He waited not very hopefully. When no one spoke, he sighed again. "You don't want to admit you were out of bed yourselves, I suppose. Well, maybe you'll tell me later, alone. Look here—" he leaned forward, peering intently into each face "—you know how important this is, don't you? It may mean the difference between life and—this." His eyes returned to the body lying on the hard-packed snow. Hard-packed, but not too hard for impressions. The snow in the trail was thickly studded with footprints. He looked quickly at Michael. "You found him. Did you look for tracks?"

"I looked," said Michael. "But I saw what you're seeing now. You know how the trail gets when we haven't had new snow, a mess of every-which-way tracks. I couldn't tell one from another."

F. Millard forced his eyes back to the sickening thing in the trail. "They used the hatchet just the way they used the knife the other time—someone standing a little behind the victim, with the hatchet under his coat, or up his sleeve. The victim turns his head, and the murderer lets him have it. The body fell forward both times, and the weapon went too deep for spurting blood; it would mostly be internal."

Kilkenny shuddered.

"I'm sorry, my dear," he said gently, "but we have to figure things out. We can't just let it go on."

"Do you think the same person killed Guy and my father?"

"The law of averages wouldn't let two people out of this small group be killers, would it?"

"How about Rudolph Schrenk?"

"The law of averages still holds good. If he did the first murder, it's reasonable to think he did the second. But when the second murder took place, Rudolph Schrenk was tied up. It's no pleasure for me to insist, Kilkenny—" F. Millard's voice was tired "—but we haven't any out: the murderer must be one of us."

Someone, he thought, his glance swiftly touching each face, that Guy knew and felt he could trust. But after living ten weeks with these people, whom didn't he know and trust? The scalelike glitter of marbled paper slithered into the grocer's mind. However well Guy had known them all, was there one of them that he trusted? Before going so far from the cabin at night, he must have thought he had nothing to fear. Then he couldn't really have known who the killer was, or he'd have known there was something to fear. All that buzzing last night, those heads close together—that must have been when the plan to meet was made.

The killer had been smart to lure his victim here. Suppose something had slipped up, the hatchet missed its aim, or Guy turned in time to see it coming? Down here, beyond the promontory, who could have heard a scream? Or the threshing about of a fight? F. Millard shuddered. A fate like this he couldn't wish on even the author of the notes.

Red broke the long silence in which they had stood staring down at the body. Staring at the body, F. Millard wondered, so they wouldn't steal sidewise glances at each other? "Well, fellas," the pilot said matter-of-factly, "We'll have to start the fires again."

The fires—more ground must be thawed for another grave under the spruce trees. The four men bent to lift the body of Guy Fletcher, while the close white hills and the far white mountains watched.

Hope opened the door to the Senator's cabin, and went on home with Kilkenny, while the men carried Guy inside. By the limited light from the open door, they blundered their way to the bunk, where six weeks before, another body had awaited burial. The birch poles creaked beneath their newest burden.

Tony struck a match and reached for the lamp.

"Hey!" Red blew out the flame. "You're wasting kerosene." He twitched down the blankets from the windows' "Poor old Guy won't need them to keep off drafts."

"I hated to mention it before the girls," said F. Millard, "but he's pretty stiff. I wonder if that's rigor mortis or freezing."

"You and Flatfoot Flannagan may be up on rigor mortis—" Red managed a crooked grin "—but it wouldn't take long at forty below for a dead man on the ground to freeze."

"Where's the key to the suitcase?" asked Michael. "We'll have to take care of that hatchet."

For an instant his eyes met F. Millard's, and the grocer remembered Michael bent over the open suitcase with the bloody handkerchief in his hand, his defiant words: "I found that key where you dropped it, and you can't prove anything else."

F. Millard fumbled inside his shirt and produced the key on the fishline around his neck.

Red whistled. "You weren't taking any chances."

Again F. Millard's eyes met Michael's. "Murder isn't anything to fool with," he said simply.

"You thought all along it was one of us, didn't you, Smyth?" demanded Tony, with narrowed blue eyes.

The gaze of the other three converged on the little grocer. He groped for words and found Red's. "I wasn't taking any chances."

They kept on staring. F. Millard tried not to shiver. Each pair of eyes was cold and distrustful. His hand slid to the pocket with the automatic.

Michael turned away. "We'd better get those fires going."

A pathway had to be cleared from the blueberry patch to the two graves under the spruce, and a six by three rectangle of frozen ground scraped bare. Two fires had to be built, and flattened kerosene can reflectors placed above them, before the men could return to their interrupted meal. Shuddering, F.

Millard wondered if they'd be able to eat. While Hope warmed the coffee and gathered up cold biscuits to toast, he wrapped the hatchet in a canvas sack—that hatchet that was still as sharp as when he had first examined it, but now no longer bright—and locked it in the suitcase with the mumblety-peg knife and handkerchief. Once more they sat down at the table. They all ate something, even the girls, and tried to talk and act as usual. Breakfast couldn't be called a gay meal, but they didn't seem stunned as they had when the Senator was killed. Was it because Guy left no daughter behind him, or was it—they acted, the little man caught himself thinking, almost as if this murder was something expected, as if they had braced themselves for it. He choked over a bite of biscuit—what if he wasn't the only one who'd been getting notes from the Mayor? Guy might have been no more popular with the others than with himself. Again, he remembered the whispering last night. But they couldn't have ganged up on Guy, not people like Kilkenny, Hope, Red, Michael, Tony! His first idea must be right. Otherwise, it was too pat: Guy's murder coming right on top of finding the peephole at the Senator's window.

"The last few times I woke up in the night I didn't hear Guy's snores," F. Millard said aloud. "Does any one know when they stopped?"

Michael answered promptly, "No."

Red tried to be jocular. "Fella, when I sleep, I sleep, I don't keep my eye on watches."

Kilkenny glanced at the empty rocker by the stove and shivered. "Poor Guy. I'm sorry now I used to curse his snoring the times it kept me awake. But it's queer about last night; I slept unusually well."

"Then you didn't see or hear anything?" F. Millard persisted.

Kilkenny shook her head.

"I heard plenty," said Hope. "I only slept in fits and starts. I didn't get up," she added hastily, "but it sounded like everyone else did. I heard steps and the door squeaking, and once I thought I heard voices."

"What did they say?"

"They were too faint. I wasn't even sure it was voices, but I thought so."

"And the snoring?"

"I don't remember when it stopped. My watch doesn't have a luminous dial, and I didn't light a match to look."

"What about you, Tony?" asked F. Millard.

"Everything we say will be used against us, I suppose?" Tony raised blond eyebrows. "Well, I didn't time the snoring, and I didn't get up… Have we any hot water, Hope? I'm going to shave."

"To tea dance at the embassy?" Kilkenny gibed.

"You said yourself we shouldn't go native. And now more than ever—" his glance found Guy's empty chair "—we have to keep up our morale."

"Darling, of course!" Kilkenny was contrite.

F. Millard's eyes traveled to the shelf by the mirror where the old-fashioned razor lay. They came back to the breakfast table and caught Mick's watchful gaze.

"Yes," said the Congressman clearly, "I was thinking of that."

"Thinking of what?" demanded Red.

Every face turned toward Michael.

"Senator Lee was killed with a knife and Guy Fletcher with a hatchet." The Irishman paused. "Is it safe to leave a razor lying on a shelf?"

Once more F. Millard heard quick, indrawn breaths.

"No, by God!" roared the pilot.

"But what shall we do?" cried Hope. "Will you have to stop shaving?"

"I think Tony was right about our morale," said F. Millard, "we shouldn't give up shaving. But I agree with Mick about the razor. Can't we keep it in the suitcase? That's the only thing that locks."

"And *you* have the key!" Tony's voice was unpleasant. *"And* the gun," Red added.

F. Millard set his jaw. Whatever happened, they mustn't find out they could upset him. His hand slipped into his hip pocket, and he straightened his shoulders. "I have the key and gun," he said firmly.

"Why should Smyth have the gun?" demanded Tony. "My right's as good as his."

"A gun might be handy in this joint," drawled Red. "I wouldn't mind having it myself."

"I've already put in my bid," said Michael.

"Why shouldn't I have it?" asked Hope. "I don't know much about guns, but I'd feel a lot safer with one."

"Well, I know how to use them," declared Kilkenny. "You could give it to me without a struggle."

"Look here, Smyth!" Tony walked close to F. Millard. "I want that gun."

Mick moved up. "After me, brother. After I'm through with it."

"How do you get that way?" growled Red. He stepped to F. Millard's other side. "Gimme, Bud."

The grocer swallowed. These three men could jump him and take it, the way they'd done with Schrenk. But, by gracious, they wouldn't get it for nothing! He backed off, his fingers closing over the butt of the automatic.

He'd have one more try at persuasion, unless things got too thick. "Wait a minute, boys! We had this out when we got the gun. You all agreed I should have it, as detective in charge of the case."

"But that," broke in Kilkenny, "was when we thought Rudolph Schrenk was the killer. We thought we had everything under control. It's different, now we know—"

Her voice trailed off while her eyes made a brief inspection of everyone in the room. F. Millard caught each answering glance, guarded, suspicious, swift. The men moved nearer.

"I warn you, fellows, anyone who tries to take this gun is going to get hurt. I don't want to shoot, but if I have to—look here, you agreed once to let me have it. If things have changed, why not put it to a vote?"

The girls and Mick were willing. Red said nothing, darting a quick glance around the room.

"How do we know," demanded Tony, "that F. Millard Smyth, the guy with the gun, isn't the murderer himself?"

"You don't," F. Millard admitted. "I could tell you I'm not, but each one of you'd claim you weren't either." He could tell a whole lot more, that the threads on the Senator's bunk poles were black and his own clothing gray, but he wasn't ready to show his hand; it might spoil everything. He wouldn't show it, even if they got the gun. "Suppose you pass out papers, Kilkenny, and we'll vote."

"What shall I use for paper?"

F. Millard surveyed the room. His eyes fell on the row of books. "Any flyleaves left?" His mind recoiled—the mottled paper—Guy—"No, don't! Can't we write on the face of the cards?"

Kilkenny dealt one to each person. They wrote briefly. She collected the cards and gave them to F. Millard.

Clearing his throat, he read his own card first. "F. Millard Smith." He turned over the next. "Red Bailey." The next. "Michael O'Hara." Then the other cards. "Kilkenny Lee. Hope Mullen. Anthony Webber."

Kilkenny began to laugh. "Everyone voted for himself. I know I did. But I'll admit I want the gun."

"You ought to have it," muttered Red. "Guess I can take care of myself. You need it. Let's vote again."

F. Millard deliberated. Suppose Red voted for Kenny: if the others kept voting for themselves, that would give her the gun. If they took it from him, he'd rather she had it than anyone else. But he wasn't going to let it out of his possession without a fight, not even to Kilkenny. Lovely Kilkenny Lee, often as she figured in his dreams, was still the owner of the perfume on the bloody handkerchief—Kilkenny who needed money—neither of the killings had required great exertion of strength. It couldn't be Kilkenny, he insisted, but he had to keep the gun.

"All right. Pass out some more cards. But there's one condition: If anyone votes for himself, it won't be counted. I won't vote. I'm prejudiced."

"We're all prejudiced," said Michael.

"I can afford to be," returned the grocer. "I've got the gun." His voice, to his own amazement, was steady. For the first time in his life, he intended to play dirty. There was a strong possibility, with no one allowed to vote for himself, that F. Millard would be the most innocuous prospect. If the vote was for him, his object was achieved; if against him, he'd keep the gun just the same. He had to; this game was for life or death.

Once more Kilkenny passed out the cards, once more the pencils wrote, this time reluctantly. The score stood two for Kilkenny, in Tony and Red's handwritings; three for F. Millard Smyth.

A long breath sighed over the room, the longest from F. Millard. He settled the gun more firmly in his pocket, once more opened the suitcase, and locked the razor inside.

"Has anyone—" Tony's voice was ice-cold "—decided how we're going to shave?"

Michael gave him a wry grin. "First, get Smyth to unlock the vault. Second, at least two of us will stand by while anyone uses the razor. Third, lock up again. Right, Smyth?"

F. Millard flushed, but answered sturdily, "Right."

* * *

The thawing fires had to be replenished and another coffin built out of floorboards. By the time the ground was soft enough for picks, daylight had long been lost, but rather than put off their unpleasant task another day, the men hung lanterns on the spruce boughs, and in that wavering, shadow-twisting light, they dug a grave for Guy Fletcher.

As they lowered the new coffin while the shadows jerked and lunged, F. Millard had never been so conscious of the close-pressing hills, of the barrier mountains beyond. Now, in the dark, with lantern flickers hiding stars and blotting out the snow-pale sweep of hills, he felt the pressure of those hills and mountains more strongly than when he could see them—the pressure, the power, the immensity, and loneliness.

The Senator had gone first, Guy was the second to escape from the rotting cabins and snow-weighted hills; death broke trail for him too.

Tony heaped on the last spadeful of earth, and the grocer unhooked a lantern from a bough, and blew out the light. Red reached for another, Mick the third, and Tony the last. As the lights winked out and the four men followed the girls to the blueberry patch and up the trail to the cabin, F. Millard saw once more the starlit hills, and the stars. Northern lights were leaping in the sky—yellow torches, red torches, green, they streamed across the black, starry dome above three lonely graves.

Back at the cabin, the four men leaned shovels and picks near the door. Kilkenny stood staring at the tools.

"What's the matter, Kenny?" Red asked softly. "We'll fill up the pit tomorrow and do our best to see that those picks never have to dig another grave."

"I was thinking—" her voice rose in the quiet night while sky-torches flared overhead "—that hatchets and razors and knives aren't the only things to be feared. A pick could kill a man. Or an ax."

Everyone stood still. All eyes whipped to the cabin and the implements tilted against it.

Tony broke the silence with a grating laugh. "What about your suitcase, Smyth? Will it hold four picks and an ax?

"You may think that's funny—" F. Millard gave a quivering sigh "—but I wish we could stretch it to hold them. It's a chance we'll have to take. At least no one can hide a pick the way he could a knife or a hatchet, while he's pretending to enjoy a little chat. At least we'll have some warning."

Chapter Twenty

The cabin seemed strangely empty that night without Guy's snores to fill it. At bedtime more snow began to fall. The hush the falling snow brought to the out-of-doors and the hush Guy's absence brought to the room kept F. Millard wide awake. He wondered how many of the others lay as he did, staring into the dark. Tonight, he heard no sound of footsteps. A few sighs and the creaking of birch pole springs quivered against his taut eardrums. But anyone who was awake stayed circumspectly in bed. He wondered if everyone guessed that he lay with his hand on the automatic.

Next morning, regardless of the falling snow, the men filled in the pit. Like—F. Millard caught himself thinking and tried to stop—like closing another grave.

Michael stamped down the last shovelful of frozen clods. He tossed up his pick and caught it. "And that, fellow citizens, is our second payment on murder insurance."

"Second payment?" asked Kilkenny from the doorway.

"Murder insurance?" asked Hope.

"What's the use locking up things like razors, with a ten-foot drop outside the door? How long would a murderer pass up a chance like that? And now—" the Congressman twirled the pick and stopped in front of F. Millard "—I suggest we gather these lethal weapons and shove them all in there." He nodded toward the Senator's empty cabin where snow was fast filling the trail.

"What's to prevent someone's going in to get them?" demanded Red.

"Footprints, brother. If we don't shovel the trail, even if it only snows a foot, no one's going to get into that cabin without leaving enough evidence to hang him."

"You've got something there, Mick," approved Tony. "Too bad we can't put the ax in too."

"It'd sure save the killer a lot of trouble if we did," remarked Red. "Without any way to chop wood, Old Man Winter would polish off the rest of us in no time."

They waded through loose snow to the cabin. Each man deposited his pick. As F. Millard came out and shut the door, he found Michael waiting for him.

The Congressman spoke softly. "Let me go with you when you take in Schrenk's lunch. I want to see you."

The grocer's eyes brightened. Did Michael have something to tell about Guy or the night he was killed? But when the two men went across the street with a steaming plate, untied the prisoner, and moved to the farthest corner of the room while he ate, the subject the Congressman brought up in low tones had no direct connection, if any, with Guy's death.

"I've been thinking over what you asked about the Mt. Zion tunnel."

F. Millard jumped.

I'm afraid you have the wrong impression. Perhaps I should have explained it. But I didn't think anyone up here knew about it except the Senator, and your question startled me. Besides, the whole thing has very painful associations."

Michael paused and cleared his throat. When he spoke again his black brows were pulled together. "My first job when I got out of college was clerk for the Mt. Zion tunnel commission. When they called for bids for timber, they naturally accepted the lowest. I didn't know anything about it, but when the stuff came, it didn't look good to me. The chairman of the board was there when the cars were unloading, and I called his attention to it. He asked me what I knew about timber, and when I admitted I'd never had anything to do with it, he said it might be a good idea to get a clerk who had; that the stuff looked all right to him."

Michael took out his handkerchief, grimy and unironed after more than two months in the wilds, and rubbed it over his face.

F. Millard waited.

"That was early in the depression." Michael shoved the handkerchief back in his pocket. "Men were losing jobs right and left, and hardly any of the kids just out of college with me were able to get them. Naturally, I buttoned up my lip. I wasn't going to expose my ignorance again."

In the quiet cabin F. Millard heard the young Congressman gulp. "No use prolonging the agony." His hands knotted into fists. "The timber was poor, all right. The tunnel collapsed, and twenty men were killed."

"Oh, no!"

"Oh, yes." The younger man's voice was bitter. "And I got the blame for allowing that timber to pass! They said ignorance was no excuse. Someone muttered about a bribe from the lumber company, and someone else said it was damn funny that they knew how low to bid."

F. Millard gave a noncommittal cluck.

"Well," said Michael briskly, squaring sturdy shoulders, but the grocer heard him swallow again, "then I went into politics. But whenever the heat's turned on, I've had to do things for some of that board ever since."

"You say Senator Lee knew this?"

"He was on the board."

At the other end of the room something creaked. F. Millard whirled. Rudolph Schrenk was stealing toward them. The grocer pulled out the automatic, and Michael came to life. The German shrugged and returned to his bunk. Michael tied him, picked up the tin plate, and turned, with F. Millard, toward the door.

With his hand on the latch, the Irishman asked suddenly, "How did you find out?"

"About Mt. Zion?"

Mick nodded. "The Senator was dead."

F. Millard's swallow was nearly as loud as Mick's. Until the grocer asked about the Mt. Zion tunnel, Michael had thought the Senator was the only one here who knew —and the Senator had been killed. But Guy had known about it too—and now Guy Fletcher was dead.

"Well?"

"G-Guy told me," F. Millard stammered. "I suppose the Senator told him."

Back in the communal cabin, Michael and F. Millard found drama. Hope sat stiffly erect, her eternal mending on her lap, the workbasket on the floor beside her. Kilkenny, Red, and Tony all stood facing her.

As the door closed, four pairs of eyes appealed to the men who came in.

Mick grinned. "Okay. Get it off your chests." No one spoke.

F. Millard felt uncomfortably that the eyes were directed at him. "What's the matter?" he asked gloomily.

Hope's hand disappeared beneath the mending in her lap and reappeared with the scissors. "These!"

"Scissors can kill people!" cried Kilkenny.

"You bet they can," endorsed Red.

"Why not keep them in the suitcase?" asked Tony.

"How'll I get my mending done?" fumed Hope. Her yellow curls quivered above indignant blue eyes. "You'll all be the ones to suffer. No one else does any mending around here."

"How do we get our shaving done?" countered Tony. "Every time a man wants to shave he has to hunt up a couple of witnesses and F. Millard Smyth to unlock the suitcase."

"But I use the scissors a hundred times a day! You only shave once. Mr. Smyth, you tell them I won't do any scissor murders!" Hope's cheeks were on fire.

"Darling," soothed Mick (F. Millard started; it used to be Kilkenny Mick called "darling"), "it isn't you. I'm sure no one expects you to do any scissor murders. But someone here might. Someone here doesn't care what he uses for weapons, just so they're sharp enough."

"You mean you think—" she hesitated.

"Yes." It was F. Millard who answered. "I think they ought to be locked up, even if it is inconvenient. I'm sorry, but we don't dare take any more chances than we have to."

"I hadn't thought of scissors," Michael mused. "There might be other things. How about pocketknives? Does anybody have one?"

F. Millard's hand slid into his change pocket; Red's dived for his.

Michael grinned. "Fork over, lads. Hope has to give up her scissors. I don't have a knife. Do you, Tony?"

"Not since I was a kid."

F. Millard flushed. Was that superior secretary making fun of him?

Michael collected the scissors and both knives. Reaching the suitcase down from the shelf, he brought it to F. Millard.

Hope made a final protest. "You might as well say table silver's dangerous."

"If you could call it silver," Kilkenny murmured.

"And could cut steak with the knives," said Tony adding, "if we had a steak."

"I doubt if the knives are as sharp as the spoons" agreed Michael. "Anyway, short as we are in the food department, we'll have to keep them for it. Anyone think of anything else to go in the suitcase?"

That was the last F. Millard saw of his pocketknife until the ritual of shaving. That ritual: the little grocer unlocking the bag, standing with the other men while each took his turn at the razor, one hand in the hip pocket with the gun, while *Flatfoot* jutted rakishly from the other— was to become as much an established habit as the daily trip to the lake.

For two days after the second murder, F. Millard had no time to investigate the note he had found in his pocket the day before Guy died. But beneath every activity of those two days an insidious question nagged him: *Ask Kilkenny Lee what she knows about the handkerchief found on her father's floor.*

It couldn't be true, of course, the implication in that note. Yet all of Guy's notes had been disconcertingly based on fact. Red's first plane had been bought with Irv Cramm's money and crashed with Irv in it. Whether or not that crash was intended by Red was something else again. There was something queer about Tony's not being drafted; his heart seemed good enough for anything except to join the army. Hope's aunt's profession was no credit to a schoolteacher. But whether Hope's refusal of assistance made the aunt continue that profession was something else again also. And Mick— what he knew about the Mt. Zion tunnel was plenty. He might have been as innocent as he claimed, but the smoke the note had raised certainly had fire beneath it. What would F. Millard find out when he interviewed Kilkenny?

His chance came the next day. Since they no longer needed a guard at the cabin, everyone but the prisoner joined in shoveling out the trail and clearing off the wings of the plane. When Red pulled out the fishing tackle, Kilkenny asked to use it. The pilot's face brightened. F. Millard began to chop out the thinner ice at the bottom of the fishing hole. From the corners of his eyes, he saw the others shoulder their tools and start back up the trail. Red touched Kilkenny's elbow, raised his sandy eyebrows, and jerked his thumb at F. Millard.

"Thanks a lot, Red," said Kilkenny clearly. "Mr. Smyth will help me. Be seeing you."

F. Millard turned away to hide a grin. Over the smashing of the ice he heard the pilot's disgruntled retreat. The grocer's grin abruptly faded. Kilkenny didn't know he wanted to talk with her. She must have arranged the whole thing in order to talk with him.

"That's big enough," she said. "It's only a fish we want to haul through, not a man. Not—a—man," she repeated slowly, eyes wide with sudden horror. "You couldn't lock up a hole in the ice inside the suitcase to protect us."

"It's hard to believe the number of ways you can think of to kill a man," said F. Millard chattily, "if you put your mind to it."

As she stared, the horror left her eyes, and her lips shaped their wide smile. "You *are* sweet, F. Millard Smyth. I'm almost glad we voted you the gun. By the way, what does the F. stand for? 'Mr. Smyth' is so formal and 'Millard' so sort of bald. And you just can't call a man 'F. Millard.' "

"I—I wish you wouldn't ask me that," he stammered. 'My mother wasn't given to jokes, but she certainly played one on me when she gave me that name."

"Lord, another mystery! Well, if you must keep your guilty secret—toss me the bait, will you?"

"Red calls me Bud," he suggested.

"Bud it shall be," she smiled, and dropped her line into the water.

That leopard coat would never look like a parka, F. Millard thought indulgently, or Kilkenny like an Eskimo woman, if she fished through the ice all winter. Her personality was as apparent in her very clothing and mannerisms as in the spirit that refused to be broken by the endless undulation of prisoning hills that rose behind her to mountain walls.

But she hadn't sent Red away to ask F. Millard about the F in his name. Yet the grocer himself was equally hesitant to start his own inquiry. "Have you known Tony long?" he began at last.

"Ever since he's been Dad's secretary—seven or eight years. Why?"

"Did you know he had a bad heart?"

"A bad heart? Seems to me that was why the draft board turned him down. Though anyone who looks less—"

"But muscles like his—Kilkenny, have you ever wondered—?"

"Muscles to play contract and dance the conga? But I shouldn't say that; whatever I used to think, Tony's worked as hard as any of us since we've been stranded."

"Whatever you used to think?"

"Oh, just that social things were all that mattered to him. I thought he was working my father for more than a job. But since we've been out here, he seems different."

Different, F. Millard wondered? The old motif of the secretary in love with the boss's daughter? Or would Kilkenny's inheriting the Senator's fortune have anything to do with it?

Kilkenny pulled out a fish. F. Millard detached it and rebaited the hook. She leaned over the hole to watch the line hit the water.

Abruptly he could wait no longer. He couldn't beat about the bush and fence with this enchanting girl as he had fenced with Tony and Red. He had to ask his question—two questions, get his answers, and bear them, whatever they might be. If Kilkenny was implicated in murder—

He'd put off Guy's note till the last. "Kilkenny, why did you want more money? Why did you ask for five thousand dollars cash, and pad your bills?"

Her eyes flew to his. Then he saw her brace herself and her chin set a little more firmly. "I'll tell you all about it, Bud. I—I really think it'll be a relief. I've been so upset. For six months before we left Washington, I was nearly crazy. And then, after Dad—after we'd been here a month or two, and I came to know you better—yes, you, Bud! You're not afraid to face things. You're not afraid to bring them out in the open. I wished then I'd told Dad about it, before it was too late."

F. Millard made a soft sound of encouragement.

"Maybe it wouldn't have made any difference. Maybe it would have been just shifting my troubles to Dad's, shoulders. Well, it's too late now. But when we go back, I'm going to face it—and beat it!"

For a flash F. Millard saw the do-it-now spirit of her father in Kilkenny.

"You may not think much of me after I tell you, but it's you, and this experience out here, that have taught me to be honest. I guess I've been kind of contrary and restless without knowing why, ever since Mother died and Dad went in for—things I didn't like, and politics. Any way, there's a roadhouse not far from Washington that has an especially bad reputation, and Dad put his foot down about my ever going there. One of the men I knew had been coaxing me to go with him, but Dad didn't like him any more than he liked the roadhouse. Well, one night I got one of those contrary streaks— what got me was Dad's figuring it was all right for him to do anything; that he could cover it up; but it wasn't all right for me—I called the man he didn't like and said I'd go out to the roadhouse. It really was a crumby place and I wished I hadn't come as soon as I got there."

Her line began to jerk, and she hauled up a fish. F. Millard unhooked it and impaled new bait.

"We had dinner," Kilkenny went on, nodding her thanks. "And of course, something to drink, not very much, but it must have been drugged. Because, when I came to, it was the next day, and I was lying on the bed in one of the upstairs rooms of that miserable—joint!"

She pulled up another fish. This one she angrily detached, herself, and slapped the hook back in the water. "I told you, you wouldn't think much of me; I didn't think much of myself. But it was really only appearances. All I'd done that I shouldn't was to go there in the first place, but how could I prove it?" She drew a long breath. "A month later I found out just how low the whole thing was. The roadhouse keeper began to blackmail me. He and the man I went with had been in cahoots. First, he asked for five hundred dollars, and then a thousand, and then—the time I asked Tony for it—he wanted five thousand dollars!"

"Why didn't you tell your father, Kilkenny, and take your medicine?"

"I couldn't—or I thought I couldn't. You know what scandal does to politicians. Dad couldn't just shrug it off as a wild daughter's escapade, because the roadhouse keeper had something on him too. The fellow told me that if I went to anyone about it, he'd prove Dad had been there twice himself, overnight with a little 'lady' from Baltimore."

"You poor kid," said F. Millard gently.

"Oh, how I hate that sort of life!" she burst out. "I wish I was back on the ranch with no prospect more exciting than marriage to a neighbor!"

"Well, my dear—" the little grocer's voice was still soft; he laid a gentle hand on her leopard-skin shoulder "—that's one nightmare less to haunt you when you go back. You said now you were going to face it and beat it."

She stared. Slowly the bitter look left her face, and her eyes came alive with gold sparkles. Impulsively she swooped forward and pressed her red lips against F. Millard's cheek. "Thanks, darling, for all you've done."

He swallowed, blinked, and swallowed again to keep back something that might have been his heart. Why hadn't he caught her in his arms? Why hadn't he told her while he had the chance? Now she was leaning over the hole watching her line again.

She gave him another smile, brighter than sun on snow. Then something like his own shyness came to her. "Do you remember we talked one night about our yellow streaks? You're helping me beat mine. I've been afraid of life and trying to be hard as nails to cover up. Why, I—I've even been afraid to marry! I thought a girl like me, wild and restless and contrary, shouldn't be tied to a man. But now—" she paused.

"Do—do you have the lucky man picked out?"

"I guess I must be coy at heart." Her eyes flashed laughter at him. "I haven't made up my mind. Red's pretty sweet, but that stubborn Irishman has his points."

Red—that stubborn Irishman—of course, he had to be young. F. Millard's madly beating heart slowed down. "I thought—" he forced himself to speak

"—I thought you didn't like politics."

Her bright gypsy face darkened. "You know how I feel about that."

Mirth, bitterness, joy, hate—as changeable as a weathervane. The Irish and Spanish in her perhaps. As changeable as the beat of his own heart. "Isn't Mick going to stay in politics?" he asked.

"Oh, I suppose so." She gave the fishline an impatient flip. "Once in politics, try and get out! I ought to know."

"But, Kilkenny, you can't blame politics for—for all you father's—acts."

"*I* can," she declared. "Whatever psychologists say. It wasn't till after Mother died, and he went into politics, and his natural kindness and friendliness petrified into synthetic pat-you-on-the-backs that he developed a weakness for women."

My gracious, had Kilkenny heard the rumor Michael had repeated to him? The rumor F. Millard connected with "and to my" on the blotter?

"Of course, I've heard the story about—Dad's other child."

F. Millard jumped. Could she read his mind?

"But at least," she plunged bravely on, "that wasn't one of these light affairs he's been having since he went into politics. Sometimes I think that's why I don't like Hope, even more than because of the way she's been working out on Mick. Hope's the kind of girl Dad used to fall for before his tastes got more sophisticated—the womanly woman!" Staring at her jerking fishline, she said grimly. "There was a time that whenever I saw a girl Hope's type— and Hope's age—I wondered if she could be my sister." The grocer gasped. "S-sister? Kilkenny, have you ever felt that Hope Mullen might really be your sister?"

"If an almost irresistible longing to beat another woman over the head with a club is a sisterly feeling, then, yes, I've sometimes felt that Hope might be my sister." Scornfully, she pulled up the line. "But I found out last year that Dad's other child was a boy."

"K-Kilkenny, have any of the men here ever acted brotherly toward you— Red or Tony or Michael?"

"Brotherly! Anything but." The splash of the rebaited hook in the water was less tinkly than her voice. "I know you'll think I've got my knife in

Hope because she snatched Mick—but have you ever thought of her for the murderer?"

"Kilkenny!" F. Millard leaned forward, took the Senator's daughter by the shoulders, and shook her. "When you talk like that, you make me think about Kilkenny cats."

"You've been talking to Hope! It isn't cattiness, just wishful thinking. She doesn't have what it takes to murder, anyway. She'd be better in the role of victim."

"That's not a thing to joke about, my dear."

Kilkenny flushed. "Of course not, Bud. I'm sorry. I told you I get wild sometimes, and contrary." She gave him a twisted smile. "Maybe it's just thinking of Hope as mistress of Mansion O'Hara."

"'Mansion O'Hara?' What on earth are you talking about?"

"Mick's place. That gentleman's estate where his family has been born for generations with silver spoons in their mouths."

"Kilkenny! I thought Michael O'Hara was a farm boy!"

"He was, but definitely streamlined. The O'Hara's got hit hard, though, in the depression. Mr. Smyth— Bud—" without waiting for a nibble she pulled up the line and dropped it on the ice, turning tensely to face the grocer "—do you think Mick's fallen for her?"

Was it to ask this question that Kilkenny had offered to fish? "Fallen for Hope?" he exclaimed.

"Seriously? Do you think he really cares?"

"Why, I—I—isn't he in love with you?"

"He used to be. He said he was. But I've never seen him like this with anyone else. He—he said maybe he'd marry a—a real woman who'd help him in politics, instead of holding him back."

"Kilkenny!"

"He must have meant Hope. Oh, well—" she threw back her shoulders; he saw her hands clench while her lips stretched into a smile "—a girl can't always be thinking of her heels."

"Her heels?"

"He's hardly taller than I am. When I wear spike heels he isn't. Who wants to marry a man as short as that?"

F. Millard winced.

"Now Red Bailey—"

"Listen, Kilkenny—" the grocer caught her arm. His question about her needing money had started a train of thought, of words and actions, still rumbling by. Now his chief question, the one he'd sought her out to ask, could no longer be sidetracked. "I'm going to tell you something. I shouldn't. But feeling about Hope the way you do—remember the handkerchief we found on your father's floor?"

Her cheeks went white, but she nodded.

"That handkerchief was scented with your perfume. If you dislike Hope so much, it may be mutual. You keep your perfume in your handbag; what if she stole it, and planted that smell on the handkerchief to make it look black for you? The morning after your father was killed, Hope asked me to bring your handbags from his cabin. What if she wanted to take your perfume bottle out of her bag and put it back in yours? What if—?"

"Oh, Bud, I wish I could let you figure it that way! But I can't—much as I'd like to prick Hope's balloon. Because I asked her to ask you for our handbags. And I put the perfume on the handkerchief myself."

"You—you had that handkerchief in your possession?"

"Ever since we came here. I found it in one of the cabins and we were so short of everything, without baggage, without even a change of stockings, that I washed and kept it for a spare. And then—that's why I couldn't say anything when you found it, all bloody, on the floor—I'd been carrying that handkerchief myself!"

"Kilkenny, don't tell me you had it the night your father was killed!"

"I don't remember for sure, Bud. But I must have."

"Oh, my God!" His words were a prayer. Into his uplifted, harassed face, beyond the curve of hills, white and jagged and harsh, the mountains stared coldly back.

Chapter Twenty-One

The rest of the day was a nightmare to F. Millard. He could think of nothing but Kilkenny's revelation. She had been carrying the handkerchief that was found on her father's floor. Her perfume was on it because she put it there. Had she used the linen herself to wipe blood off her hands? No! No! Not Kilkenny.

But money was the greatest motive for murder in the world. Flatfoot Flannagan had brought that out a score of times. Then how about "and to my"? If the Senator had another child, perhaps he'd divided his fortune. Perhaps someone else stood to gain as much as Kilkenny.

Rudolph Schrenk could hardly be her half-brother. But even if the illegitimate son of a United States senator could be a German citizen, speaking English with a British accent, a spy in his father's country, common sense said that whoever killed the Senator also killed Guy Fletcher, and Rudolph Schrenk had been tied up as tight as the string on a butcher's package when the second murder took place.

That left Michael, Red, or Tony who could be at the same time the murderer and the Senator's natural son. Each had been frank enough about his antecedents, their stories had really been frank, and not merely stories. Kilkenny said she knew Michael's people. Still—

There ought to be a pattern; that's what the mystery books said. But if there was any pattern among the hit-or-miss facts and wild guesses F. Millard had assembled, it must have been for a crazy quilt. The ravelings and the ink spot under the Senator's bunk, the fountain pen cap on the table, the books on the floor, the blotter, the broken watch—all combined to suggest one story. The notes and the shabby secrets they uncovered; the draining of the gas tanks; the finding of this lonely settlement, tin, and a Nazi agent—combined to suggest nothing. How about the Senator's strange contentment with his exile? Mick and the suitcase key? Tony's running from behind the Senator's cabin the night the statesman was killed? One after another, recollections darted into F. Millard's mind, swerved, and darted out, like a flight of swallows.

Coincidence, according to *Flatfoot,* was something to be looked at askance. Wasn't there too much coincidence in there being valuable mineral deposits, a foreign agent, a mysteriously vacated settlement, a stranded plane, and two murders—all in one infinitesimal square mile out of the vast wilderness acreage of Alaska? That much coincidence ought to make a pattern.

From the first it had seemed to F. Millard that the apparent abandonment of the village, long ago as it must have been, had more significance than the others would admit. If he found the answer to that question, would he be any nearer to finding the murderer? On the surface, it didn't seem likely, but murders weren't surface affairs. A connection between the hamlet's desertion, the tin, and Rudolph Schrenk seemed more likely. Or were they all independent matters? That circled back to coincidence again.

By a stretch of imagination could tin be back of the murder of Senator Lee? What about their flight from Fairbluffs? He rolled his frayed copy of *Flatfoot.* It had been Guy who saw the smoke. Had it been the Senator or Kilkenny who suggested landing? Out of all the cubic miles of air above Alaska, why had that route been chosen? Who chose it? The Mayor, as host of the flight? The Senator, as guest of honor? Or Red, who flew the plane?

F. Millard sighed and shoved the rolled magazine back in his pocket. Was all this thinking wasted effort? If tin was back of the murders, what about the words on the blotter? Could the Senator's natural son have any connection with tin? Surely the ink spot and ravelings were related to "and to my." But tin? And a foreign agent? And a deserted Alaskan village? Circles again, by gracious!

His mind returned to the cobwebby cabins, the knives and forks and dishes on the shelves, the interrupted card game—all pointing toward a normal existence suddenly broken off. The letter from Henry's wife had suggested two possible endings. The most obvious was starvation, with little Jud, lying under the spruce, a victim. But as Guy had pointed out, people who starve leave bones, and Jud's grave had been the only one they found.

The second way the letter pointed seemed too fantastic. Jud's mother didn't trust the natives, Indians without squaws or children led by an Eskimo. F. Millard could remember from his reading there had been no native trouble in interior Alaska since Russian days. The massacres at Sitka and Nulato were ancient history even in '99. That notion seemed too fantastic, but something had happened—not the slow way, by starvation—something sudden.

The letter, all the voiceless evidence within the cabins, were the only clues to the past. But Rudolph Schrenk was already here when the plane landed the Senator's party. He might be the connecting link between the past and present. F. Millard pulled his overcoat and hat off the caribou horns and stepped out into the trail.

Dusk was closing in about the crumbling cabins. This was the fourth day since Schrenk had been caught. After the first day, except to attend to his necessities, his captors had been too busy to pay him much attention. Tied there alone in the few hours of light and the long, long Alaskan November darkness, he ought to welcome diversion.

There was still enough light for F. Millard to see the combined eagerness and defiance with which Schrenk turned to the opening door.

"It isn't mealtime. To what do I owe this unusual attention?"

"I thought—" F. Millard was about to say, "you might be lonesome," but such uncalled for pampering would put the German on his guard. "I thought you needed more fire. It's getting colder outside."

"Outside!" The prisoner's tone was bitter. "What difference does that make to me? Cold nights, before I fell into that deathtrap of yours, I could ski down close to the cabins. I would have found it amusing to watch you through the lighted windows—two beautiful girls, one with so much fire and restlessness, always searching for amusement—cards, men, anything she could find—"

Was that how Kilkenny looked to the skulker who came at night? No wonder F. Millard had known the feeling of being watched. There *had* been eyes in the hills.

"—and one so fair and still, sitting there sewing and watching… Two girls and three young men. A big old man with a well-shaped head. I didn't see him long. I suppose he's the one in the new grave under the spruce."

The *new* grave? Then Schrenk didn't know there was a newer grave now than Senator Lee's.

"A fat man always sitting in the rocking chair. And—" the German paused; through the deepening dusk F. Millard caught the malicious gleam of his teeth "—the little gray rabbit with quivering ears, hopping from group to group."

F. Millard was glad of the shadows now.

"I would have been amused," continued Schrenk, "if I hadn't watched you gobbling up my supplies."

"It was lucky for us," the grocer mumbled, drawing up a chair, "that you had so many supplies. You must have been planning to stay a long time."

"Long enough to accomplish what I came for."

"And did you?"

Again, the gleam of teeth. "I was ready to leave."

"But how could you get away, all by yourself in the middle of winter? On skis?"

Through the dusk came a throaty chuckle. "I think, little gray rabbit, that shall remain my secret."

"But how did you get here? You couldn't have brought all those supplies in on skis! And that suitcase!" The suitcase stuck in his mind; that wasn't the sort of thing men took camping. "Did you come by plane, or dog team?"

"My secret, gray rabbit!"

For a shackled prisoner, this fellow was too cocky. There might be something behind it. But just now F. Millard was concerned with other problems. The German must have stalked them like a cat. He might have picked up some valuable information. "I believe you when you say you didn't kill my friend." He'd keep back the clinching of that belief; the second murder would be an ace up his sleeve. A little fear of the law would do Schrenk no harm. "That's my own belief, you understand, Schrenk; I can't answer for the marshal." He paused for his words to penetrate the other man's consciousness. He saw Schrenk's body tense. "You must have been hiding where you could watch us the very first day. It would help your interests as well as mine if you could tell me who drained the plane's tanks. Did you see anyone go to the plane While the rest of us were in the village?"

The German answered slowly. "You must recall that there was no snow when you arrived. I didn't have the advantage then of the only pair of skis and deep snow. Of course, I watched from the hillside, but you ran about like chickens. Naturally I was more interested in what went on among the cabins, so I chose a vantage point overlooking the village. I could see part of the trail, but the plane was out of sight."

"Did you see anyone on the trail?"

"Yes," returned Schrenk positively, "I wasn't watching the trail, you understand, but I happened to see two persons."

"And they were—?" F. Millard leaned forward.

"The blonde young lady—I saw her going toward the village—and the big redheaded man."

Red! F. Millard caught back a gasp. "You mean he was with her?"

"No. They were by themselves. He went down the trail after she came up. He was out of sight for some time before he returned."

Had it been Red, F. Millard asked himself, on whom he smelled gasoline that first day? Red? Why had he been so sure it wasn't Red? Just because you don't expect murderers to be redheaded men, any more than you expect them to be fat men, or pretty girls? At least he'd been right about the fat man; Guy hadn't been the murderer. But someone had killed Thomas Jefferson Lee, and some one had killed Guy Fletcher.

"I suppose," F. Millard said, feeling his way, "it was you who put the new leather latchstring in the cabin down the street."

Schrenk nodded. "The old one had rotted away or been gnawed. I thought, at first, I'd live in that cabin, and then I decided on this one closer to the woods. If anyone came, as your party did, I could make a quicker escape."

The bloodstained handkerchief—the letter R—Kilkenny found it here when they came. F. Millard leaned forward again. "Did you lose a handkerchief, Schrenk, when the plane landed, and you left so suddenly?"

The German's dim outline once more expressed wariness. "A handkerchief? Why do you ask?"

"Someone found one embroidered with R in one of the cabins. It wasn't old, like the rest of the clothes, and your first name is Rudolph."

Schrenk took a long time to answer. "Are you trying to connect me with the murder?" Suddenly his wariness vanished. He leaned back against the wall. "Your friend was killed three weeks after I left here. If my handkerchief was in your possession all that time, it couldn't implicate me. Yes, I left it. I was sorry, because it was embroidered by my—what you would call my girlfriend."

There was a certain satisfaction in solving even such a minor mystery as the ownership of the handkerchief. Yet it really proved nothing. It was still Kilkenny, by her own admission, not Schrenk, who had carried the thing.

The part about Schrenk's girlfriend might be worked on. "I am glad," said F. Millard softly, "that you have someone to think about, a dear one. It must help to pass the hours of darkness in this spooky place." He looked closely at the shadowy figure of the other man. A light would show his face, but confidences come out more readily in twilight.

Schrenk disregarded the lead. He straightened aggressively. "You are most inhuman to give me no lamp! Here, in this land where day is one long night, with only enough brief sun to tantalize! There is a lantern half across the room, which I cannot reach, but you light it only when you bring food. There are books in the cabin where you live, but they are not for me. What do you think I am? An ox that chews a cud?"

"It is a shame." The grocer's voice was as smooth as heavy syrup. "We fixed your rope so you can lie down or sit or stand. I wanted to give you a light, but the others say you would burn through your knots."

"Would I be fool enough to burn my hands through too?"

"That's what I told them, but they said it was running a risk. Perhaps they still think you're involved in the murder. Of course, it's our duty to turn you in for being a foreign agent, but I'd hate to see you stuck with a murder charge when you didn't deserve it." He paused again significantly. "If you happened to pay us one of your visits the night my friend was killed, and saw something—somebody—"

"Listen to me, gray rabbit!" Incredible as it seemed, with the man tied and F. Millard in possession of his gun, the German's voice held a threat. "I wasn't here the night that man was killed. I wasn't anywhere near. I know nothing about it. You're not getting me mixed up in murder. I tell you I wasn't here."

"Well, if you weren't, you weren't," F. Millard soothed. "Of course, it would be easier to prove your innocence if you could pin the murder on someone else, but naturally I wouldn't want you to invent something you didn't see. I was just thinking the others might be more favorably disposed—it does seem a shame to sit here alone in the dark in a place as spooky as this. I hope you're not superstitious."

"Why do you keep dwelling on the supernatural?"

"But surely you know the story of this settlement?' F. Millard tried a shot in the dark. "You know the old superstition about people haunting the place where they've met violent death?"

"Does your murdered friend haunt these cabins?"

"I wasn't thinking of my friend; I meant the people who built them." Drat the gloom! Now he wanted to see the man's face. But, again, the shadowy outline was all he had to judge by. Once more he saw it tense.

"Do you think the people who built these cabins met violent deaths?" Schrenk hedged.

"Yes, I think so. Don't you?"

"Did you find any evidence?"

"Didn't you?" F. Millard parried. "How long had you been here when we came?"

"Four months." A direct answer for a change. But when he heard the German's next words, F. Millard decided Schrenk's direct answer had a purpose. "There was nothing here to suggest foul play when I came—four months ahead of you. I don't believe you really know any thing about this place."

"Don't you? I'll bet I know as much as you." Miserably F. Millard knew they were behaving like two small boys swapping lies, and he was the smaller boy with the poorer lie.

"You think so?"

This time the grocer caught no gleam of teeth. He couldn't see the other man's shoulders shake, but he was certain that, in the dusk, the Nazi was laughing at him. It was time, he decided, to play his ace. "Well, I'm glad things like that don't bother you, or I'd hesitate to tell you the latest news." Schrenk's head jerked up. "A while ago you spoke of seeing a fat man with us."

"Yes."

"You haven't seen him for a few days, have you?"

"No."

"Two nights ago he was murdered."

Gott." The German sprang upright. "The Indians were right! This place is cursed! So many deaths—but they weren't in the village—" F. Millard heard the click of Schrenk's teeth as he clamped his jaws together.

Now was the time to go, on that striking exit line, leaving the Nazi with something to think about in his hours alone in the dark.

"You can't—you can't do this to me!" cried Schrenk. "You can't leave me at the mercy of a murderer! You'll have to untie me! You'll have to bring me a light!"

F. Millard stood up. "Sorry, but we can't take the chance of your getting away. I don't believe the murderer will bother you."

"But what if he does? What if he comes here? You can't—"

"Sorry," the little man said again. "I have to go now, but I'll drop in again."

He closed the door on the German's shout, astonished at his own capacity for ruthlessness, for the cat-and-mouse game he had played. As he thought of Schrenk's terror he felt faintly ashamed of himself, but ethics and necessity didn't always mix. A small-town grocer from Nebraska could hardly be expected to match wits with an international spy, and yet, this time, the small-town grocer had won. He strutted back to the communal cabin.

The Nazi agent knew what had happened to the people of this village—death by violence that took place somewhere else. How could a Nazi know what Alaskans like Guy and Red didn't? How, unless his presence here was some way tied in with the past? F. Millard almost capered through the door. Now, he felt, he was on the right track.

Chapter Twenty-Two

T hanksgiving came and passed, with only the opening of an extra can to mark the holiday.

Hope put real deliberation into choosing that extra can. She stayed behind Thanksgiving morning while the others set out to clear off the plane. From the doorway F. Millard saw how small she looked, alone in the bunk-lined room, with the fast dwindling store of food, fair and small and appealing. He stepped back inside and closed the door.

Hope glanced up, holding out a can. "What do you think, Mr. Smyth? This is the very last of the corned beef, but after all, it's Thanksgiving."

The grocer took the can and returned it to the shelf. "We'll have to save something for Christmas."

"Christmas! Don't tell me you think we'll be here then! Do I have to put up with that girl's cattiness another month?"

F. Millard sighed. Evidently Kilkenny's feeling was returned. "I wish you girls got along better—only two of you, hundreds of miles from the rest of the world."

"Maybe that's what's the matter." Hope sighed too. "I could like her so much—if she'd let me." Her voice was wistful. "You know about my aunt. You know what's been in my background. As a teacher, I've achieved respectability, even social standing, in Alaska. But that's not enough. It doesn't make up for what I've missed. I want what that girl's always had— just because she was born Senator Lee's daughter."

"But Hope—"

"I suppose you think respectability ought to be enough, after the bringing up I had. But that's the very reason it isn't. I've got to go to the other extreme to heal the hurt. Kilkenny rubs it in. She's never said anything about my aunt; so I don't believe she knows. Did you tell her?"

"I haven't told anyone."

"How did you find out? Who told you?"

"Guy. He got it from a man who met your aunt in Cincinnati. He said he hadn't told anyone else. I don't believe Kilkenny's trying to rub anything in. She's not that kind of girl. Being stuck out here so long has upset all of us. Schrenk threatened us from the hills till a few days ago, and we had those awful murders. It's enough to get anyone down. I think you've both been wonderful. Getting on each other's nerves is the very least that could happen."

"Getting on each other's nerves—it's more than that! She could give me everything I've missed—if she would." Hope stood very straight, her yellow curls the only spot of sun within the cabin. In the stillness he heard her quick short breathing. "She won't, but that's not going to stop me from earning it myself!"

Maybe Hope wanted to be a Congressman's wife more than she wanted Michael. Maybe, as Kilkenny said, she had deliberately tried to get him. But could anyone, except Kilkenny, blame the young teacher for trying, after her raw deal from life? Besides, it might really be love.

"What right has Kilkenny Lee to be stuck up?" cried Hope. "What is she anyway, but an immigrant's daughter? They talk about the Lees of Virginia, but how about her Irish and Spanish? Kilkenny Cordova Lee!" Every word was scorn. "There were Mullens in America in Puritan days!"

"Were they your people?" F. Millard thought of her aunt.

"I don't know why not!" said Hope defiantly.

He thought of Schrenk's description: "The other girl so fair and still, always sewing and watching." Beneath that charming calm, Hope Mullen was as intense as popping corn.

In haste he returned to the groceries.

Chapter Twenty-Three

November limped to a close. Every morning without a snowstorm brought its ritual of clearing off the plane. Every morning, snow or sun, the sober farce of witnessed shaving played its hour on the cabin stage. The endless searching of the skies, fishing through the ice, lugging water, baking biscuits, went automatically on. Reluctantly F. Millard took Guy's place in the contract game which continued from night to night. The game of mixed doubles continued too: Kilkenny and Red, Hope and Michael. Sometimes Hope's eyes were on Red, sometimes Kilkenny's on Mick. And always, above everything and under everything, there was watching, alertness, suspicion. A face turned quickly to meet another face quickly averted, naked distrust fast covered by lowered eyelids.

F. Millard went on with his daily visits to Schrenk, but after those two illuminating flashes, he got no more light on either past or present.

The last night in November, contract gave way to poker, and Red took a hand. How many hours of desperation, the grocer reflected, these cards had helped to fight off? Henry's wife had sought their distraction after little Jud was gone. Henry himself, and their God-fearing neighbors. Now, it was a Senator's daughter and a Congressman, a grocer, an aviator, and a secretary with diplomatic yearnings who were fighting off despair.

Toward midnight they ended the game. Red got up to bank the fire. F. Millard collected the cards, fluttering their edges like *Flatfoot's* tattered pages. His eye caught his own name staring up from the antiquated deck, and his heart gave a startled jump. Then he remembered the voting day they all wanted the gun. This must be one of his votes. The pencil had dug into the pasteboard and left his name in a lead colored groove where the glaze had been broken. Idly he ran through the pack. His name appeared again, Kilkenny's, Hope's, Mick's, Red's, Tony's. Sitting well to one side of the lamp, he caught the shading of the groove before he saw the word. He flipped a few more cards, then suddenly bent forward.

There was no lead black on this card, but a groove where lead had been, a pencil dug in hard. He held the card to the light, tilting it this way and that.

"What's the matter?" Kilkenny raised her eyebrows. "Don't tell me you're getting fussy about the state of our cards."

"Something written—" he muttered.

"We voted on them once. Don't you remember? For the gun."

"This is different. The pencil mark's worn off, but you can see where it pressed—besides, we voted on the face, and this is on the back."

"Anything for a change." Kilkenny held out her hand. "Let's see if I can make it out."

Mick and Tony leaned forward. Hope laid down her sewing and Red rubbed his splintery hands on his breeches as they joined the others.

Tony laughed apologetically. "This shows what we've sunk to, if a word on the back of a card can put us all in a dither."

"It's dug in hard," Mick pointed out, "like someone was in a scramble to get something down."

"It isn't one of our names," said Kilkenny. "That looks like a small letter s."

"It must have been written when the cards were young," Michael murmured. "It's all worn off from playing."

"S-a-1—hey, it's salmon!" cried Red.

"Salmon!" echoed Hope.

'W-w-was there a p-p-pencil on the t-t-table?" stuttered F. Millard. "Can anyone remember if there was a pencil on the table when we found the cards?"

"You mean with the old game? The one the people left?"

"Why couldn't it have been written then? The worn-off lead shows it's old." F. Millard's eyes were shining. "She said—Henry's wife said in her letter they were watching for the salmon run."

"You mean—?"

"Remember the letter said they had natives posted to watch? What if they'd been playing cards when the news came in that the salmon were running? They'd jump right up from the table—the way they did—and start out."

"And they never came back," said Kilkenny softly.

"But would anyone take time to write where they'd gone, if they were in such a hurry?" Hope asked doubtfully. "Would it even occur to anyone to do it?"

"Henry's wife!" cried Michael. "You remember she was suspicious of the natives. She'd want to leave a clue. You can see it was written in a tearing hurry."

"It looks like her writing too." F. Millard could hardly keep from stuttering again. "Of course, with just one word, and that scrawled, you can't tell much. But it slants the same way hers does."

"To think that it took forty years to discover her clue." The Senator's daughter was off on one of her seeing-back sprees.

"Forty-two," corrected Hope.

Kilkenny came out of her trance to frown.

"But does it seem reasonable—" Tony interposed—"it must have been night or the men wouldn't have been home playing cards; they seemed to be working against time for a reason, but there were four hands on the table, you remember; so Henry and the neighbor's husband must have been playing too—does it seem reasonable to think that in the middle of the night the whole village—men, women and children—would rush out to catch fish?"

"It sure does," declared Red. "How would you feel if the lake was fished out, and the food kept getting lower? By the time you were down to the last pound of beans and half sack of flour, if someone came in and said the streams were thick with salmon, wouldn't you rush out in the middle of the night and take your wife and kids to catch as many fish as you could? Don't be a sap. Besides it's daylight all night in July."

"But then—then what happened?" Kilkenny's voice was so low it was almost a whisper. "Why didn't they come back?"

"Maybe they drowned," suggested Michael flatly.

Red gave another snort. "They wouldn't all drown. Some of the men would manage to swim ashore."

"If they crossed the lake," argued Tony, "to get to the salmon stream—and it must have been the outlet at the other end; that's the only stream around here that would reach the ocean—suppose they tipped over in the middle, they could have drowned."

"You don't suppose the Indians—" Kilkenny's words died away.

"Nonsense!" Red must be feeling contrary, F. Millard silently noted, to contradict Kilkenny. "Show me an Indian massacre since Russian days in this neck of the woods, and I'll eat it."

"It's a mighty queer thing," said Michael slowly.

"What do you think, Bud?" Red turned to F. Millard. "You're the detective."

While the others speculated, the grocer had been thinking. Several times he started to speak and held back. There might be no reason, and yet—having kept to himself this long what Schrenk had inadvertently told, he might as well keep it till he could fit it in with the other clues to make a pattern. "I hardly know—" he began. '

"Listen!" broke in Red.

F. Millard glanced up. This wasn't the "listen" Red used for argument. The pilot's head was up, his body tense. Gradually each of the others took on his breathless quiet. Then F. Millard heard it—faint, faraway, a throb.

Red leaped to his feet.

"Motors!" choked Michael.

"My God, a plane!" cried Tony.

"Where's the lantern—quick—quick!" Red's bright head flashed from wall to wall.

"Oh, why did they come at night?" gasped Hope.

"Stop them! We've got to stop them!" cried Kilkenny.

F. Millard could only gurgle.

They tore about the room, bumping each other, shoving boxes, overturning chairs to find the lantern. "It's coming fast!" cried Tony.

"Oh, what if it goes by?" Hope wailed.

"I'll carry out the lamp," growled Mick. "It can't do any more than blow up!"

"It's coming down!" shouted Red.

"It acts like it knows where it's going," Michael muttered.

"There's a lantern in Schrenk's cabin," F. Millard remembered.

"Get it, Bud!" yelled Red. "Grab your coats!"

"Here's the lantern!" screamed Kilkenny. "Under—"

"Get the other, Bud," ordered Red. "Don't forget your coats. Come on! He's almost down."

"Where? Where?" begged Hope.

"The lake! He knows about the lake!" Red's big hands struck a match, fumbled with the chimney.

"My God, won't we ever get there!" gasped Tony.

F. Millard plunged outside. The roar of the plane was like thunder. The wilderness shook. It must be landing. He couldn't see in the black murky night. He clawed at Schrenk's door, burst it open, crashed against the table where he'd seen the lantern.

"Gott in Himmel, let me loose!" bellowed the German "I'll give you anything—a thousand dollars! Ten thousand! Quick—"

"Don't bother me," snapped the grocer. His hand found the lantern. He struck a shaking flame.

"Cut the ropes. Don't wait to untie them. I'll give you—"

At last, the wick caught. The chimney flopped down. F. Millard dashed through the door, slamming it for the second time across the Nazi's howls.

The other light was halfway to the blueberry patch. F. Millard ran, his lantern bobbing madly.

The noise had changed, softened. It was earthbound now, like a truck. The plane must be down, taxiing toward the spur. As he listened, the motors ceased. In the sudden silence he heard the pounding of his own running feet. Confused thuds and grunts came back from the runners ahead.

Their light swept around the spur. In a few seconds his did too. He just missed a crash. The others had stopped—huddled, tense, in the trail. Wildly he looked for lights on the lake: the plane or swinging lanterns from disembarking men. No gleam was in sight. The lake was as black and still as the night Guy Fletcher was killed.

Suddenly out of the darkness came a guttural voice. A brief, commanding sentence in a language F. Millard didn't know.

"Who are you?" Red hailed sharply.

An explosion of sound broke out on the lake—hisses and strange, fast chatter. Then a clicking, like wood on wood, a heavy thud, and light thuds like running feet.

"Hey!" shouted Red.

"Wait!" shrieked the girls.

F. Millard's lantern was steady now. In its light he saw Mick trying to climb the snowbank.

"You—you—" the Congressman spluttered.

Tony pulled him back. "You know you can't make it. I'll answer their German." He raised his voice in the guttural sounds the first unknown voice had made.

No answer came out of the dark. The thuds stopped. There was a brisk, metallic clatter, a bang like a slammed door, and the motors roared in their ears.

"Wait!"

"Hey!"

"Help!"

"God damn you!"

—Yelps like pebbles falling on pebbles compared to the pulsing din that thundered across the lake; up, up toward the hills; came back defiantly above their very heads. Shattering sound, but still no light, only the arrogant, fierce drums rolling out the passage of the winged monster that didn't have to stay on the ground, the cursed ground of this village.

No light on the plane, no moon, no stars, no northern lights, nothing to see but the black curve of sky and the dim gray of snow-weighted hills.

The throbbing grew fainter and fainter. As it died away, F. Millard thought he heard it again beside him in the trail. Was the plane coming back? Then abruptly he knew that the sounds in the trail were sobs. Kilkenny was sobbing wildly. By the dim light of the lanterns, he saw Red's arms circle her quivering shoulders. The grocer's heart gave an extra bump.

"Damn! Damn! Damn!" Hope exploded as rhythmically as the motors—Hope, who never swore.

His face flaming, Mick slid down the snowbank. "It was German they spoke first, wasn't it, Tony?"

F. Millard saw the big man force himself to relax, deliberately open his fists. "He said, 'Why weren't you here? You shouldn't keep us waiting.' Yes, it was German." '

"And the second time? What was that other language?"

"Japanese."

F. Millard gasped and heard another gasp near him "I don't know much Japanese," said Tony. "I only made out something like 'What's happened?' 'Other people,' and 'Two lights,' before they scrammed."

"There are advantages in studying for the diplomatic corps," the Congressman murmured.

"And there are advantages in being a Nazi agent, if you're not caught," said F. Millard. "You don't see any planes dropping out of the night to get us."

"You mean," gasped Hope, "they came to get him?"

"Who else? They didn't want us."

"I wonder," said Michael slowly, "what that means? Why they came to get him now?"

"If—" Kilkenny had stopped sobbing; she leaned forward, lips parted, while Red hovered near "—if that means war?"

"Or if it's about to mean war. This is November 30th. Anything could have happened by now."

Hope drew a shaking breath. "I know what should have happened. What that plane should have meant. It should have been a rescue plane for us."

"It should have been," agreed Michael. "But it wasn't; so we'll have to forget it. Come on back to the house. He tucked his hand beneath Hope's elbow.

Red's hand scooped up Kilkenny's. Tony glanced at F. Millard and matched his step to the grocer's. Silently, morosely, so different from the eager, pelting anticipation of half an hour before, the six exiles filed back up the trail.

Chapter Twenty-Four

The days following the tantalizing appearance and disappearance of the plane were wrapped in gloom even deeper than those following the murders. Then, at least, there had been activity to plunge into: hunting the mystery man after the Senator's death and collecting whatever could be used for weapons after Guy's, and there had been two graves to dig, two coffins to construct. Now there was nothing.

Next morning, after the few minutes it took Red to examine on skis the snow on the lake, to note the broad tracks of airplane skis, and the crisscross webbing of snowshoes left by the strangers, there was nothing for the frustrated castaways to do but be sorry for themselves. Even finding chickenlike scratches and a deep depression in the snow, where one of the men had tangled his snow shoes and fallen in his hurry to escape two lanterns and a gabble of unknown voices, gave the exiles only transitory pleasure. They returned to their daily routine bitterly conscious that rescue had been almost in their grasp, and deliberately withdrawn.

The fact that rescue hadn't been intended for them, that the plane was not bound for Fairbluffs or a landing field in Alaska, only gave them more worries. Poison was being distilled for their countrymen under their very noses, and they were powerless to break the retort. No pacing up and down the trail, no chopping wood, no card games could make them forget the nocturnal flight of the unlighted plane that had landed and flown away.

The stranded Americans might be tantalized and upset, but Rudolph Schrenk faced tragedy. He had been arrogant in the knowledge that escape would be provided. Now escape was cut off, the plane come and gone.

Rudolph Schrenk had been abandoned. His alternating fits of confidence and sullenness merged into one mood—despair. Even F. Millard gave up his daily visits; there was no information to be had from a man who only sat and stared at the table.

A week dragged by. Daylight on December 7th spread over the jagged eastern mountains, late but clear, to promise another dull Sunday. Evening broke the promise.

It was Red's turn to take in Schrenk's dinner. "I'm black and blue from bumping into that damn table with the lantern," he grumbled.

"I still think it's silly that whoever carries the plate doesn't wait at the door till I find the lantern and light it." As armed guard, F. Millard accompanied each meal across the street.

"And you've still got the only gun in camp." The one meal after dark had brought up this argument before. "I know it's not reasonable for him to get loose. But when you tie and untie a set of knots as often as we do his, any thing can happen. It's a damn sight better to risk dropping the plate than that fellow's getting the gun."

F. Millard shrugged. "I'm not the one that gets bumped."

Red grinned. "Okay, Bud. But now that we've found the other lantern, why not light it here?"

The grocer grinned too. "I never thought of that.".

The lantern stood by the door. The girls were washing dishes. Michael and Tony were playing honeymoon bridge on the newly cleared table. Red and F. Millard had the end of the room to themselves.

As the little man put his hand in his jacket pocket, memory turned a switch. This was the pocket where he had always found the scandal notes. For the last few weeks of Guy's life F. Millard had been almost afraid to put his hand in it. He sighed. Unfortunately, it was also the jacket in which he kept his matches. He hadn't had to use any lately. The fire never went out, and someone else always happened to be nearer the lamp when their brief daylight turned into dusk. The only time he'd struck a match, since lighting the lamp in the Senator's cabin the day he found the last note, was the night the plane had landed. That night there could have been pie in his pocket and he'd never have known the difference, providing he found a match.

His fingers chose one now. Then his hand flew out of his pocket. He forgot the man beside him and those across the room. With both shaking hands he clawed at the folds of a scrap of marbled paper.

It couldn't be—not possible—Guy Fletcher was dead! On the plain side of the fluttering paper, he saw writing— that crabbed, uphill scribble! A dead man couldn't write notes! Guy had been dead for three weeks. Three weeks! And yet F. Millard had just been telling himself that he'd struck only one match since the day before Guy was killed. It could be possible. It could have happened. Any way, it had!

He tried to steady the paper, reached up to settle his glasses. Suddenly a big hand shot out and closed on his wrist. His small hand holding the mottled paper stuck out past Red's as helpless as a doll's.

"What's that?" Pitched too low to carry across the room, Red's voice stung like jerked rope. "You got one of those soon after the Senator died. This time I'm going to see it!"

The pressure on his wrist was so tight that F. Millard's fingers uncurled. Red snatched the scrap of paper and held it open. Both heads bent above it.

Red Bailey lies about being born in Alaska. He was a New York foundling. Ask him what happened to his radio man.

Both heads rose. Eyes clashed.

"Where'd you get this thing? What the devil—Red stopped. "Come outside. We can't talk here."

F. Millard reached for his overcoat. Red opened the door.

"You haven't got the plate," called Hope.

"Back in a minute," growled the pilot.

The door shut behind them. Light streamed through the window on the snow, one small gold square in an immensity of star-pricked dark and shadow-streaked silver snow. An immensity that held two men: one small and middle-aged, one young and large and angry. On this same trail five hundred yards away, a man had been murdered; next door, in the cabin ten yards away, another man had met death.

F. Millard clenched his teeth so they couldn't chatter. But this was different from the night Guy had gone out in the dark and hadn't come back. Everyone had seen F. Millard leave with the pilot. If Red returned alone—suddenly the little man hiked up his overcoat. His fingers closed on the automatic they had taken away from Schrenk.

"Well, Red," he said confidently, "what do you have to say?"

The pilot released a long breath, slowly. "How come you had that paper?"

F. Millard let his coattail drop; Red had hold of his temper.

"Who wrote it?" the pilot demanded.

"Guy Fletcher."

"You been carrying that thing around ever since he was killed?"

"I must have, but I didn't know it."

"Talk sense," growled Red.

"I think Guy felt he'd been slighted and was trying to get even (one way our being stranded got him—remember how his disposition soured?) or else he was a natural born troublemaker. I've been getting those notes ever since the middle of October."

"Trying to do me dirt?"

"They weren't all about you. There were notes about everyone except Guy himself—and me. I've been wondering if he sent notes about me to the rest of you."

"You mean—even notes about Kilkenny?"

"One of them was."

"Son of a bitch! Did you save them?"

F. Millard jammed his hands hard into his gloves, so they wouldn't make any telltale gesture toward his breast pocket. "We can't get even with Guy now; he's out of reach."

"Maybe that's why he was killed. Maybe he sent notes to someone else."

"Maybe," agreed the grocer. "The worst of it is, there was something true in each one."

"Say, was that why you asked me all those questions that day about Irv Cramm?"

F. Millard nodded. "That was it. I never heard of him till I got the note."

"And I'll bet you heard it all wrong, if this note's any thing to go by. What'd

Guy say about the others?"

"What's wrong with this note, Red?" the grocer countered.

"Only about everything—except the facts."

"The facts are true?"

"Mom hates it; so I never mention it. But Dad told me I was adopted from a New York orphanage when I was a few months old. If she wants people to think I'm their own kid, it's okay by me. It'd be something to be proud of."

"Then the note was right."

"Not the way he put it: that I lied. Damned if I'd call that a lie."

"But the fact was true," F. Millard repeated. "How about the other part: what happened to your radio man?"

"I don't know what Guy was driving at. Bob got sick before we left."

"Left for where?"

"Here. That's why Hope took the radio."

"What happened to him? What kind of sick?"

"Oh, flu, or whatever it was they were having an epidemic of before we left. He was just like everybody else throwing up—fever—stomachache."

"You say there was an epidemic in town?"

"Yeah. They have them every now and then. I don't see why there was anything funny about Bob's getting sick when there were so many others sick too."

"I don't either, if there was an epidemic in town and his illness was just like it. Had he been sick long?"

"Hit him the night before we left. He was all right up to ten or eleven, and then, bang—no good for work. Lucky Guy and Hope were both there; so we could fix everything up."

"Guy and Hope and the radio operator and you were all together?"

"And Hope's roommate. Bob's kind of sweet on Hope's roommate. And I—well, Hope and I went around together some." Red's voice turned gruff. "None of us were pally with Guy though; I was surprised when he asked us to dinner. If I'd known what kind of a skunk—oh, well, as you pointed out, he's dead."

"And you shouldn't speak ill of the dead?"

"Speak all you want to, but you can't do anything about it."

"Guy asked the four of you to dinner?" F. Millard prodded.

"We were having it together anyway. Bob's girlfriend asked him and me to the girls' apartment; so when Guy asked all four of us, it just meant the girls didn't have to cook."

"Did you go to his house?"

"No. We went to the restaurant. And up to the girls' place later and had more coffee and chewed the rag. Bob didn't get sick till time to go home."

"Did he have anything different to eat?"

"We all had the same: steak and French fries and corn-on-the-cob and—God, when I think of that dinner, and the whitefish and beans we're living on now!"

F. Millard swallowed extra saliva. "Try not to, and, for gracious sake, don't describe it! It couldn't have been anything he ate, then, that made him sick, if you all had the same thing."

"The very same. It was just flu, I tell you, Bud."

"Funny, Guy thought it worth putting into one of his notes. If there's no more truth in his other notes than there was in this—"

"There was sure no truth in whatever he said about Irv Cramm, if he claimed I was up to anything. Why, Irv was my best friend! We were partners."

Partners, F. Millard reflected; that was how Red could collect the insurance. Because his partner had died, Red was able to buy a new plane and start the business right.

"I guess things didn't look so good, with me on a bender. But I swear to God I was innocent. My God, how could I send my own partner up to—to get what he got, unless I was drunk as a skunk? How could I—"

Red broke off. The only sound in the wilderness night was the squeak of their steps on the dry, hard-packed snow of the trail. Overhead the aurora quivered and flared in varying shades of rose.

But F. Millard spared only a glance at the sky. Red had been adopted. How about "and to my"? No one would send his partner out to meet death unless he wanted insurance money more than he wanted a partner. Anyone who'd do that would hardly think twice about killing a father he'd never known, if the inducement in the will was great enough, and then killing the man he thought was a witness. Whoa, F. Millard cautioned himself, Red wasn't the only one. And if there was anything fishy, about the sudden illness of the radio man, as the note implied, Red still wasn't the only one he had to consider.

"Who suggested flying out to this lake?" F. Millard asked suddenly.

"You mean before we left?"

"Yes, in Fairbluffs. Whose idea was it?"

"Lord, I don't know. We just came this way, and when the radio went out, I said to choose your lake, and we'd land and fix it. Don't you remember? You were there. I don't know who picked the lake; I got my orders from Tony."

"Who suggested flying in this direction?"

"The Senator. He said he'd like to go westish, but not to Nome. 'Westish' was his word, not mine. He wanted to fly over pretty country, with trees and water—'uncharted wilderness,' he called it. He got his wish. Too bad he didn't live to enjoy it. This sure is wilderness, and judging by the planes that don't fly over, I guess it must be uncharted too."

So, the Senator had chosen the route! The Senator, who became so strangely satisfied with exile. Had coming here been his own idea, or could the seed have been planted in his mind?

"When your radio operator was taken sick, Red, was Guy upset?"

"Why, n-no. I wouldn't have said so."

"Was Hope?"

"Only the way a girl would be if her roommate's boyfriend got sick in their apartment. Running around with cold cloths for his head and offers of hot-water bags to counteract it." F. Millard could hear the grin in the other man's voice.

"Who suggested that Hope take his place?"

"Guy did. He said, 'If Bob's not all right tomorrow, why not give Hope the radio?' It knocked me for a loop."

Again, the squeak of their footsteps was the only sound in the night. They had reached the end of the trail. Ahead loomed their useless plane, a wide-winged shadow under the stars, tinged with rose from the northern lights. To their right brooded the spur that cut off the cabins. They had passed the place on the beach where Guy's body had lain, without even thinking about it.

"Looks like we've covered the situation pretty completely," drawled Red, "as well as the trail. I'll bet our prisoner's hungry. We might as well take him his supper."

Chapter Twenty-Five

"Ever since Bud found that word, I can't play decent contract; I forget the value of the cards, looking for more words." Kilkenny's slim hand left a fan-shaped trail of cards across the table.

It was two days after F. Millard had found the last note. He sat with the contract players at the freshly scrubbed table. Red stared moodily into the darkness through a window reflecting the game. Hope, for once without her mending, rocking in Guy's chair by the stove, turning the pages of *Arctic Village,* now nearly memorized.

"You could hardly expect them to leave a signpost with mileage," gibed Michael. Most of his conversation with Kilkenny these days was a give and take of gibes. Even at cards, the Congressman and the Senator's daughter now played on opposite sides. "Henry's wife left her clue, and it's up to us to make something of it."

"I still think they were done in by the Indians," said Tony.

"Hell!" Red turned around. "I tell you that's out! Besides, the letter said their leader was an Eskimo, and Eskimos are friendly, peace-loving people. More so than Indians."

"But you're speaking of the stereotypes," objected Michael. "Individuals may be different."

"Isn't there some sort of theory," Hope asked idly, "that Eskimos are descended from Japanese? You could almost believe it from these pictures." She held up the open book. A reproduced photograph showed the broad, dark face, the wide nose, slanting black eyes and coarse black hair of an Eskimo.

"That one looks Japanese." Tony got up and bent over the book in Hope's lap.

"It's a funny thing—"

"I'll bet they drowned."

Words spattered around him, but F. Millard sat without speaking. Eskimos looked like Japanese. Eskimos—a cog in his mental machinery found its complementary groove. The wheels began to turn. Eskimos looked like Japanese. The leader of the Indians feared by Henry's wife had been an Eskimo. Rudolph Schrenk knew about the fate of the village. The wheels were turning faster—faster—whirling. F. Millard gripped the edge of his chair. Pictures flashed by, crowding, pushing, flattening those ahead.

"What's the matter, Bud?" Red asked curiously. "You're shivering."

The grocer blinked. That was Red lounging loose limbed by the window, Kilkenny and Mick still sitting at the table, Hope and Tony bending over the book by the stove. The five familiar persons with whom he had lived for three months. The five familiar faces looking just as they had ten minutes ago. But now one of them looked different.

"I—I felt a breeze." F. Millard was shivering violently. He walked over to the stove and stood with his back to the heat, his back to those five faces, He must control himself. They mustn't guess. He fixed his eyes on the well-known lines of his bunk, no better known than the faces he was avoiding.

He mustn't get so excited. He mustn't let it show. If the missing piece of the jigsaw puzzle could make one face look different to him, how could he hide his own knowledge from a pair of eyes that must be always alert, sensitive to suspicion, ready, if necessary, to direct a pair of hands to act—again. F. Millard bit down, tooth against tooth, as hard as he could bite.

"It is kind of chilly," said Red.

Behind him, F. Millard heard the pilot throw another log on the fire. In the three months they'd been stranded, he and these five persons had come to know each other better than in a lifetime of normal acquaintance. They knew him as well as he knew them. If his mind could follow theirs, why couldn't theirs follow his?

Suddenly F. Millard was afraid. He hadn't yet thought the thing through. Images had flashed before him like previews on the screen. It wasn't consecutive, logical thinking. He mustn't take that step, frantically as his mind clamored to fit each piece in its hole. He couldn't. It wasn't safe. Of the five pairs of eyes behind him, he could feel the demand of one.

He made himself reach out his arms in a normal, bedtime stretch. "I feel like I'm catching cold," he made himself say, and made himself turn around. That would explain the shiver, any fever in his eyes or cheeks. He didn't dare look at the faces now. He mustn't let anyone past his guard.

Kilkenny stood up. "Let's all go to bed. If we keep on talking. Bud'll stand there till he gets pneumonia for fear he might miss something."

She smiled and stepped behind the blanket shutting off the girls' corner. Hope followed. In a few minutes the cabin was dark.

Did he dare let himself think now? Or could one mind reach out to another, one mind very sharply attuned? Nonsense, he told himself firmly. But they all knew each other too well. They must have seen he was upset. Was each one willing to accept his explanation of a cold?

The mystery books said there ought to be a pattern. He hadn't seen it till tonight. With the key piece in his hand, all the others fitted—the salmon run, the abandoned village, the Nazi agent, the emptied gas tanks—F. Millard began to remember. Little things he had let slip by crowded in, big things to which he had given wrong significance. But what could he do? He had no proof to justify an arrest. He couldn't stay awake all night, every night, with his hand on the automatic. What would happen to him, and to the others, if he went the way of the Senator and Guy, and the murderer got the gun?

His grasp on the weapon tightened. Then he gave a convulsive jerk. The pattern he was putting together would fit more than one person!

He sat straight up in bed. It didn't have to be the one he had thought it was. All the little arrows, all the angles of the puzzle pointed just as plainly toward another. Another!

He gave a snort of disgust and flopped back under the covers. He couldn't have two murderers! He'd have to decide between them. But this piece fitted here, and that piece fitted there. Which—? And either way he had no proof.

If pictures had whirled through his head before, he felt as if the head itself were whirling now. How was he going to look after the gun and protect the innocent from the guilty if he let himself get in this state?

The thing to do, he told himself sternly, was to forget it, forget all about knives and hatchets and people who used them. Suppose there had been no murders, that Guy still snored in the cabin across the street where Schrenk was now tied to the bunk that had once been F. Millard's, that the Senator and the girls still slept in the cabin next door. Suppose none of the six persons now breathing the air of this room need be imprisoned—or hanged. If their only worries were rescue and food, what about Kilkenny? Surely, after months of being marooned with three attractive young men, she would choose one in the end. Tony, he felt, had no more chance than he did. In the darkness he sighed, once for Tony, and once for himself. She had more in common with Michael—highhandedly F. Millard disregarded Hope—but with Red she could escape from politics. Would the Senator's daughter be happy as a small-town pilot's wife? According to Red's story, he knocked over little tables, swept off vases when he talked, and might want to chew tobacco—not an indoor man. Michael stood for the things Kilkenny was used to, Red stood for adventure. But Kilkenny Cordova Lee, the femme fatale, remained as unpredictable in F. Millard's dreams as in life. He smiled and closed his eyes.

When he awakened, the room was as still as the day they had found it. Only now it was shrouded in black. Inside the cabin and out, the night was so dark that all F. Millard could see was a line of light from a crack in the stove that looked like a glowing string. He wished he hadn't left his glasses on the table; then at least he might have seen the shape of the windows. The room seemed unnaturally quiet. Surely the breathing and turning of six men and women should make some sound in the dark some rustle or sigh to show the room wasn't empty. But no sound came out of the night.

His hand slid under the blankets to the automatic. He pressed the envelope of clues between his shirt and chest. He felt for the key to the suitcase on the fishline around his neck. Everything was all right. The room must be all right too. But his scalp still faintly prickled, his ears still strained for a sound. No sound; no sight but the string of fire; black velvet hush closed him in.

His thumb itched for the comforting flick of *Flatfoot's* pages. Eyes hard on the crack of light, F. Millard started to reach for the chair by his bunk. Just one flick of the tattered pages—

The string of fire was gone! He froze, with his arm bent under the blankets. Something—someone—was between him and the stove. Someone who moved in silence. He felt a tiny jar on his bunk poles, hardly more than a touch. Then something stirred his blankets stealthily on the side next to the wall—the blankets over the gun!

Circulation rushed back! F. Millard grabbed. As his hands closed on the automatic, he felt, through the blankets, the pressure of other hands.

The pressure was instantly removed. An indefinable ripple of air, and the crack of light reappeared.

F. Millard snatched his coat off the chair. If he could strike a match before the prowler got back to bed—

In the dark his shaking hands couldn't find the pocket. One hand popped into an opening—wrong pocket! Drat the coat! A shower of pygmy staccato notes—the matches poured on the floor.

"For gracious sake!" While the darkness quivered with the sound of his voice, F. Millard groped over the side oi the bunk. Captured a match. Dug into the boards. The thing refused to ignite. The other end! Light sputtered feebly in the big dark room. He cupped the flame with both hands. It steadied. He held the match up like a torch.

Red sat up in the next bunk, wild haired. Beyond him F. Millard saw Kilkenny standing wrapped in her coat in the middle of the room. Had all his calculations been wrong? The match burned down to his fingers, and he didn't feel the hurt.

"What's the matter?" Kilkenny's tone was sharp. "What's happened?"

No! No! He couldn't have been wrong! The pieces made a pattern. Everything fitted. But why was Kilkenny out of bed? It shouldn't have been Kilkenny the match revealed.

"What is it, Bud?" she asked again more sharply.

"Wait till I get my pants," he mumbled. Jerkily he pulled them on; leg holes were easier to find than pockets. His bare feet upcurled on the chilly boards, he felt his way to the table.

By the time he lit the lamp, everyone was roused. Red was up and in his breeches. Hope had come out of the girls' corner. Michael and Tony were sitting up in theirs, the Congressman rubbing his eyes.

"Whatever is the matter?" Kilkenny asked impatiently.

"I see everyone's accounted for, so it wasn't another murder."

"What were you doing up?" F. Millard steadied his hands on the table.

"I don't really know. It sounds crazy. But I woke up feeling something was wrong. I didn't hear anything, but I felt I had to get up and stop something dreadful from happening. Did—did something happen, Bud? Why did you light a match?"

Maybe it was all right. Kilkenny must be telling the truth. She'd had these psychic spells before. But she'd lied before too; at first, she'd said she never saw the handkerchief that was found on her father's floor. Still, there had been time during those frantic seconds while he tried to light a match for whoever had been at his bunk to get back to bed and appear to be wakened by the commotion.

He said briefly, "Someone was after the gun."

He saw the girls' eyes widen and the men's narrow. Each person took a quick survey of the others and returned his gaze to F. Millard.

"You needn't think," growled the pilot, "because you found Kilkenny up—"

"I couldn't tell who it was," the little man interrupted. "But I think we'd better sleep with the light on."

"Every night?" cried Kilkenny.

"What about kerosene?" asked Tony, suddenly practical.

"We'll just hope it lasts till we're rescued. If it doesn't, *we* may not either."

Once more that keen exchange of glances traveled about the room. Then the girls raised their curtain and stepped behind it, Red returned to his bunk, Tony and Michael pulled up their covers. F. Millard screwed down the wick as low as he dared and took his icy feet back to bed.

Why did it have to be Kilkenny who was caught in the flare of the match?

She had her coat on too, making her look more than ever like a gypsy with her black hair hanging down, that smart leopard coat flung over—whatever she wore for sleeping; F. Millard boggled at thinking that out in too great detail. But Hope had worn a coat too. The girls would naturally throw something around them before coming out in the room. Just because Kilkenny was up and wore a coat didn't prove she had been the one who bent over him for those paralyzing seconds. Anyway, he'd slept all he wanted tonight. He lay staring at the lamp-

In the morning F. Millard was conscious of curious glances. Red was still truculent, keeping close to Kilkenny and glaring at everyone else, especially at the grocer.

After breakfast F. Millard took his courage by the hand and led it up to the shelf of supplies. One shelf held every thing now, one corner of one shelf. In a few more weeks that would be empty. They were lucky there were fish in the lake. Henry's wife said—he swallowed—the lake had been fished out once. What if that happened again? He blinked and shook his head. It was the kerosene supply he'd come to look at.

A case—no, half a case—one five-gallon can. He pushed the box back on the shelf.

"Pick it up," said Hope grimly.

He tensed his muscles to lift a five-gallon weight. The can almost leaped from his hands. It wasn't full. He shook it and heard only a hollow slosh.

"It sounds nearly empty." His voice sounded hollow too.

"It is," Hope corroborated.

"Do you still want to keep the lamp burning all night?" demanded Tony.

F. Millard whirled. They were all lined up behind him— Kilkenny, Hope, Tony, Michael, Red—each face hostile. "We've got to," F. Millard said simply. "If we want to stay alive."

Clearing the path and sweeping off the plane were accomplished that morning with more than usual vigor. The top of the wings of the useless plane sparkled beneath the brush brooms. Fishing was unusually popular; the six men and women hung around the hole in the ice as if loath to return to the cabin. By noon, hunger, cold, and a full box of fish drove them in.

It was after lunch before anyone asked for the razor. Then Tony stripped off his shirt. "We'll have to shave by lamplight if we don't do it now. And this spotty old mirror is dim enough in the sun."

"It gets dark God-awful early these days," commented Michael.

"What do you expect this near the Arctic Circle?" Red, took up instant arms for Alaska. "Today's the 10th of December."

F. Millard caught his breath. The days were still getting shorter. More darkness—less kerosene. The can was almost empty. How long would it be before they'd have to spend hours in the dark, straining their ears for suspicious sounds, each tense to catch the killer, before the killer caught him—all of them, but one.

Mick and Red had their shirts off now, and F. Millard opened the suitcase. The girls, long accustomed to undershirt shaves, continued washing dishes.

The Congressman heard it first. He stood by the back window, farthest from the clatter of plates. Red was scraping his copper wire beard. Tony and F. Millard were arguing the merits of electric and safety razors.

Michael grabbed Red's elbow.

"Christ's sake!" the pilot yelped. Blood began to ooze through the lather.

"Come on!" shouted Mick. "There's another plane!"

Tony choked off his sentence. A tin plate dropped at the sink. They could all hear it now—a distant drone, as unmistakable as the throb of the Japanese plane ten nights ago.

Red swiped a towel across his face. "Thank God it's daylight this time!"

"Thank God we swept off the plane!" cried Hope.

Tony and Kilkenny missed the stove and crashed into each other.

"Don't forget your coats," yelled Red.

The grocer ducked under the pilot's arm and tore outdoors.

A bird-shaped gray speck soared over the western horizon.

The trail in front of the cabin was alive with crazy figures—jumping, shouting, madly waving.

F. Millard jerked the automatic out of his pocket and fired three rapid shots into the air.

"My God, they can't hear you, Bud," snorted Red. "Stoke up the fire! Make more smoke! Build a bonfire in the trail! Right overhead they can see the flames. We've *got* to stop them!"

Hope and Michael broke for the cabin.

"I'll wigwag from the plane," shouted Red. "We've *got* to attract their attention!"

He jerked the upright skis from the snow and careened down the hill, Kilkenny and Tony behind him.

The plane was larger and louder.

Mick burst out of the cabin with an armful of wood. "It's an Army ship!" he whooped.

Hope flew out with shavings and kindling.

Mick dropped his load, snatched hers, and lit a match. He piled sticks on the crackling fire.

They left nothing undone today—tried everything they hadn't thought of the other night.

"The stove!" F. Millard gasped. "Did you leave the draft open?"

"God, yes. Shut it off, Bud! It ought to be going good now."

The grocer dashed into the cabin. The stovepipe was red with the fire roaring through it. He slammed in the sheet iron strip that cut the draft and dashed out.

The bonfire in the trail blazed high.

"He saw us!" yelled Mick. "He wobbled his wings! Come on!" He grabbed Hope's hand and they tore down the trail. F. Millard ran behind them.

When they reached the lake, the plane was circling to land, its Army insignia clear. As the broad skis passed over his head, F. Millard remembered the flash of the mystery man's skis the night he had leaped the trail with the grocer goggling in it.

The wide skis hit the snow. The plane roared across the lake, turned and taxied back, almost to the edge of the clearing beside Red's stranded plane. Two soldiers tossed out snowshoes, dropped into them, and hurried across the remaining stretch to the ragged jumping jacks in the trail.

"My God!" cried the first man, springing down the bank, "Congressman O'Hara! And—" he wavered toward Kilkenny "—isn't this Miss Lee?"

One long breath sighed from the waiting group.

Michael spoke first, a hoarse croak. "I won't try to say we're glad to see you. I'll leave you to guess for yourself."

"Where's the Senator? You must be the pilot." The stranger's bright eyes picked out Red. The mustache on his boyish lip fairly vibrated as he turned to Hope. "And you're the teacher."

"You seem to know us, Lieutenant." Michael's voice was more normal. "I haven't had the pleasure—"

"Sorry. Of course. Alvin Rogers, Lieutenant, U.S.A. Sergeant Matt Brown on the bank. But who wouldn't know you people, with your pictures plastered over every paper in the country, and planes out searching for months?" He glanced up the trail. "Where's the Senator?" he asked again.

Silence fell on the lake. At last Red cleared his throat. "The Senator's dead," he said gruffly.

Lieutenant Rogers looked shocked. "Oh, I'm so sorry. A—a landing accident?" He glanced diffidently at Kilkenny.

"No accident," said Red shortly.

"What do you mean?"

"Senator Lee was murdered."

F. Millard saw the young lieutenant's Adam's apple jump.

"Suppose we go up to the house," Red suggested.

"Can't you take us back to Fairbluffs?" burst out Kilkenny.

"One of you. There isn't room—we're on reconnaissance—"

"You can send a message, can't you," asked Red, "and get them to shoot out a plane?"

"S-sergeant, radio back to Fairbluffs that we found the Senator's party, and the—the Senator's been killed, and get them to send out a plane for eight—no, seven people.But there's only six of you!"

The sergeant saluted smartly, made an unwieldy turn on his snowshoes, and lurched toward the plane.

"I came to Fairbluffs after you were lost. Which one of you's the Mayor?" The lieutenant's eyes turned to F. Millard.

The Mayor's gone too," said Michael.

CHAPTER TWENTY-FIVE

"You don't mean—?"

"Mayor Fletcher was also murdered."

"Wait a minute, Sergeant! Congressman O'Hara, what's been going on here?"

Explanations burst out in a babble. Everyone talked at once. The sergeant came back and hung over the bank above his superior officer.

"You found a Nazi agent in this God-forsaken hole? And tin? He didn't do the killing? You don't mean—you don't mean it was one of you?"

Another silence fell. F. Millard broke it. "Yes. It was one of us."

"Which one?" gasped the sergeant.

Again, they all waited for F. Millard. He couldn't just fling out an accusation. He didn't even know whom to accuse! He needed proof. And what about last night— Kilkenny in her leopard coat, caught by the match flare in the middle of the room?

"One of you a murderer?" Incredulity looked out of Lieutenant Rogers's eyes. "You can't—surely you don't mean—?" His voice hoarsened: "Which one?"

"We are not prepared to say," returned F. Millard stiffly.

Another concerted long breath rose in the cold air like smoke.

"Sergeant," barked Lieutenant Rogers, "send your message—accommodations for six passengers. Stay with the plane. I'll go with these people."

The sergeant started once more for the plane.

The lieutenant turned back to the others. "This is the biggest news since Pearl Harbor."

"From where I'm sitting," remarked Kilkenny, "Pearl Harbor's a place, not a piece of news."

"Not a piece of news! Do you mean—? Why, you people don't know we're at war!"

Walking up the trail to the village, the castaways heard for the first time the story of Pearl Harbor.

In a daze F. Millard saw the charred remains of the bonfire Hope and Michael had built n the trail. In a daze he noted that the cabin was still stuffy from the roaring fire in the stove, even with the draft closed. Pearl Harbor—

the Axis—his country at war—

His aimless feet suddenly stumbled. F. Millard was shocked from his stupor. When they heard the plane, all domestic activity had ceased; whatever anyone held he had dropped. At the sink, knives, forks, and plates were helter-skelter; the razor lay on the floor by the open suitcase. In the scramble to stop the plane, F. Millard had forgotten the suitcase. Breathlessly he bent over it.

Someone else hadn't forgotten—the mumblety-peg knife was gone!

Chapter Twenty-Six

F. Millard jerked toward his cabinmates clustered about Lieutenant Rogers.

"Who was the last one in the house?" he demanded.

"You were," said Michael. "Don't you remember when you went in to close the draft?"

"What the hell's the matter now?" scowled Red.

"Just one thing—" the little grocer hoped his voice was scathing "—the knife that killed the Senator is gone!"

Commotion broke loose in the cabin—clamor and scurrying as frantic as the night the Japanese plane came. But a knife was so much smaller than a lantern that even the beds had to be torn apart in the search.

"You and Hope were in here just before I was, Michael," F. Millard grunted, shaking blankets, "when you filled the stove and got wood for the bonfire." He lowered his voice. "You tried to get that knife once before."

"But I had a witness this time," the Congressman retorted. "Hope was with me. You came in alone."

"What does it matter who came in last?" said Kilkenny impatiently. "Or who was alone? In that mad scramble to stop the plane the whole suitcase could have been emptied without the rest of us seeing."

"It may be in the lake by now," F. Millard sighed.

"The lake's frozen!" pointed out Lieutenant Rogers.

"We'd just been fishing," the grocer explained. "The new ice at the bottom of the hole wouldn't be strong enough to stop the knife if someone threw it in."

"The worst of it is—" Kilkenny's voice was husky "—it may not be in the lake. Maybe someone's planning to use it—again."

By the time the hunt for the missing knife was given up, the day had begun to darken. The cabin had been combed, each person, going into the girls' curtained corner with one of the others, had been searched.

"Going back today, Lieutenant?" asked Red.

Alvin Rogers's eyes traveled slowly around the circle of strained faces. "Looks like it's up to the Sergeant and me to wait till the plane from Fairbluffs gets in tomorrow morning. I can't leave a murderer running around here loose with a knife."

"I guess he's been that way, except for the knife," drawled Red, "for weeks. We're used to it by now."

F. Millard blinked. A plane from Fairbluffs coming in tomorrow—one more night to spend in the cabin, one more night of watching and marking time. With rescue in sight, no one could say they mustn't squander kerosene. Unchallenged, the lamp could burn all night, and at least keep that from happening which had almost happened last night. But with only one more night in the village, there was only that night left in which to catch the murderer.

No reflection on the forces of the law. F. Millard excused himself as hastily in his mind as if his thoughts had been spoken. The marshal, of course, could do a better job of catching criminals than a grocer who read detective stories. But within these crumbling cabins lay the bond between past and present. If the murderer was not caught here, could anything ever be proved? Some thing had to be done tonight, and it was up to F. Millard to do it.

As the others begged for news of the outside world, a plan began to form in his mind. He stood at the window, where he had stood so many hours, trying not to hear the absorbing conversation, trying to fix his mind on the plan on which so much depended. Darkness would be necessary. Soon it would be dark. But that subtle element called atmosphere was equally important. However dark a December afternoon might be in Alaska, it would be better to wait until night. Both murders had happened at night; the salmon run, so many years ago, had come at night, one of those daylit summer nights of July. With a sigh, he set another chair in the circle around the stove.

The talk had returned to Pearl Harbor.

"As soon as we get back," announced Red, grim lipped, "I'm going into the Air Corps."

"And I—" all the color receded from Tony's ruddy face "—I shall enlist in the Navy."

"What about that heart of yours?" Michael's voice had an edge.

Tony's color rushed back, deepened to magenta. "The Army turned me down, not the Navy. Must have been a temporary ailment. I'm feeling okay now."

"Went up for your physical too soon after flu, I suppose?" The Congressman's tone was more cutting.

"Don't quarrel now," Kilkenny broke in. "Don't you know we're leaving tomorrow? Getting away from all this. Do you know what I'm going to do?"

"Get a permanent and facial, I suppose," remarked Hope. "And, of course, a manicure."

The other girl changed her gathering frown to a smile. "I won't scratch back tonight, Hope. As I just said, we're getting out tomorrow. I meant about the war. In two months, I'll be twenty-five—and I'm going to run for Congress."

"Congress!"

"Kilkenny!"

"You in politics?"

"I'll be more useful doing a job that has to be done, that most people don't know and I do, than if I took up knitting, or tried to be a nurse, or drove a truck. And I'd release a man for work, maybe for the Army."

Michael leaned forward, his eyes as bright as hers. "I wish you'd take up residence in my district, Kenny." He hadn't called her Kenny for weeks.

"Are you going, Mick?" she asked softly.

"To the war?" whispered Hope. No one heard her but F. Millard.

"What does an Irishman like better than a fight?" grinned Michael. "Of course, I'm going. I never heard of a bigger one."

The Congressman and the Senator's daughter sat staring at each other.

"I wish I could manage your campaign, Kilkenny," said Tony wistfully.

Hope gripped the arms of the rocker, her rounded pink cheeks flaming. "You all talk so big about your contributions to the war—going into the service or politics—as if *that'd* be a sacrifice! None of you'll be giving up what I will!" She stopped, with her eyes on Michael.

The eyes of the room that had been centered on Kilkenny, now turned to Hope.

Into F. Millard's mind came a picture of the Senator with his shaggy, magnificent head, sitting up in his bunk, playing mumblety-peg on a board; a picture of Guy in the rocker where Hope sat now, his small, black eyes almost lost in cheeks that stayed plump in spite of short rations. He heard again Guy's voice: "Take off your rose-colored glasses. Find out the kind of folks you're dealing with."

It was Guy's voice that spoke through F. Millard now. "All very noble and patriotic sounding. But you've forgotten something. One of you won't be allowed to do those things. Because one of you is a murderer."

Then he gulped and wished he'd kept still. The young lieutenant had visibly started. But the five men and women who slept in this cabin, who ate at this table, at whom his words had been thrown, stolidly gave back his stare.

Dinner did little to relieve the tension, though the girls both tried to be gay. Recklessly they opened the only can remaining out of all the German's supplies, the corned beef they'd been saving for Christmas.

Kilkenny laughed almost hysterically when they took it down from the shelf. "Christmas couldn't be better than this! Tomorrow we're getting out of this dump! Tomorrow we're going home!" Then her laughter stopped as abruptly as it had begun. F. Millard wondered if she remembered, as he did, that home would be different now.

Lieutenant Rogers wasn't so adept at concealment. F. Millard caught him glancing surreptitiously at his neighbors. He wasn't accustomed to eating with a murderer. He hadn't been doing it ever since the end of September. It still had to be one of two persons, F. Millard told himself. Tonight's test should say which.

It was hard to wait. Even the corned beef didn't taste so delicious because of the ordeal yet to come.

He made himself wait till the last bites were swallowed, the plates washed, and the cabin neat. He made himself wait till they settled once more about the stove. He looked round the circle of faces. There were so many things he understood now that he hadn't three months ago, not even one month ago. He knew now, or thought he knew, why Kilkenny wanted to throw herself into politics when she'd been so bitter against it, why Hope had said that she was making the greatest sacrifice herself, why Tony had twice changed color so violently when he said he was going to enlist.

F. Millard coaxed the conversation toward the crumbling cabins and the unexplained disappearance of their builders. The men and women sitting by the stove lost the wary look that slid over their faces whenever the murders were mentioned and sprang into a discussion that never lost flavor. Now, thought F. Millard, was the time.

He stood up, scraping his chair on the floor. "Tomorrow we'll leave these old cabins to finish rotting into the ground. Before we go, don't you want to try to clear up the mystery?"

Red grinned. "We've been trying to for three months."

But there was no mirth in Kilkenny's voice. Her words came, low and intense: "Which mystery?"

"The whole thing," said F. Millard quietly. "It's all bound up together—what happened to the settlers, and what happened to your father and Guy."

"Don't tell me that some fantastic event already white with age is mixed up with modern murder!" Hope completely rejected the notion.

"I'll show you their connection." F. Millard didn't raise his voice, but its tone of quiet conviction surprised himself. "Suppose we go over to the other cabin."

"I don't see how—" Red blustered.

"I'll show you," the grocer repeated. "You boys get the shovels."

"Shovels?" Kilkenny's voice rose sharply. "Do you mean—my father's cabin?"

"I'm sorry." F. Millard wouldn't let himself weaken, in spite of her whitening face. "When the plane gets in tomorrow, the marshal will be on it. Do you want him to arrest the wrong person?" Would he have to remind her in front of them all of the handkerchief with her perfume?

She sat for a minute, pale and tense. Then she too stood up. "I'll get my coat. It'll be cold in that closed-up cabin."

"Thank you, Kilkenny," F. Millard said gently. "If the rest of you will help too, we'll get this business over."

"Look here, Smyth." No more friendly "Bud" from Red. "Are you going to point your finger at one of us and say, 'Arrest that guy!'"

"Not unless the others agree."

"Agree! Do you think we're going to agree to hang someone we've been living with, someone who's helped us fight off cold and hunger and death itself for three months? If you do, you're nuts!"

"You've forgotten something, Red," the little man answered. "One of these very folks who helped fight off cold and hunger and death, brought death to two of us. One of these folks killed the Senator and Guy."

"And he's got the knife again!" Everyone whirled toward Kilkenny. "Bud's right, Red," she went on. "Can't you see we've got to stop a murderer, no matter how much it costs?"

For a long minute Red stared at the Senator's daughter. Then he clumped to the door.

In the bustle of putting on wraps and chopping kindling and shavings to start a fresh fire, F. Millard drew aside Lieutenant Rogers, a fidgety, suddenly formal young lieutenant with a rapidly hardening jawline.

The grocer didn't have time to explain. The others were too near, too watchful. He only had time to mumble as fast as he could, "We're all going in the next cabin and I'll explain how everything happened. I'll be depending on you—"

"I'm the one to be in charge of this investigation," the young officer broke in stiffly. "How do I know you aren't the murderer yourself? I represent the Army."

F. Millard laid a placating hand on the olive-drab arm. "Of course, you should be in charge. But—but—" his pulse rate stepped up "—you don't know the things that have happened! I've got it all figured out. When I tell them—don't you see, I'm the only one who can make the murderer show his hand?"

"You mean you don't—?"

"Someone's got to watch the door!" cried F. Millard. "Because, before I finish my story, the murderer's going to see the game's up, and try to get away."

"How can he? There isn't any—you don't mean he'll try to get our plane? By God, he'll have to get both Sergeant Brown and me first! I'll go right down there now!"

"No!" F. Millard said sharply. "That'd spoil everything! You've got to trust me, Lieutenant! Go down and bring the sergeant back with you. That'll make the murderer think the coast's clear, there's no one guarding the plane. That's the only way we can get him—when he tries to escape. We've got to let whoever it is get started, and then nab him."

"Do you mean you haven't got proof?"

"S-sh!" F. Millard gripped his arm. "I'm pretending I have."

"How many of these men can fly a plane?" demanded Alvin Rogers.

"All three," returned the grocer. "And both girls."

"Are you coming?" Red called.

"Go ahead. We'll be right with you." F. Millard lowered his voice again. "Wait till someone leaves. We've got to be sure. Wait till the door actually shuts. Give him a few seconds to get started—and then dive."

"Who? Who shall we watch?" the lieutenant whispered hoarsely.

F. Millard gulped. "I don't know."

"You don't know!"

"S-sh! S-sh!" the grocer implored, darting a quick glance over his shoulder.

Rogers turned. The others were advancing in a body. This time Tony was spokesman. "We're not doing all the work and sitting over there waiting while you arrange a getaway. That's no reflection on Lieutenant Rogers; you're a plausible talker. We ought to know, after you talked us out of the gun."

"Why, Tony—"

"We've nobody's word but yours that you're not the murderer yourself!"

With a pounding heart, F. Millard jerked the pistol from his pocket, displaying it, butt foremost, to the officer. "They voted to give me this. Does that look like they didn't trust me?"

"Oh, come on, Bud," said Kilkenny wearily. "I don't suspect you. Let's get it over."

"I'll have to ask you for that automatic, Mr. Smyth,"

Lieutenant Rogers held out a steady brown hand. "If you want to prove your good faith."

Slowly, sadly, F. Millard surrendered the weapon. If that was the only way he could make the soldiers see it—

At last, they all moved toward the door. As the others filed through, F. Millard slipped a hand beneath the officer's arm and pulled him back.

"Catch anyone who leaves!" he whispered fiercely. "Man or woman— private citizen or public! If you can't catch him, shoot! You're dealing with a murderer!"

As the lieutenant started to head for the plane, Red, Tony, and Michael cleared away the snow that had remained unbroken before the Senator's cabin since the day they shut in the picks. Inside, they lighted the lamp and started a fire in the stove that hadn't been warm since the Senator was laid by little Jud under the spruce.

Curious, the lieutenant returned and the two soldiers came into the cabin as F. Millard said, "I want everything the way it was the night the Senator— the night we found him." He tried not to shiver.

"Is this—" Lieutenant Rogers hesitated, glancing at Kilkenny "—where Senator Lee was killed?"

F. Millard had a wild desire to say, "X marks the spot." But he couldn't in front of Kilkenny, even though he felt no levity with the wish. He nodded and turned to one of the taller men. "Tony, will you help me hang up these blankets again?"

"Over the windows?"

"That's the way they were. Red pulled them down when we brought Guy here. Remember?"

"Say, what is this?" demanded Red. "A reconstruction of the crime?"

F. Millard was noncommittal. "Seeing is believing; so, I'll have to make you see it. Will someone give me a hand with the bunk?"

Hope helped him unfold and spread the blankets. He pulled them lopsided, so they hung well over the edge of the bunk.

"That's a hell of a way to make a bed," said Michael critically.

"It's the way it was that night," F. Millard returned. "Will one of you go back to our cabin and bring over the books?"

"The books!" cried Tony. "Who wants to read?"

"All the books" said F. Millard firmly. "You boys might as well all go back and bring over more chairs. This may take quite a while. Prop the bedroom door shut with that straight chair, will you, Red? This rocking chair ought to face the bunk, and the other one was across the foot, sideways. No, don't take that table away, Mick; it was pushed up against the covers."

Tony returned with an armful of books, the twelve grubby volumes the exiles knew so well. Squatting, F. Millard piled them in two neat stacks side by side, one touching the blankets, one a leg of the rickety table. He looked to make sure the mumblety-peg board was still on the chair near the bedroom door. Then he surveyed the room.

"Does someone have a fountain pen?"

Michael took his from an inner pocket. F. Millard unscrewed the cap and laid both parts on the table.

The Congressman reached forward, then drew back his hands. "Since we're leaving tomorrow, I guess it's all right to let the ink evaporate. These hoarding habits we had to learn will leave their mark for the rest of our days.

Hoarding habits weren't the only mark their stay in the village would leave, F. Millard thought grimly. His hand moved toward his own breast pocket and quickly dropped. "Does anyone have a sheet of paper and blotter, or an envelope the size of a blotter?"

Again, Michael supplied him, removing a letter from its envelope and handing them over, both covered with bridge scores.

F. Millard laid them on the table. "Now a handkerchief on the floor, and I think everything's ready. My gracious, I nearly forgot the watch!"

Red tossed down a grimy rag where the handkerchief had been found, and the grocer took out the old-fashioned watch that had been his father's. He stood turning it over in his hand.

"Don't use that, Bud," said Kilkenny softly, "if you're going to do what I think. Didn't you say it was your father's? I'll go find something that won't break."

As she shut the door, he felt a nudge, and met the sergeant's raised bushy eyebrows. His lips formed soundless words: "Shall I follow?"

F. Millard shook his head. But minutes passed and she didn't return. His hands began to sweat. After all, it had been Kilkenny the match revealed last night, it had been Kilkenny who carried the handkerchief that had lain where Red's lay now. Kilkenny needed money—

Then the door opened, and she stepped in, carrying a tin cup. F. Millard drew a shaking breath. He laid the cup on a corner of the table, swallowed through the dryness in his mouth, and turned to face the others.

"I guess everything's ready. You must be wondering— let's begin at the beginning."

"There is a beginning then?" asked Tony sarcastically. "Back in 1897 or '98, when the men who built these cabins found tin."

"Tin!" Lieutenant Rogers echoed.

"Still hell-bent on digging up the past!" sneered Red.

"That's when it all started." F. Millard's voice steadied. "Suppose you let me tell it. Remember the letter we found told how anxious the men were to go on with their work? We assumed it was gold they were after, because that's what Alaska was known for. But what Henry and his friends were taking out was tin."

"How do you know?" broke in Tony.

"Mick did some prospecting before the snow came. Outside of that old shaft and a few traces of gold, all he found was tin—lots of tin. All Schrenk had in his canvas bags was tin ore."

"That's right, drag him in too!" jeered Red. "Go ahead and claim a tin strike in 1898 brought over a Nazi agent forty-three years later and caused the death of a U.S. Senator and a small-town Mayor."

"I do," said F. Millard firmly. "Both directly and indirectly. Can you folks keep still long enough for me to give you the picture? Assume for the moment I'm right about the tin. All right, here's this little faraway community—you know how faraway it is today and think how much worse it was when they had to depend on their own legs or canoes in the summer, and man-pulled sleds in the winter—"

"What about dog teams? Don't you read Alaska stories?" mocked Tony.

"When they had so little food that one of the children died, what would they have to feed dogs?" cried the grocer eloquently. "No, they had to depend on themselves. Here's this little community, even more isolated then than now, running out of food—"

"But the cabins," interrupted Kilkenny, "why did they take time to build such good cabins, if they wouldn't stop their work long enough to get food?"

"These folks were different from the usual stampeders. Remember their books—three Bibles, and a hymn book, and—"

"We remember them, all right," Michael said wryly.

"Well, these folks weren't just looking to make a quick fortune and then clear out of Alaska. They wanted the fortune, all right, I guess, but they were evidently a religious sect that wanted to make their home here. That's why they built things tight and firm and bothered with rock foundations. Someone in the group must have made the strike in '97 or '98. All right, they must have spent the first year getting ready. Then, in 1899, they began intensive mining. But they made a big mistake: To keep the place to themselves—the village as well as the tin— they were too close mouthed, and that signed their death warrants. If there'd been enough white men in the settlement, what happened here couldn't have happened. But there must have been one leak, and it trickled in the wrong direction. They made another mistake too, common to Cheechakos then or now—they didn't allow enough food."

He had them now, thought F. Millard, pausing for breath. No one offered to interrupt. They leaned forward in their chairs, every face intent.

"We're back now to where we started—the little, isolated settlement running low on food. The men were anxious to take out as much ore as they could in the short summer season, but of course, for anything as necessary as food, someone would have had to make the long trip to the post—one of those cautious trips where you're careful not to give yourself away, careful to seem sociable and do enough talking, but never say the wrong thing—a miner would have had to go, if it hadn't been for what they thought was a lucky break. A party of natives showed up in the early summer and camped nearby. They didn't eat the villagers' supplies; they hunted and fished for themselves. Finally, they must have made some sort of dicker with the settlers to take over the hunting and fishing for the whole community, so the white men could go on mining. They showed the women where to find berries and made themselves generally solid. Of course, the natives being there helped fish out the lake that much sooner, but that was just one of those things. Otherwise, everyone thought their being there was a break—everyone but Henry's wife, for little Jud's death had made her unnaturally sensitive. Anyway, when the food got low and the game and fish got scarce, instead of taking a white man off the job and cutting down production, what could be more natural than sending two or three natives to the post for supplies?"

F. Millard paused. Every face was alive to the problems of the men who had built the cabins now slowly decaying, the cabins that had given much needed shelter to themselves.

"Go on," Kilkenny urged.

"But the natives sent to the post were late getting back. The Indians camped at the village brought in less and less game. The lake yielded fewer fish. It was getting time for the salmon run. The leader of the natives—an Eskimo, you remember, and able to talk English, I'm sure—assured the white men their troubles would be over as soon as the salmon ran, even though the supplies were late. This Eskimo was very helpful and showed so much concern that he even posted runners at the outlet of the lake, so they'd get the news immediately as soon as the salmon came… All that was right there before us, if we'd ever stopped to piece it together. Last night I got the missing link."

"Missing link?" Michael's heavy eyebrows met.

"Did you ever stop to think that it wasn't only because of the war that Japan needed tin?"

"What do you—" began Tony.

"It wasn't the *war* that gave them the shortage. That made the need greater, but tin isn't one of their natural resources."

"F. Millard Smyth!" burst out Hope. "You're surely not trying to say—?"

"You gave me the clue, Hope. Last night when you were looking at the pictures in *Arctic Village* and said that Eskimos looked like Japanese."

"My God!"

"Bud!"

"You don't mean—?"

Hubbub broke out around him. In spite of himself, F. Millard couldn't keep back a pleased grin. *Have your grin now,* he humored himself; *you won't feel like it later.* At that thought, his smile vanished.

"All right, folks, take it easy. Remember I said these men who were so mum about their tin strike let out one little slip too many? The Japanese must have had their agents in this country even then. First thing the next summer, the summer the men started mining, before any returns could leak out to the general public, the Indians arrived with their Eskimo leader. Henry's wife was right; it *was* a funny thing for a bunch of Indians to have an Eskimo leader. And it was harder to believe in view of what happened later. You remember Red said Eskimos are a peace-loving lot? But the Japanese aren't. They traded on the likeness between the Eskimos and themselves. They collected a bunch of renegade Indians, and their leader was Japanese, safe in the knowledge that he could pass for an Eskimo in Alaska.

"I know we discarded the Indian massacre idea. For one thing we couldn't figure out a motive. But look at it this way: The white settlers have kept still about finding tin. For all the other Alaskans know (and mighty few of them even knew of this settlement's existence), they're a group of settlers finding enough gold to make a living, but not enough to cause a stampede. And it's a hard place to get into. Well, when an Indian or two drifts into the post with a story of a fishing accident, a sudden squall on the lake—what is there to get excited about?"

"Fishing accident?" queried Michael.

"The folks at the post may have sent down the commissioner if he happened to be handy, or a deputy marshal, if he was, as a matter of form—"

"But, Bud, there was only one grave!" cried Kilkenny.

"What about this fishing accident?" repeated Michael.

"What about the mining operations?" demanded Red.

"The settlers had one little gold mine, the old shaft Mick found, as a blind in case any strangers came that far off the beaten track. Well, the Eskimo-Japanese and his gang would leave that to speak for itself and cover up every thing else."

"Including the settlers?" Mick asked dryly.

"The fishing accident took care of that."

"*What* fishing accident?" growled Tony.

"The night of the salmon run. Of course, you know this is just a guess; I wasn't an eyewitness—but it could have been like this: The Indians come tearing in to say the salmon are running. And the men, and maybe some of the women, go tearing out to get them. The quickest way to reach the outlet of the lake is by boat. The settlers would want to go the quickest way. The Indians would be waiting with their canoes. When they got to the middle of the lake, what's simpler than tipping over a canoe?"

"They drowned the white men!" gasped Hope.

"Henry," whispered Kilkenny, "and maybe Henry's wife."

"The men would put up a fight," Red objected, but F. Millard saw that even the skeptical pilot was shaken. "Maybe some of the Indians were drowned too, but there'd be a lot more Indians than white men."

"Wouldn't the white men have guns?" asked Lieutenant Rogers. "As soon as they saw what was going on, they'd shoot."

"They wouldn't take guns along to catch salmon with friendly natives. Gaffs, probably, or nets, but not guns."

"And then," Michael took up the story, "the natives came back and finished off the women and children. Perhaps, they buried them without the formality of marking graves, or they might have dumped them in the lake with the others. Then the renegade natives helped themselves to the things they wanted. That's why we only found one knife and razor (they were under other things, remember?), and no guns or axes."

"That's why, I think," agreed F. Millard.

"But you ought to *know!*" said Red sharply.

"I guess the details are something we'll never know, but you can check the facts with Schrenk," the grocer offered. "He knew death struck the settlement. He gave it away, and then shut up like a clam. But if the authorities put pressure on him, I'll bet he'll talk. He must have got the story from his allies, the Japanese."

"No wonder the natives say this place is cursed," Michael said slowly.

"No wonder everything was left the way it was, and Henry's wife's letter was never mailed to her sister," Kilkenny murmured.

"The fiends!" Hope whispered fiercely.

"All because Japan needed tin," Tony finished.

A sigh rustled over the room.

F. Millard took a fresh grip on the edge of the table. "And now—" he cleared his throat "—we come to the murders."

Chapter Twenty-Seven

very figure stiffened.

"To make you understand it, I'll have to show you what happened. Remember, the night the Senator was killed, Kilkenny came to fix the fire at 9:15? The latchstring was in, and they never pulled it in except at night. She had to wait for her father to open the door. By then, say 9:17, he was apparently alone."

"Look here," growled Red, "you said you were going to show some connection between that 'fishing accident' back in 1899 and the recent murders. How about it?"

"I'm getting there. But I have to go in a roundabout way. Just give me time."

"Let him alone," said Michael suddenly. "Let's see what he has to offer. We don't have to agree, you know."

"There was no one in sight when Kilkenny got in," F. Millard went on, "and the bedroom door was propped shut with the chair on the Senator's side. She pushed the latchstring back through its hole. Except for that, the only thing unusual about the room was the table's being cleared of everything but her father's watch and the cap of his pen. The books were on the floor, weren't they, Kilkenny?"

"I suppose so." Her voice was strained. "At least they weren't on the table."

"You didn't notice whether they were stacked up or toppled over?"

"I didn't notice at all," she insisted. "Yet I think if they'd been in a mess, I'd have noticed and straightened them up."

F. Millard returned to his story. "So she fixed the fire and went out again—

would you say in about five minutes?"

She nodded.

"That would make it 9:22 when she left the cabin. And the Senator's watch stopped two minutes later."

"We know all this," Red broke in impatiently.

"But I have to show how it fits. Just think—the murderer wasn't in sight when Kilkenny left this room, but eight minutes later Mick found the Senator dead, his watch broken, and an unidentified bloody handkerchief lying on the floor!"

Red sprang to his feet. "You're not saying—"

"Wait till I get through." F. Millard held up his hand. "Why didn't the Senator want to be interrupted? There was ink on his fingers, but if he wanted to hide anything he'd been writing, he could have thrown something over the table. But if he and *another person* had been writing something together, that would be different. Suppose they wanted to keep it to themselves. The table was pulled right up to the bed where the Senator could reach it, the rocker close by. Suppose there'd been someone in the rocker when Kilkenny knocked at the door. Think of them —the Senator sitting up writing, this other person in the rocker. They look wildly around the room. No one could hide in the bedroom; the voice at the door was Kilkenny's, and she might go in there. There's only one possible place. The Senator blots the paper, the person in the rocker jumps up, grabs the paper and pen, but doesn't think about the cap—and dives under the bed."

"Under—" Kilkenny shuddered "—was there someone under the bed when I came in?"

"That's pretty farfetched," objected Tony, "and I doubt if there'd be time. Kilkenny didn't hear any scramble. With the bunk built into the corner, and the table up against it the way you have it now, and those books stacked by the table, no one could just roll under. It'd take some maneuvering to get there without any noise, and be out of sight by the time the Senator crossed the room."

"I'll show you. If one of you'll take the part of the Senator, I'll be the murderer." F. Millard looked over his audience. He mustn't choose one of the soldiers; their job was too important. "Suppose you do it, Mick."

The Congressman's eyes narrowed. "I wouldn't mind having you gone over again for the missing mumblety-peg knife."

F. Millard snorted. "If I wanted to kill you, I wouldn't choose such a public place. Besides, I've had a gun for a month. I'll ask someone else."

"I'll do it." Michael stood up quickly. "Do you want me to get into bed?"

The grocer nodded. "Take off your shoes."

Red said impatiently, "What does another stain on the blankets matter—" He broke off, his eyes flying to Kilkenny. The first stain on the blankets had been made by the Senator's blood.

"We're going to do this right," declared F. Millard. "Give me your coat, Mick."

He hung the Congressman's overcoat on a nail beside the door.

"But Dad had his on that night when he came to the door," said Kilkenny.

Red turned on F. Millard. "Do you think anyone as hipped as he was on the subject of drafts, with all these blankets hung over the windows, would get out of bed in his underwear and walk to the door for his coat?"

"He'd already been up to pull in the latchstring. Perhaps he'd left his coat over here," suggested Mick from the bunk.

"Someone else pulled in the string." F. Millard's voice still held conviction. "But Red's right; he'd never have gotten out of bed without something on. Someone else gave him the coat, before diving under the bunk."

"That much more time would be used," argued Tony.

"I'll show you, and do it without any noise," the little man insisted. He sat down in the rocker by the bunk. "Now, Mick, when I say 'Go,' knock on the wall and call out, 'Just a minute.' Then blot that letter. When I toss you the coat, fling it on, shove on your shoes—don't tie them—and walk slowly to the door. By the time you get there and raise the latch, I'll be out of sight." He took a deep breath. "You might lean toward the table and write on the back of that letter just to show it can be done."

Twisting at the waist, Michael began to write, but no ink showed on the paper covered with penciled scores.

"Never mind if your pen's gone dry," said F. Millard. "Pretend to blot it after you knock. Ready? Go!"

Michael twisted the other way, poising a muscular fist. Through the stillness of the Senator's cabin thundered a knock.

F. Millard tensed. Everyone, he thought, must have felt the same shock. For an instant he stared at Mick as the murderer must have stared at the Senator.

"Just a minute!" called out Michael.

The little man leaped to his feet, glaring about the room. For this moment he was the murderer. "Under the bunk!" he hissed. "You'll have to let her in!"

Soundlessly, he ran on his toes across the floor, jerked down the coat, ran back, tossing it to Michael, snatched up the paper and pen. "The blotter—" he whispered. "Stick it in a book! Open the door."

He turned toward the head of the bunk and dived beneath the overhanging blankets. As his heartbeats slowed, he heard Mick's shuffling steps.

"I'm at the door," the Congressman called.

"All right!" F. Millard's voice under the bunk sounded muffled and sepulchral. "Can anyone see me?"

He crawled forward and stuck his head out beyond the books. Michael stood by the door. Everyone else sat frozen.

"Now you know it can be done," he told them. "Everything's just the way it was when Kilkenny came in—the watch and pen cap on the table, no one in sight, and the bedroom door propped shut—but someone was there just the same, where I am, under the bunk!"

No one stirred.

"Now I'll show you what happened after Kilkenny left. Sit down, Mick; we won't need to act this out." How could they before the victim's white-faced daughter? "With the table and books in front of the bunk, the person underneath is decidedly cramped. He—" F. Millard stopped "—please understand, when I say 'he,' I don't necessarily mean a man." Both girls started. He saw them exchange swift glances. "I can't keep saying 'the murderer' or 'the person under the bed.' 'He,' in this case, is something quite indefinite— though I don't mean to imply that it ought to be 'she.' Oh, dear, this is getting involved. I just want you to remember that as far as we've gone, it could be anyone. I'm using 'he' for convenience."

He felt a maddening flush creep up to his face. His voice lost its impressive ring. His position on his stomach, peering out under the edge of the blankets, didn't help. He drew a deep breath and held it till he had himself in hand.

"Let's go back where we started—the murderer's style cramped by the things in front of the bed. Going in at one end, he'd crawl out at the other, as he's headed in that direction. With the rocking chair sideways across the foot of the bunk, he'll have to come out where I am now —headfirst, and he'll have to wriggle. As he wriggles, his elbow or knee or foot strikes the first pile of books, topples them against the other; that hits the rickety table, and off goes the watch. Like this." He raised his elbow.

"But the books weren't toppled over," Hope demurred. "I remember those two neat stacks beside the bunk when we—when the Senator—"

"The murderer straightened them," the grocer returned. "He'd never leave that evidence to give himself away. Now watch."

He flopped his elbow. One stack of books jarred the next, and then the table. The tin cup clattered to the floor.

"Very clever," remarked Tony, "but he might have turned around under the bed and come out at the other end."

"It wouldn't have made any difference," F. Millard insisted. "He could have jarred the table itself and the watch gone over just the same."

"That's what you were doing, Bud, wasn't it, the time we saw the light in here?" Kilkenny exclaimed. "The day we caught Schrenk. You were just coming out from under the bed, and there was a broken saucer on the floor. But you didn't have the blankets on the bunk."

"I was just finding out if it could be done."

"Not a complete reconstruction," jeered Tony.

"The murderer staged a reconstruction scene of his own that afternoon," said F. Millard, "when I had a light in here and someone saw it through the snag in the blanket. He found out for the first time that he might have had a witness the night he killed the Senator. Remember how we dug away the snow and each of us looked through the hole?"

CHAPTER TWENTY-SEVEN

"Except me," said Red. "I was collecting the stuff from Schrenk's camp."

"You didn't look then," admitted the grocer. "But we didn't have snow for several days; the path to the window stayed open."

"But that was the night Guy was killed." The pilot's tone was triumphant. "We put him in here that morning, and I pulled down the blankets myself."

"After you'd had all night to look! I woke up often the night Guy was killed, and I never heard so many foot steps and opening and shutting doors." F. Millard thought again of the whispering before they went to bed, the rustling and creaking, the restless sounds all night, Guy's snores that had stopped toward morning. "The murderer found out what he wanted to know—someone *had* been standing at that window, someone he had to kill."

"And that night Guy got the hatchet," Michael finished softly.

"In the neck," someone murmured.

F. Millard broke the silence that had fallen over the room. "Let's get back to this case. There's something I want to show you before I come out."

"Just a minute," broke in Tony; "if you say the murderer knocked over the books and then picked them up to keep from giving himself away, why didn't he pick up the watch too?"

"I imagine he did, and when he found it wasn't ticking, he laid it back on the floor. Its stopping would have to be accounted for some way, and the Senator himself, the murderer must have reasoned, could easily have joggled that wobbly table and knocked off the watch."

"Do you mean to say he did all this while the Senator sat looking on?" snorted Red. "Picked up the watch, listened for its tick, and dropped it back on the floor?"

"No, that would be after he'd—finished. Here's what must have happened: The murderer comes out from under the bunk." He started to wriggle out. "But wait, I was going to show you something while I'm here. If any of you still has any doubt, come and look under the bed."

All but Kilkenny came forward, squatting in front of F. Millard.

He held up the blankets and struck a match. "On the floor, way back by the wall, you can see an ink spot."

"There is one, all right." The lieutenant verified his report. "You can see it."

Tony pointed toward Michael's pen clutched in F. Millard's hand. "He probably did it right now."

"Mick's pen's dry," retorted the grocer, "and so is the spot."

"You might have done it that other time we found you here."

"Well, I didn't! I left my pen on the hotel bureau in Fairbluffs the day we started. And remember something else—the Senator's pen leaked."

"He's not kidding us, Tony," said Michael thoughtfully.

Under the bunk F. Millard gathered about him what dignity he could. He struck another match. "Notice some thing else while you're here—how low the bunk poles come."

"No room for a fat man," agreed the Congressman. "Anyway, Guy was killed himself."

"All right," said F. Millard, "if you'll get out of the way, I'll explain the rest."

They returned to the row of chairs. Tony stood leaning on his. Red fiddled with the stovepipe draft till it sent out a puff of smoke. Hope and Michael sat down.

"We're back now to where Kilkenny fixes the fire and leaves. Her father gets up again and pulls in the latch string, so the murderer can come out of hiding.

"But the Senator was sick," objected Hope, looking sick herself. "Would he be running around like that?"

"There's quite a large question in my mind about how sick he was," began F. Millard.

Kilkenny's words twanged like arrow shots. "Have you forgotten what he looked like—his color—his fever! How can you talk like that!"

"My dear, I didn't mean he hadn't been sick. No one who saw him could doubt it. But don't you remember, in a few days the cold was gone; he looked better and said he was all right, but we were all afraid to let him get up? By the time we were willing, he wanted to stay in bed. The question is: Was he really weak, or had he some reason to pretend it? I think I can show you, in a little while, that he had a reason."

Kilkenny walked to the window by the door and raised the blanket. Red took his hand off the chimney draft and ranged himself beside her. Tony sat down slowly.

"Let's get back to where we were," said F. Millard. "Since the two in the cabin were up to something they wanted hidden, they wouldn't take any chances on someone popping in just as the murderer was coming out from under the bed. The Senator would pull in the string. Alright, let's suppose the string is in, and the Senator's back in bed. Now the murderer can come out." F. Millard crawled out and stood up, stretching cramped muscles.

"Now then, quickly, before anyone else comes to the door, the Senator must finish his paper. It won't take long. He was almost through when he had to blot it to let Kilkenny in. The paper done, the murderer hides it on his person. Then, on the plea of making things look normal to the next visitor, he suggests a game of mumblety-peg. When he crosses the room to get the mumblety-peg board and knife from the chair by the bedroom door, he stops by the outside door and raises his hand. The Senator assumed he put out the string."

F. Millard walked across the room, paused at the front door, and picked up the bloodstained board from the chair by the bedroom wall.

"Now then—" he returned to the bunk "—the murderer lays the board on the Senator's lap, and stands close beside him, a little behind, while he opens the knife."

"There'll be fingerprints on that knife," broke in the Lieutenant.

"Not now," Red contradicted. "That's the knife that was stolen."

"But it wasn't stolen to wipe off fingerprints," said F. Millard. "The murderer would rather have a gun, but a knife is better than no weapon." He paused. "The way I figure it, the only prints on that knife would be the jumbled ones left by all the mumblety-peg players. When the murderer opened the knife for its final use, he held it in a handkerchief."

"The h-handkerchief!" stammered Hope. Both small hands gripped her chair arms.

"Rudolph Schrenk left it when he cleared out of the village, and Kilkenny found it. The murderer stole it from her to throw us off the track. But we guessed its use wrong," the grocer continued. "We thought he used the handkerchief to wipe off his bloody hands, but I believe he had it wrapped around the knife when he plunged it into his victim."

No one spoke. In the hush he heard someone swallow.

Michael cleared his throat. "What was this document they tried to keep so secret?"

"What motive could anyone here have for killing the Senator?" cried Hope, leaning forward tensely.

"What about this ancient tin discovery you were going to connect with the murders?" demanded Tony.

Red and Kilkenny stood still by the window.

"When I tell you what the document was, two questions will be answered. The Senator wrote his will."

Kilkenny took a step forward. Red followed. The others straightened in their chairs.

"No will written under duress would be good," Michael pointed out.

"It wasn't written under duress," said F. Millard. "He wanted to write it."

"Do you have the will?" snapped Tony.

"No, but—"

"Wouldn't it be a boomerang for the murderer?" Lieutenant Rogers asked. "It couldn't come up for probate without exposing him."

"How about it, Mick?" asked Red. "You're a lawyer."

"It wouldn't prove anything except that the Senator made a will in favor of that person," answered Michael. "Of course, it would show a motive, but—there may be other motives in this crowd—and it certainly wouldn't prove that the legatee killed the testator."

"But there'd hardly be time," exclaimed Kilkenny, "between my going out and your coming in, Mick, for anyone else except the man under the bed to—to have done it."

"The time would be incredibly short," the Congressman agreed, "but incredible things do happen."

"Anyway," said F. Millard, "the murderer's plans may be changed. I think he expected to blame the Senator's killing on Schrenk, but when the need to kill Guy arose, Schrenk was out of the running. Now it's more important to get off with a whole skin than a fortune, so he may destroy the will rather than risk presenting it."

"There's another angle worthy counsel hasn't mentioned," remarked Tony unpleasantly. "The Senator might have been killed because this will threatened the murderer's interests. He might have been killed and the will destroyed so it *wouldn't* be effective, instead of to make it effective."

Slowly every face turned toward Kilkenny.

Seconds passed before F. Millard could trust his voice. "I didn't say that was all the evidence I had."

Quiet slid over the room.

Kilkenny sank into a chair. Tony got up and walked to the front window. The lieutenant's keen eyes followed.

F. Millard took a deep breath. "The murderer left concrete evidence behind—ravelings from his clothes."

Sitting or standing, immobility struck every figure. "—from his clothes!" Kilkenny whispered hoarsely.

"I showed you how little space there was beneath the bunk. While the murderer was there, he caught his clothes on a splintered pole. When he pulled loose, he left some threads behind."

"What color?" Michael croaked.

"Black."

Every pair of eyes swung around the room, to Kilkenny's black suit, Michael's and Tony's black mixed tweeds, Hope's black sweater.

Red's knuckles were big on the back of Kilkenny's chair. "These plaid breeches let me out, but if you think—" he leaned protectively above the seated girl.

"I'm let out too!" Hope sprang to her feet. "Because I didn't snag my sweater till last week. I remember thinking how lucky I was, with all the casualties to the rest of our clothes."

"Neither of you are let out," said F. Millard quietly. "The day after the murder I saw a snag square on the line of black in those plaid breeches, Red. Turn around and I'll point it out."

The pilot didn't move. He glared back at F. Millard.

"And your sweater, Hope," the grocer went on, "was mended in the back. I saw that too."

"That clears me then," she declared, "you're saying my sweater was mended. I may have torn it in Fairbluffs; I don't remember. But you say yourself it was mended. Don't you remember the night the Senator was killed, Kilkenny and I slept over in your cabin, and I didn't even have the workbasket till I came back here to get it the day of the funeral—to mend Kilkenny's jacket." She paused, her eyes sought the other girl, and stopped in calculation. Then she turned back to F. Millard. "You were here when I came for the basket. I remember how you jumped when I opened the door." She drew a deep breath and sat down.

F. Millard ignored the reference to jumping. "That doesn't let you out, Hope. You carry a mending kit in your handbag. And you asked me to get the bag for you the day of the Senator's funeral. You could have mended your sweater then. You and Red aren't cleared any more than anyone else with black clothes."

He looked directly at the soldiers, glanced down significantly at his own gray clothes, and back at the lieutenant. Slowly Alvin Rogers nodded. F. Millard let out his breath. "But Hope's sweater and Red's breeches are neither here nor there, because the ravelings themselves will show whose clothes they came from."

In the room's electric stillness, F. Millard gulped. He hoped an expert could tell what garment those shreds of black fuzz belonged too. He had grave doubts himself, but the murderer mustn't know how pitifully scant the evidence actually was.

Hope sat with her hand at her throat, her eyes as big as Kilkenny's. Red began pacing the floor. Tony remained at the window, tense and very still. Michael's knuckles on the arm of his chair stood out as big as Red's.

F. Millard rammed one hand in his pocket; the other he steadied on the table. "Guy, of course, was killed because he knew too much, or the murderer thought he did. I believe myself he made a mistake. If Guy had actually known who the murderer was, he never would have gone with him to the lake in the dark.

"And now that you understand about the recent murders, I'm going to relate them to the first ones that happened in the village—the wholesale murders, back in 1899."

The sergeant gave a grunt of satisfaction.

"And then—" F. Millard paused "—you'll know who the murderer is."

Michael got up and walked around his chair. Instead of sitting down, he leaned across its back. Hope stepped to the stove and fiddled with the draft as Red had fiddled half an hour before. Red still paced the floor. Tony stood tense and quiet by the window. Kilkenny huddled down in her chair.

"Have you ever wondered why, out of all the trips there were to choose from Fairbluffs, this route was chosen?" F. Millard asked. "Rudolph Schrenk knew what happened in the village. How would he know—a man way off in Europe—if his allies, the Japanese, hadn't told him? Rudolph Schrenk isn't the only Axis agent in the country. He said himself there are operatives in all the large towns."

Hope made a poor adjustment of the draft, and smoke puffed into the room. She and Michael, near-by, broke into a fit of coughing. Michael muffled his in a grimy handkerchief. Hope pawed vainly through her coat pockets, then hurried to bury her face in the blanket at the window behind Tony. Red stopped his pacing by the door.

"The way I understand it," the grocer continued, "these agents don't know each other, but they know where other agents are. The agent in Anchorage, or Nome—or Fairbluffs, would know there was an agent here. He'd know there'd be a supply of food in this isolated place. He'd know that if he wrecked the radio, and drained the gas tanks, the odds would be a thousand to one that he'd have all the time he wanted to get the Senator to make a will, and then he'd make that will effective. He'd know—"

The door closed softly.

Both soldiers sprang to their feet.

"Wait!" F. Millard's voice shook. "We've got to be sure."

For half a minute he stood, shivering. "All right! Go!" he gasped.

The two soldiers leaped through the door.

"What's going on?" yelled Red. "What are you—"

F. Millard jumped in front of the door as they all rushed forward. "Wait!"

Outside they heard a shot.

"Hope! Hope!" screamed Kilkenny. "Where's Hope? What are they doing?"

F. Millard laid his hand gently on her arm. "Don't feel bad, my dear. They had to do it."

"But what—my God, Bud, what are they doing to Hope?"

"Don't feel bad," he repeated softly. "Hope killed your father."

Chapter Twenty-Eight

F. Millard sat very still in his cushioned seat in the rescue plane as they roared above forest and tundra. Death and the crumbling cabins were hours behind them now. Soon, Red told him, they could begin to look for Fairbluffs.

He peered at Kilkenny across the aisle where she'd sat on the outgoing trip. Her position and the clothes she wore were the only things about her unchanged. Of the five returning from the Senator's party of eight, Kilkenny had changed the most. The restlessness, the brittleness, had disappeared. Something glowed through her now —peace, and the warmth he had felt before trying to break through her protective chromium plate. It showed even in external details—no predatory nail paint, eyebrows grown out of their sophisticated arch. Was Kilkenny Cordova Lee, F. Millard asked himself with a melancholy smile, at heart a womanly woman? That made him think of Hope, and his smile vanished.

Hope, who wasn't with them, whose body still waited in the village with the soldiers, and Schrenk, and the marshal, who had come on the plane from Fairbluffs. Hope's body in the cabin, and the bodies of her two victims still in the frozen ground. Today another fire burned over those graves, and tomorrow another plane would bring back the living and dead.

It had seemed strange when the plane they were in rose from the frozen lake, leaving three waving figures to shrink smaller and smaller by the fishing hole and Red's stranded plane, while they, who had been bound so long to those shores, soared above their prison fence of white hills.

Kilkenny turned her head. She leaned across the aisle to pat the grocer's hand. Surely, he thought, there would never again be malice in those glowing golden eyes.

"Don't feel too sorry." Her voice was soft even over the roar of the motors. "It isn't all to be regretted. Good has come from it too. My warped view of politics has straightened, and Mick and I are going to play it clean in the time he has left before going into the Army. Because I had some unlucky breaks and a lot of misunderstandings doesn't mean all politicians are crooked. I was too self-centered and stubborn to think of that before, but Mick and I—after we're married—" she paused to give the grocer a radiant smile.

Michael turned around, holding out his hand. She shamelessly laid hers in it. F. Millard sighed. In the seat ahead of him, he caught Red's rigid profile determinedly facing the window. This business of Kilkenny and Mick was harder on Red than on himself. If only he could lay a hand on that set, broad shoulder and tell Red his pangs were shared—

Behind Kilkenny Tony bent forward. "We were all so excited last night and everything so mixed up, I'd like to get a lot of things straight this morning. How did you ever catch on it was Hope? I was scared to death you thought it was me."

"I had plenty of reasons at first to think it was you," said F. Millard.

Across the aisle of the plane the two men stared at each other. Scared to death, the little man's mind repeated, that summed up Tony Webber. He remembered the no longer imperturbable secretary's stammering words last night, the few shamefaced explanations, and thought of the timid "decayed gentlewomen" Tony had always lived with. Now F. Millard understood his contradictions. As big and muscular as the red-haired pilot, the blond secretary was physically a coward. First in muscular exercise, while it was only exercise, when danger appeared, he hung back—just as he'd hung back when they trapped the mystery man until Red and Mick had safely overpowered him—just as he'd run away from a man coming out of the woods instead of running toward him, the night Do-It-Now Lee was killed— just as his heart was good enough for any physical feat, but not good enough for the Army. F. Millard had heard about drugs that made hearts misbehave. And yet, when his country was actually threatened, Tony was man enough to throw himself into its service.

Across the aisle, his gaze still locked with F. Millard's, the blond man flushed hotly. The grocer smiled and held out his hand. "I guess those reasons are between us, Tony, now that you're in the clear. Mick and Red looked mighty suspicious too."

"Red was spoiling for a fight because he thought you thought it was Kilkenny, wasn't he?" asked Tony.

F. Millard answered uncomfortably, "I guess so."

Kilkenny's gaze was gentle on the back of the red head across the aisle. Her glance returned to the others, and she demanded indignantly, "Why did Mick look suspicious?"

"You'd have suspected something yourself," returned the grocer, "if you'd known he stole the suitcase key, and caught him with the bag open, about to destroy the evidence."

"Mick, you didn't—?" Kilkenny exclaimed.

"He didn't, because I caught him," said F. Millard, still a little grim.

Michael grinned sheepishly. "It did look bad. But if you had smelled your best gal's perfume on the fatal handkerchief, wouldn't you have tried to destroy it too?"

Before F. Millard could find an answer, the Congressman went on, "But I wouldn't have touched the knife with a ten-foot pole! That knife was the only real evidence we had! I knew there must be some innocent explanation for the perfume on the handkerchief. But I wouldn't take any chances on Kilkenny's getting involved." His Irish eyes were tender, resting on the girl he loved.

F. Millard and Kilkenny sighed romantically together.

Tony turned back to the grocer. "Was that Hope I saw in front of the Senator's cabin, that hunched figure that looked like someone peering in the window? Did I come along just as she was leaving?"

"That must have been Guy having his peek through the hole in the blanket. Hope must have left just before he came along or just after you scared him away, while you and Mick were—mmm—running around in the woods."

"Then maybe Guy saw her. Maybe she had to kill him."

"That's what she thought, of course. Because she crossed the room in front of that window to get the mumblety-peg board and knife. But I believe he was killed out of panic. He looked wise when I asked if he saw any one, but I'm sure he didn't, because when he looked in, the mumblety-peg things were already gone from the chair. He told me that without realizing what he gave away. But I'll bet Hope didn't know it. Poor Guy, his desire to be important killed him."

"You didn't suspect Hope yourself, did you, Mick?" asked Tony. "Whenever I think of the way you and she—"

Michael looked embarrassed. "I wondered about her at first. But I couldn't see any reason, and—well, I completely gave up the idea. She seemed like such a nice girl."

F. Millard saw Kilkenny try to withdraw her hand. "I don't believe you ever suspected her, Mick, even at first," she said coldly.

"*Only* at first," he amended, "but I think, instinctively, you did, Kenny, all along." His voice deepened. Wincing, F. Millard knew that he must have squeezed her hand. "Surely there was more than what one good-looking gal feels toward another in the way you felt about her."

"Don't give me any credit, Mick. I thought you were taking too much interest, and anyway, her type was unpopular with me, the type Dad sometimes got involved with."

The three men exchanged swift glances.

Michael spoke quickly. "What started me wondering was that Hope really had the best opportunity to jimmy the radio and drain the gas tanks when she stayed with the plane while the rest of us went to the village. Of course, there was time for any of us to have slipped back and done it after she left, but she had a real excuse for being there."

"By the way, what did happen to the radio?" asked Tony. "Did she really wreck it?"

"I don't know much about radios," said F. Millard, "so I may not have this straight, but I don't believe she sent a single message back to Fairbluffs. I think she just pretended, without having the transmitter on; then if any one discovered it was off, she'd have said she forgot. While she had the plane alone to fix the radio, she burned out the generator. Or she may even have done it before we left, and then if anyone noticed, she'd have said it just happened."

In the seat ahead Red turned long enough to say grimly, "She fixed the radio, all right!"

"By the way, Mick," F. Millard asked, "what were you doing in the woods the night the Senator was killed?"

"That snow flurry scared me into bringing in the tin ore I had cached in the old mine shaft."

"I'd like to say," the grocer volunteered uncomfortably, "that I accept your explanation of the Mt. Zion tunnel matter."

"Thanks, Bud." This time it was Michael who held out his hand.

"And yours, Red—" F. Millard touched the pilot's shoulder "—about those things we mentioned."

Red gave him a grimace meant for a smile and turned back to the window.

"I was sure I smelled gasoline on someone that first afternoon," said the grocer. "Now that I know it was Hope, I know why I couldn't remember. Since she'd been working on the plane, it would be natural to smell gasoline on her, and pass unnoticed."

"She was a damn smart girl," Michael said emphatically.

"You know," said Kilkenny slowly, "I didn't like her, but I hated to think, there at the end, that anything was going to happen to her."

"She never could have stood life imprisonment," F. Millard added, "and I'm glad she didn't have to be hanged. A girl with an ambition like hers is someone to be pitied. I'm glad I didn't have to shoot her, and that Lieutenant Rogers only shot her in the leg. It's much more fitting that she killed herself with the knife she'd used for murder."

"I wonder where she had that big mumblety-peg knife when I searched her," mused Kilkenny.

"In the flour sack," Tony answered. "The knife and will, both had flour on them."

"I told you she was clever," said Michael. "She was the cook. She could lay her hands on either one whenever she wanted. She must have pinched the knife while I was making shavings for the bonfire."

"You haven't told me yet, Bud," Tony reminded the grocer, "why you suspected Hope."

"The funny part of it was," F. Millard admitted, "when I finally got on the right track, Red was the one I suspected."

The glum pilot turned around. He hesitated, avoiding Kilkenny's eyes, then he leaned forward to join the huddle.

"Incidentally," F. Millard began, "Hope had no idea what she was doing when she pointed out that Eskimos looked like Japanese. And to do her justice, I'm sure she was as much in the dark as we were about what happened in the village so long ago. I'm sure she only knew there was another agent here; she may not even have known about the tin. But when she remarked that Eskimos looked like Japanese, and everything started clicking into place, I knew it could only be another Nazi agent who would know about this spot, isolated enough for her purpose, with supplies already here to maintain existence. I knew then that it had to be one of the Alaskans in the party, and I naturally thought of Red. I would have thought Guy if he hadn't been killed. And it wasn't till the middle of the night that I thought of Hope at all."

"You spoke about Hope's purpose," said Kilkenny thoughtfully. "Do you mean she—knew Dad before she came to Alaska?"

"Oh, no," said F. Millard quickly. "You were all in Fairbluffs a week or two, and it wouldn't take a girl like Hope long to see an opportunity, and she had just as much chance to poison Red's radio operator as Red did."

"Poison my radio man!" ejaculated the pilot.

F. Millard nodded. "If she couldn't get it in the restaurant food, it was easy to slip in the coffee they had later at her apartment. I'm sure there's some sort of drug that would cause reactions like flu. We can check with a doctor when we get back. Just a small dose, you know, not enough to kill him. I don't think she intended to kill, at first."

"You're all hiding something from me!" burst out Kilkenny. "I was glad last night when you kept me away from Hope. I haven't seen the will, but there was some thing between her and Dad that you're trying to conceal, and I have a right to know. Was she—were they—?"

"She does have a right to know," agreed Michael. He picked up Kilkenny's small, tight fist and gently straightened her fingers. "You know your father's reputation, Kenny. To Hope an immensely wealthy, susceptible widower must have looked like a golden harvest. I believe she thought that if she could get him alone, away from other interests and competition, she could make him offer marriage."

"You must remember, my dear," said F. Millard as gently as Michael, "that a girl brought up the way Hope was could very understandably feel that the only way she could ever make herself superior to girls like you would be through the possession of money. Money was something Hope had never had and always wanted."

"Then why didn't she wait till we were rescued, and marry him—instead of killing him? If money was what she wanted, wouldn't she get more that way? Because even if Dad fell for her, I know he'd never—never forget about me." Her voice broke, but her teeth clamped down firmly on her full, red underlip.

"Because" F. Millard answered, "something came up Hope didn't count on. She fell in love with Mick."

"Oh!" Kilkenny gasped.

"Bud!" exploded Michael.

"Sorry, Mick." F. Millard gave the Congressman a feeble grin. "Even Hope found the biological urge was almost as strong as ambition. But not quite. She figured out a way to get a large slice of the Senator's fortune and Mick too, providing her charms were as effective with him as they had been with the Senator. And it wasn't for lack of trying that they didn't work. Sometimes I think if it hadn't been for Kilkenny—"

"You make me feel like a particularly choice worm between two birds!" scowled Michael.

F. Millard ignored him. "You remember a few days after we got stuck, how the Senator's attitude changed? All of a sudden he stopped stewing, seemed satisfied to stay in the village, even looked younger?"

Red finally spoke. "You mean that's when he fell for Hope?"

F. Millard nodded. "Her scheme worked all right. Everything would have been sitting pretty if she hadn't developed a heart interest of her own."

"But how did she ever get him to write a will in her favor?" Red looked bewildered.

"By threatening to expose the whole sordid mess. I'm sorry, Kilkenny," F. Millard said softly, "but you know such things do happen. The Senator could have had no idea what was in her mind, he must have thought the will would merely regularize her position in case—well, in case we were marooned a long time and they couldn't be legally married. That's what she must have told him."

F. Millard saw Kilkenny's shiver of distaste. Then he saw her slip back the woman-of-the-world mask she had discarded. "What about the will?" she asked quietly. "What did Hope get him to do?"

"Her share will come back to you, of course, under the circumstances," Michael assured her. "He left certain sums to Tony and a few other long-time employees. The bulk he divided between you, as his daughter, and Hope, as his future wife."

"That 'and to my' from 'and to my future wife' certainly had me fooled," F. Millard admitted frankly. "I found 'and to my' on the blotter your father used and stuck in a book while he was writing the will the night you came to the door. I thought of every relationship in the world except wife."

"That's why you were so interested in—in my half-brother, wasn't it, Bud?" Kilkenny asked bravely.

"I don't suppose you ever heard, Kilkenny," said Tony quietly, "but he died almost a year ago."

"Oh" Her voice was gentle. "I never even saw him."

They all sat for a while without speaking, with no sound but the beat of the motors. When F. Millard looked back at Kilkenny, her face had regained the peace and warmth he wanted to see.

Michael was watching too. He turned gaily to the grocer. "If you could reconstruct a will from three words like 'and to my,' you're as good as these anthropologists who reconstruct whole animals from one bone."

"The trouble is, I didn't reconstruct the right will." F. Millard's smile was rueful. "But I thought it must be a will."

"Bud!" Kilkenny cried. "Was that all bluff too—that hair-raising reconstruction in the cabin?"

"A lot of it was," he admitted. "But I couldn't think of any other way to get the proof."

"F. Millard Smyth! Darling, I salute you!"

She meant it too, the grocer saw; that shine in her eyes wasn't laughter. He hunched down into his collar, though it didn't hide his blush. But this time he didn't care, his chest was so pleasantly warm.

"By the way, Red," he said to the pilot, "you did something that looked bad, and you never did explain it. That first afternoon, the day the gas was drained from the plane, Schrenk saw you go down to the lake after Hope came away. He couldn't see the plane, but you were gone long enough to empty the tanks before he saw you come back."

"Boy, I'll bet that set your bloodhound nose twitching." But Red's grin wasn't the all-out flash of his usual grins. "I really didn't go to the plane at all. I thought Hope was still there, and I started back to see if I could help her. Then I got thinking about how upset she was over her first radio job going sour, and knew she'd never forgive me if I insisted on helping. I knew Hope. She might look no more ferocious than a baby bird, but I'd seen her angry once or twice, and I'd hate to have it turned on me. She was a gal that held a grudge too. But it was important to get the radio fixed; so I just stood there by the hog back, trying to decide what to do. I thought if I heard her struggling, I'd go on and offer to help. But I didn't hear anything, so I decided she had everything under control, and turned around and went back."

"The way she managed the whole thing was mighty smart," said F. Millard, "like that business about her pride being hurt if you didn't let her fix the radio herself. And then the matter of how we came out here in the first place—she managed it so the Senator was the one who suggested flying this way, probably filled him up with lies about this part of the country. If we could only check with the Senator and Guy, I'll bet we'd find her guiding hand behind every move that was made—you know how perfectly she timed reporting the radio out of order. When Hope's looked up, I wouldn't be surprised if they found that aunt of hers belonged to the Bund. Hope must have grown up under that influence, and all that talk of hers about the Mullens being among the first families of America was pure red herring. She rather overdid the matter of spitting on Schrenk when we caught him, but of course she was trying to cover up. Do you remember how upset she used to get when we talked about the Germans joining the Japanese to attack us? And when we got the news of the war, do you remember what she said —that she was going to give up more than any of us? I think she meant her salary as a foreign agent, and with Hope, giving up money would be the greatest sacrifice. When she took on the job, we weren't in the war, but I think she was afraid to go on, with us in it."

"I'm sure you're right, Bud. Let's talk about happier things." Kilkenny smiled at Michael.

F. Millard was forlorn again. In the seat ahead he saw a muscle tighten in Red's cheek. Both men turned abruptly to the window.

Far off in the distance the mountain range they had seen so long from the other side flung its ragged scallop against the blue sky. All the land below them—high hills, low hills, trees and tundra—was white with snow, the same land that, on their outward trip, had been green and brown, and splashed with red and yellow autumn colors. Red and yellow, gypsy colors for Kilkenny. F. Millard stifled another sigh. Kilkenny would soon be gone, offwith Mick to that Washington world that was only fable to the grocer. And it wasn't just Kilkenny he'd be losing, soon he must leave Alaska. His carefully gathered dollars wouldn't have kept him here this long if he hadn't been forced to stay. In the little time he had left he certainly couldn't travel on planes. Better look his fill while he could.

He leaned closer to the window. Where were all the rivers and lakes he remembered? Frozen now, of course, covered with snow like the ground. White, white wilderness—and he'd been in it, living like the pioneers. He'd wanted Alaska long before he'd heard of Kilkenny. Well, even if he had to take the next train, he would have had these three months.

In the seat ahead, Red waved his arm. "Fairbluffs!" he shouted. "Look, Bud—that speck way over to the left —that's Fairbluffs!" He turned to the others, once more alive, awake. "Listen, you guys, there's something I'm going to do before I enlist. I'm going to hop a plane and travel all over this gol-durned Territory before Uncle Sam puts me to work."

F. Millard beamed. He'd just been telling himself that Alaska was an older love than Kilkenny; how much truer that was of Red. A last tour of the places the young pilot loved—how grand for him to have it.

Red's big hand crushed the grocer's shoulder. "All around the Territory!" he boomed. "With Bud Smyth for my guest!"

Safety belts were flung aside, and F. Millard engulfed in handshakes and shoulder claps. When, blinking and dazed, he finally emerged, to wipe off his glasses and focus his eyes, he found he still couldn't speak. Happiness smothered him in beating wings.

Kilkenny's laughing face was misty. What was she saying? "Now that all the rest of the mysteries are cleared up, how about the last one?"

"Another mystery?" he asked weakly.

"What about the F in F. Millard?"

Blood surged to his face. "You—you don't really want to know, do you?"

The answer came in chorus: "Yes!"

"My—my gracious," he stammered. "If I tell, will you promise not to tell anyone else? You—you understand my mother was a very romantic woman, and our little town didn't have much to read in those days." He paused.

"Go on!" Kilkenny urged.

"The next year it took the country by storm, but my mother was a fan from the first. The book wasn't published till 1886, but it started in *St. Nicholas* the year before, a month before I was born."

"Bud Smyth!" cried Kilkenny. "What *is* your name?"

"She—she named me Fauntleroy."

The men whooped before they could stop, but Kilkenny put her arms around the grocer's neck and kissed him full on the mouth.

"Strap on your belts!" yelled Red. "We're going to land!"

About the War

Perhaps those of us who live on the West Coast feel especially close to the war, but I can't believe there's an American—east, west, north, or south— who doesn't want to help. We aren't all fitted to be truck drivers or welders or nurses' aides—we women, but every time we flatten a tin can, or pick up a nail off the sidewalk, or pour hot gravy fat into the "defense grease" bowl instead of making gravy, in our small way we're helping the war effort.

Over a period of years my mother has been accumulating things for a mythical mountain cabin. When the war came along, the hardware for mother's cabin went to the front—brass hinges and doorknobs, window catches, cupboard latches have gone to war. When it's over, she'll start collecting again, and she'll have rubber and gasoline then, to take her to the mountains.

I'm not doing as much as the women on the production line in airplane factories and shipyards, but morale is important too, and that's my job. When I get to stewing about my small contribution, I pound another page of a mystery story out of my typewriter. I write about Alaska because I lived there twelve years, and maybe you'd like to read about Alaska because your son or father, your boyfriend or husband, your brother or cousin, is a soldier in Alaska now.

Acknowledgements

I want to thank the following people who have helped me bring *Murder Breaks Trail* back. My literary lawyer, Paul Rapp helped me regain the publication rights. I also want to acknowledge the guiding hand of Alan Rinzler who suggested republishing Eunice's earlier works. Special thanks also go to Eunice's nephew, Harry Watson Mays and her grandnephews John and Kirk Rademaker and their sister, Erica for their support and permission to publish these novels.—Elizabeth Reed Aden, goddaughter

Elizabeth Reed Aden

About the Author

Eunice Mays Boyd (1902-1971)

Eunice Mays Boyd was an award-winning mystery writer during the Golden Age of Agatha Christie. Her books are intelligent, cozy whodunnit murder mysteries with many twists and turns. She loved to read mysteries and prided herself in identifying the murderer well before the end. After graduating from UC Berkeley in 1924, she moved to Alaska where she based the F. Millard Smyth mystery series: **MURDER BREAKS TRAIL** (1943), **DOOM IN THE MIDNIGHT SUN** (1943), and **MURDER WEARS MUKLUKS** (1945). A fourth book in the series, **ONE PAW WAS RED,** will be forthcoming. She co-authored **THE MARBLE FOREST** that was made into the movie "Macabre" (1958). Eunice's new vintage murder mysteries were discovered fifty years after her death. **DUNE HOUSE** (2021) and **SLAY BELLS** (2021) are set in San Francisco. **A VACATION TO KILL FOR** (2022) takes place in France.

SOCIAL MEDIA HANDLES:
    Facebook: Elizabeth Reed Aden Author

Twitter: @eliz_reed_aden
Instagram: elizabeth_r_aden

AUTHOR WEBSITE:
www.eunicemaysboyd.com
www.elizabethreedaden.com

Also by Elizabeth Reed Aden/Eunice Mays Boyd

Dune House (2021) with Elizabeth Reed Aden

Slay Bells (2021) with Elizabeth Reed Aden

A Vacation to Kill For (2022) with Elizabeth Reed Aden

Previously published F. Millard Smyth mysteries to be republished by Level Best Books:
   Doom in the Midnight Sun (1944)
   Murder Wears Mukluks (1945)

The Marble Forest (co-author) (1951)